PRAISE FOR *DUST TO DUST*:

"Paranormal romance done well."

—*Kirkus Reviews*

PRAISE FOR *ASHES TO ASHES*:

"A beautiful novel about the power of love over life and death."

—Alex Flinn, *New York Times* bestselling author of *Beastly*

"Intense, suspense-laden, and full of surprising twists.
This story will haunt you in every sense of the word!"

—Sophie Jordan, *New York Times* bestselling author
of the Firelight series

"An appealing and sometimes-poignant blend of savvy
adolescents, young romance, and paranormal evil suggests
there's no escaping teen drama—even in the afterlife."

—*Kirkus Reviews*

"Walker infuses standard romance with larger issues
of mortality, afterlife, forgiveness, and morality."

—ALA *Booklist*

Dust to Dust

MELISSA WALKER

KATHERINE TEGEN BOOKS
An Imprint of HarperCollins Publishers

Katherine Tegen Books is an imprint of HarperCollins Publishers.

Dust to Dust

Library of Congress Cataloging-in-Publication Data
Walker, Melissa (Melissa Carol), date
    Dust to dust / Melissa Walker. — First edition.
        pages   cm
    Sequel to: Ashes to ashes.
    Summary: After surviving a tragic accident, sixteen-year-old Callie McPhee wakes up from a coma with knowledge of the afterlife where she met Thatcher, the spirit who protected her, and can help her save the people she loves from the menace of evil spirits.
    ISBN 978-0-06-207738-7
    1. Coma—Juvenile fiction.   2. Future life—Juvenile fiction.   3. Ghost stories.
4. Spirit possession—Juvenile fiction.   5. Love stories.   6. Paranormal fiction.
7. Charleston (S.C.)—Juvenile fiction.   [1. Coma—Fiction.   2. Future life—Fiction.
3. Ghosts—Fiction.   4. Spirit possession—Fiction.   5. Love—Fiction.   6. Supernatural—Fiction.   7. Charleston (S.C.)—Fiction.]   I. Title.
PZ7.W153625Du   2015   2014030717
[Fic]—dc23   CIP
                                                                                                    AC

Typography by Ellice M. Lee
16 17 18 19 20   PC/RRDH   10 9 8 7 6 5 4 3 2 1

First paperback edition, 2016

For Barbara Walker, my favorite niece

One

MY FATHER SAYS THAT people in comas experience all kinds of visions—neurons fire, new pathways open in the brain. I don't know the science behind all that, but I've been concentrating very hard on staying in the present, and only seeing the things that are right before my eyes. Now that I'm finally at home, that's getting easier.

The wooden swing on our wraparound porch goes back and forth, back and forth without a creak. To the left, I see our manicured front lawn, all flush with emerald-green grass and violet larkspurs, and to the right there's the bend in the Ashley River that has always been my backyard. My father installed this swing with his perfectionist's touch, and I know he did it just for me. I can picture him out here toiling with hammer and nails in the hot July sun. He kept his mind on solid wood and hard work instead of me, his only daughter, lying comatose in the hospital.

As my toe touches the ground to keep the swing moving, I wince at the sight of the long, jagged scar on my leg. My meds are wearing off and I'm starting to feel that familiar tingle that signals the edge of pain throughout my body. I take a white pill from the pocket of my shorts and place it under my tongue before swallowing it with a sip of lemonade.

I've been home from the county hospital for two weeks, and I've spent most of that time in this porch swing, surrounded by yellow-and-white-striped pillows. There's something about this swing, its motion, that's familiar. Like I'm being held and rocked by something. Or someone.

I remember his soft blond hair, the way it curled around his ears. I remember the blue of his eyes, the tiny scar on his chin. I remember the way his gaze never wandered from mine, the slightly crooked smile.

Shaking my head, I clear the "memories" that I've created in some deep, coma-induced fiction-loving part of my brain.

I look down at the white-painted planks of my porch. What I should focus on is all the living I have to do, the little things that make life worth missing. Like the gentle relief of the wind that touches my skin as the ceiling fan turns the hot Charleston air, the sound of sprinklers in our yard as Dad tries to keep the grass from browning in this sweltering heat, the slow rumble of Mrs. Nute's car as she drives by and gives me a wave and a thumbs-up.

I smile and wave back, my arm completely healed from its break.

Everyone's giving me a thumbs-up these days. Callie McPhee, the girl who came back from the dead.

Except I wasn't dead.

When I crashed my shiny new BMW into a truck on Route 52 in June, I almost lost my life. What I understand is that I was in a coma, alive but unresponsive for weeks. That gave my body time to heal.

I get what happened to my body. It's what happened in my head that I can't understand.

I think my synapses worked overtime, because I remember so many things: the sound of his voice, like velvet; the shadow of stubble around his chin; the way one blond lock of hair fell onto his forehead when he leaned close to me. And his name: *Thatcher.*

He was my ally. He protected me, kept me from something dark and sinister that I can't quite place. The world I was in, the Prism, wasn't all light and happiness—it wasn't Heaven—but the moments with Thatcher . . . they were. I have the urge to call for him, to lean my face into the sun and search for him in the invisible heat of summer.

I turn my head toward the river and watch its placid surface shimmer in the sunlight. I took the pill but I still feel some phantom sensations inside my body, echoes of the brokenness, I guess. I wonder if I'll ever feel whole again.

A Carolina wren lands on the porch railing in front of me and looks into my face, cocking its head. For a moment it seems like its eyes, deep and blue and familiar, are trying to tell me something, like they know me.

"Thatcher?" I whisper.

The bird flies away quickly, up into a tree and out of view.

I lean back against the back of the swing and laugh. *What am I doing?* Talking to a bird? Imagining that it's this ghost boy who doesn't even exist?

"Callie? Can I bring you a blanket?"

My father's voice booms from the front door, which he's opened up a crack.

"Daddy, it's like one hundred degrees," I say. "Do you think I'm one of those crazy old ladies who needs a blanket no matter what?"

He smiles. "I just thought that with the fan on—"

"With the fan on it's *almost* bearable out here," I tell him. Then I tap the swing. "Come sit."

He does.

We're silent for a couple of minutes, and I can feel him tensing up. My retired-navy father, who never used to have time for anything impromptu, who lived his life with military precision and a schedule that was as airtight as a submarine, is having trouble sitting without looking at his watch.

"Pretty day," I say, hoping to help him relax.

"Gorgeous. Makes you appreciate things." He looks at me then, and I know what he means by "things." Being alive, being together. He may not be able to express it quite yet, but I can tell that he's trying to do things differently now that his daughter has faced death.

He took the week off from his job at the Citadel. He teaches physical science during the year, and he usually goes into the office all summer—research and writing and all that professorial stuff.

Since I've been home from the hospital, though, he's been hovering, tending to my needs (both real and imagined, like the blanket).

"How're you feeling?" he asks.

"Good," I say, patting my pocket. "Just took a pill."

"Still having visions?"

My face goes red at the mortifying thought of my stoic father seeing me talk to a bird. When I was in the hospital and kind of out of it, I told him that I'd seen another world called the Prism. I wish I hadn't, but he doesn't seem to judge me for it. He, of all people, knows it was just the pain meds talking.

"Less and less," I tell him. The truth is that when I take a pill, I feel more at ease, and not just physically. My mind relaxes, too. The Prism is a lovely name for a place that doesn't exist. And Thatcher? He's not real.

But the guy pulling into my driveway is.

"Hey, hey." Nick gets out of his beat-up sedan and strides up to the porch with a bouquet of sunflowers under his arm. My dad stands up to shake his hand.

"Captain McPhee," says Nick with a nod.

"Mr. Fisher."

Relations between my father and my boyfriend used to be chilly, but since the accident there's been a slight thaw. Before, my dad wanted a lot of things for me: a perfect GPA, the right college, a proper career path. Of course, he still wants those things, but first and foremost, he wants me to be happy.

And when I can shake the visions from my head, I am.

I look into Nick's soulful brown eyes as he bends down to hand over the flowers and give me a kiss on the cheek, and I can't help but feel like a lucky girl. The pill is working—my soreness is gone for the moment.

"Ahem." Dad coughs into his fist.

Nick's face reddens and he looks at me, his eyes a little panicky. I realize he's wondering if my dad found out that he's been sneaking into my room at night through the upstairs window.

"Daddy, hush," I say, swatting his arm playfully. "Don't embarrass Nick."

I give Nick a smile to let him know that our secret is safe, and he visibly exhales. Dad stares at him for a moment. My father may be attempting to show a softer side to me since the accident, but he's still Captain McPhee with everyone else.

When I start to stand, both Dad and Nick put their hands out to help steady me, but I shoo them away.

"Y'all, I'm not an invalid," I say, though I do need to hold on to the porch rail to get up. I've been doing physical therapy every day and I feel stronger and stronger—I can see muscle tone returning to my legs, and the therapist said it's good for me to walk around and stand on my own. What I really want is for everyone to back off and treat me normally.

"Nick, do you want a lemonade?" I ask, stepping slowly toward the front door.

"I'll get it," he says, but I push my hand into the center of his chest in a *Stop* motion. As an added bonus, I get to touch his tight muscles.

"No, *I* will get it," I tell him with a flirty grin. Then I turn my head. "Daddy?"

My father is looking at me like I'm a withered flower that's been crushed under a cow's foot. "Let me, honey," he says.

"Good gracious, will everyone just relax?" I say, shaking the sunflowers at them for emphasis. "I am capable of pouring two glasses of lemonade."

"Make that three, Callie!" says a bright voice from behind me. I turn to see Carson, my neighbor and best friend, making her way up the porch steps with a big picnic basket under her arm.

She raises her heart-shaped sunglasses onto her head and winks at me. I give her a grateful smile—Carson is the only one who treats me like I'm an able-bodied person these days. She grabs the sunflowers from me and says, "Hurry up now! The potato salad's getting warm."

As I set up the tray with three glasses, ice, and a pitcher of lemonade, I feel extra glad that I haven't told Carson about my visions. Not because she'd think I was nuts, but because she'd want to hear every single detail. Carson's really into "the other side" and all of Charleston's ghost lore. She's been dying for me to remember things about when I was in the coma, but I've told her it's all a blank. I feel bad lying to my best friend, but I don't want to make the illusions I created in my head feel more real by discussing them with Carson. Only my dad knows, and he's already dismissed everything as coma-induced brain misfires. Just like I have. Mostly.

I carry out the tray and exit through the back door to meet

Carson at the wooden table by the water. Our housekeeper, Carla, comes three times a week, and she set up the patio umbrella this morning when I told her we were going to have a picnic tonight. It'll guard us from the evening sun, and I swear it's ten degrees cooler in the shade. Carson is setting up the deviled eggs, and she already has Nick's flowers in a mason jar she brought with her and filled with river water.

She smiles at me. "I got another call from that *Good Morning Charleston* producer."

I glare at her. "Carson, I already told her *no*."

"Oh, but Callie, it would be so much fun!" She looks at the sky and her face lights up in the way that tells me she's about to rush down a talking highway at full speed. "They said they'd send a car to take us to the studio! And you wouldn't have to make up anything—if you don't remember what it was like to be in the coma, you can just say that. The producer said that everyone just wants to see you, the girl who almost died. People are really interested in these kind of stories, you know. And maybe you'll even remember something if they ask the right questions and—"

I've been giving her a *no* face this whole time, and she finally pauses. "Cars, I don't want to sit on a couch and smile for the cameras. What happened to me is personal."

She gives me a sad smile, and I can't tell if she's accepting what I'm saying. I hope so. I mean it. The truth is, I don't understand my time in the coma, and I certainly don't want to try to figure it out on television.

"All right," sighs Carson. "I give up . . . for now." Then she glances up at the house. "So things are okay with your dad and Nick?"

I turn back to the porch to see my father showing Nick the remote control he uses to turn the sprinklers on and off. Dad is frowning in concentration and Nick's face is slightly red.

"It's still awkward, but I think they're both trying," I say, happy to change the subject.

"It's cute to watch them together," says Carson, smiling at their stiffness. We break up into laughter and then she gestures at her table. "So what do you think?"

Carson's setting is total Martha Stewart—white tablecloth, Nick's flowers, a tiny votive candle in the center of the table, and sturdy paper plates filled with cole slaw, potato salad, and cold fried chicken. "Wouldn't I make a great girlfriend?" asks Carson, throwing back her glossy brown curls and laughing as she waves Nick and my dad over to dinner. "How did *you* end up with the perfect guy while I'm still as solitary as ten miles of bad road?"

I grin at her. "Just lucky, I guess." But as I watch Nick walk across the grass toward me, I feel uneasy, like I'm forgetting something that's between us . . . or someone. The phantom pain echoes inside me again and I fish in my pocket for another pill—I have one more left in today's dosage and I'd better save it for bedtime.

When we all grasp hands to say the prayer, my dad bows his head as we close our eyes.

"Thanks be to God for this table, this food, and the friends who are sharing it. Our eternal gratitude for Callie's second chance at life, Carson's loyal friendship, and Nick's pure love of our girl."

Carson squeezes my hand and I almost giggle and break the silence—embarrassing!—but when I open my eyes, Nick is smiling at me. It's a nice moment, one I can't imagine having had at the beginning of the summer, when my dad was telling me I was too young for a boyfriend. Back then he hardly ever made time for a sit-down meal; I fended for myself at night with leftovers that our housekeeper tucked into the fridge while he got home past dinnertime, and our conversations consisted mostly of him setting boundaries and me nodding dutifully with my fingers crossed behind my back.

Before the crash, I looked for this sense of contentment in all the wrong places—in the rush of wind as I drove too fast, in the free-fall sensation of jumping off a too-high cliff into a swimming hole. I put myself in danger just so I could feel something. I used to need a thrill to feel alive, but now this will do.

It's a whole new world since I almost died, and everyone I love is sitting around this table.

Well, almost everyone.

Two

WHEN I SAY GOOD-BYE to Nick and Carson after a full meal and a "Happy Recovery, Callie!" cake, complete with rose piping and near-perfect pink script (Carson's practicing her frosting skills), Nick whispers in my ear, "See you later."

This is the first night that I insist my father not help me up the stairs to my room—I'm ready to live my life again, on my own, and it only takes a little bit longer than usual for me to navigate the steps. He's still there with a glass of water, though, to tuck me into bed and give me a kiss on my forehead.

"Daddy," I say, when he stands up to leave my room. "You know I'm not eight years old, right?"

His eyes crinkle up around the edges for a moment, and I wonder if he's getting emotional, but then he clears his throat. "Yes," he says. "Believe me. I know I missed that time."

He's not wrong to have regrets about the way he walled off his grief and stopped connecting with the world, including me, after Mama died when I was six years old. He did miss a lot.

"Well . . . good night," he says. And it's just a word, but the way he says it is softer than usual, like he's trying to convey something deeper. I smile at him in the doorway, hoping he can tell that I appreciate his efforts to show me his affection.

As my father's footsteps echo down the hallway, though, loneliness creeps in. Looking around my room, at the wide window seat, the soft yellow curtains, the photos on my antique-looking desk, something is . . . out of place. A flash, a memory, races through my brain—I'm in this room, but it's not real. It shimmers, just out of reach. I can't touch anything; there's nothing solid. *I'm not solid.*

But he was. *Thatcher.* He moved at my side like an opposing magnet, never quite touching me but always close, always watching, always protecting me from . . . what?

I've been having nightmares since the accident. Just this morning I woke up with a jolt, and a lingering image of my bedroom—this very room—ransacked and destroyed, its contents scattered and broken as if a tornado had ripped through it. And I remember a voice, *his* voice, telling me to be careful, to stay alert. In the journal next to my bed, I wrote down Thatcher's words so I wouldn't forget them. I'm almost afraid to look at them now, but when I open the page, I see my own shaky handwriting and I can hear him saying, "I'll find them. I'll protect you."

I grab a pen quickly and scribble out the words. They're nonsense. They're the fog my dad was talking about, the haze of the pills and the misfired synapses in my post-coma brain. But it's strange to me that it's only in the early morning, when my pill is wearing off, that these visions and voices—these nightmares—come.

A small bead of dread settles into my stomach, so I close the journal and put it back in its place underneath the books in my nightstand's top drawer. Then I quietly lift up my comforter to step onto the floor. The feeling of the soft tufted rug under my feet does a little to ease my worries and ground me back in my world. This is real. I am here.

So why, for a moment, did it seem like I was somewhere far away?

I hear the leaves on the oak tree outside rustling. I walk to the window, carefully moving the dangling glass prism that Nick gave to me in the hospital aside before I slide it open.

In one motion, Nick moves from the thick branch that reaches toward my house into my room, stepping onto the window seat and then softly to the floor.

"What are you doing out of bed, young lady?" he asks me.

"I wanted to greet you right," I say, taking his hand and leaning into his chest—strong, sturdy, tangible.

How silly of me to think there's nothing solid here. Nick is the most solid thing of all.

It's the other boy who invades my thoughts, *Thatcher.* Who isn't here. Who doesn't exist. And when Nick is around, Thatcher doesn't invade my dreams.

I shake my head to knock away the crazy, and Nick steps back, putting his hand under my chin. A trickling sensation of near-pain blurs the edges of my body and I break away from his touch, sitting back on my bed as I swallow my last pill of the day.

Nick perches beside me. I watch him reach into his pocket.

"I've been meaning to return this to you," he says, and he hands me a heart-shaped amber pendant on a silver chain. I take it into my palm and finger its smooth edges. Nick had given it to me as a gift last year, a replacement for a heart-shaped jade charm that my mother gave to me once upon a time. When I lost the jade piece, I was devastated—it felt like I was losing Mom all over again. I told Nick about it, and he bought the amber heart to remind me that other people loved me too.

A notion, maybe a memory, settles behind my eyes. Nick took this pendant while I was in the hospital; he held on to it so he could have a piece of me. I remember seeing him with it . . . I remember . . .

I shake my head. I'm making things up again.

"I took it after . . . ," Nick starts. But he pauses. "Anyway, that doesn't matter now," he says. "This heart is yours again."

He smiles at his own cheesy words and I grin back at him.

"Thank you." I open up the clasp so he can put it around my neck. I want it close to me.

After he fastens it, he kisses the top of my head and I lean into him with a sigh. "I'm so tired," I say.

"Don't overdo it." Nick looks around pensively. "I probably shouldn't even be here, Cal."

"You should," I tell him. "That's not what I meant. I want you here. I love you here."

We snuggle into position on my double bed—Nick sitting up

against the headboard and me resting my head on his chest. Since I've been home from the hospital, Nick has snuck in to be with me whenever he can make an excuse to his parents. I fall asleep more easily with him near. Without him, my dreams are filled with dark echoes of the imagined world I created, the Prism—it's foggy and uncertain, a glimmering gray space that feels part peaceful and part menacing, like a place among the clouds where both warming sun and threatening thunderstorms hover. But with Nick, I'm not in the clouds. I'm firmly on the earth.

Today has been a good day, and I smile as the pill takes effect. No more phantom sensation, no more paranoia about a world that doesn't exist, no more false memories—just two sixteen-year-olds alone in a bedroom. I look up at Nick with sleepy eyes and whisper, "Kiss me."

He does, more passionately than I expect. His familiar lips move over mine and he reaches to touch my hair and the sides of my face as his tongue explores my mouth. It's the first time since the accident that he isn't treating me like I'm fragile, and my body responds to the delicious touches as his hand moves down the front of my soft cotton nightgown, brushing my chest and working its way to my hips.

My mind flashes for just a moment to another world, one where touching was discouraged, where connections were supposed to be more than just physical. But with Nick's breath in my ear, his hands on my body, that thought is quickly dismissed. I'm tired of the weird ways my brain is wandering; I want something normal and grounded—I want this.

Nick pulls me closer, and I wrap one leg around his back so I can be as near to him as possible, my breath ragged in between kisses. My nightgown slips up to my waist and when he runs his hand up my thigh, my entire body lights up with sensation. I haven't felt this kind of touch in so long.

A moan escapes me and I kiss him harder, so ready to feel alive again, ready to take things even further than we ever have—I wanted to go all the way before the accident, but Nick held back. Maybe tonight's the night. I put my hand under his shirt and trace the hard contours of his back as Nick lowers his lips to kiss my neck, pressing his body against mine so I can tell how much he wants this too.

But when I move my other hand lower, Nick pulls away suddenly, standing up and looking at me with confused eyes.

"We shouldn't," he says. "I'm sorry, I—this could hurt you. You're not ready for something this . . . physical."

When we stop, I feel half disappointed and half relieved as the passion I felt drains out of me. I flop back onto my pillow with a sigh. "When will everyone stop treating me like I'm a broken little baby bird?"

Nick tilts his head to one side teasingly. "You kind of are a broken little baby bird," he says. So I throw a pillow at him.

He catches it and sits back down on the bed.

"Come here," he says, holding up his arm.

I pout at him.

"Callie, we'll get back to that stuff soon enough," he says. "It just doesn't feel right now."

"Okay," I say quietly.

I lean into him again and he gives my arm a gentle squeeze. The moment is gone, and I wonder where it went. *It just doesn't feel right*. Nick's words echo in my head as I close my eyes and try to fall asleep.

The aliveness, the sensation of touching and kissing and feeling, is so very right. But Nick isn't all wrong. Something seems off to me too. Nick is warm and familiar with his soft brown curls and warm, smooth cheeks and smiling, kissable lips that used to move so well with mine. And yet I can't shake this uneasy feeling I have sometimes when he and I are alone. A feeling that I've let go of him, and I've already said good-bye in my heart.

I wake up in the middle of the night and Nick is gone. My phone says it's just after three a.m. I turn onto my side and face the window, slowly closing my eyes again.

Crack! I sit up, startled, and find myself staring at the newly fractured glass in my bottom windowpane. Shakily, I stand to inspect it. It's a single line, not like the spiral spiderweb that would happen if someone threw a rock—more like a break created by extreme pressure. I trace my finger along the ridge of it, and as I do, a low thrum of energy rattles my body.

My pulse quickens as I hear a loud, familiar sound. A guy's voice, deep and boisterous, rings in my ears. *"Callie . . . we're heeeere."*

Then a girl's voice follows, higher and less jovial. *"You're so cheesy,"* it says, seeming to address the first voice. But then, her focus shifts to me. *"We are here, though. And we're very interested in renewing our friendship with you, Callie May McPhee."*

I whip my head around, trying to see where the voices are coming from, but all I see is my room, trashed. Destroyed again like the image I can't rid my mind of, as if a storm blew through it and destroyed it piece by piece—curtains flying, rug shredding, framed photos smashing against shimmering walls.

"Who's here? What do you want?"

"Wait, you don't remember us?" says the girl's voice in a fake pouty tone. *"I'm hurt."*

"Yeah, Callie," says the guy, his voice growing deeper and more menacing. *"You were such a dear friend."*

Then something grips me by the throat and I can barely breathe.

Three

I SIT UP IN bed with a start, sweat on my forehead. My eyes adjust to the dim light of the early morning, and my shades are drawn. My room is fine, neat and tidy. It was a dream. But my heart is racing and when I raise my hands in front of me, they're shaking. Those voices sounded so real.

I hear a low crackling sound, like static from a radio, and I scan the room to find my old alarm clock in the corner—the one I used to have before I started using the alarm on my phone. I stand up and walk over to it. The numbers that tell the time are blinking and the radio is tuned between stations. That's weird. I probably haven't turned this thing on for years. I shut it off and open my laptop to see if there was a power surge or something.

There's a blank page open on my screen—a Word document that hasn't been written yet. I don't remember starting anything.

I'm about to shut it down when I see the cursor move on the page—right to the center, as if someone has hit a tab. Then, the typing starts:

No more pills. Clear your mind.

I look over my shoulder quickly, heart starting to race. No one's there. *Stay calm, Callie.* Could someone be logged into my network somehow, like with a shared screen? The letters are in bold italics, strong and urgent.

What if it's him?

Thatcher. I feel my mind start to spin, whirling with excited panic. *Could he talk to me this way? Can he reach me across worlds? Is he real, and really here?* And if he's here . . . were *they* here? My "dear friends" from the other side? Whoever they were?

Glancing back at the window, I reach over to open the shade. Slowly, my hand shaking, I pull back the bottom corner. It's there. I see it. A long, jagged crack.

I drop the shade quickly and slam my laptop closed, hurrying into the bathroom that's attached to my room, where I turn on all the lights and run the faucet, splashing my face with water. *Wake up wake up wake up.*

I stare at myself in the mirror, wild-eyed and wet. These pills are turning me into a crazy person. Ghosts, poltergeists, another world. Maybe I'm hallucinating because of the meds.

I take a deep breath and dry my face, still flushed. My dark-blond curls are wild, so I pull them into a knotted bun.

After another moment of willing my heartbeat to slow down, I walk back into my room and open the laptop. The blank page is gone—there's no evidence of it ever existing.

I walk over to the window and throw up the shade. I wince. The crack is there, clear as day. I take a deep breath. It's probably from a bird that hit the window or expansion from humidity or something, but I must have seen it and created a nightmare around it, complete with ominous voices.

I shake my head and pull on a sweater to deal with my father's over-air-conditioning habit. It's comforting, in a way, that my dad still keeps our house as cold as a morgue. Consistency is nice, even if it means I have to wear long sleeves inside at the end of summer.

I start to make my bed, pulling up the comforter and fluffing the pillow back into place. When I pick it up, for a moment, I catch a whiff of something familiar. Thatcher. He had a smell, like fresh-cut grass, and I inhale to find it there, in my pillowcase. God, I really am insane.

On my nightstand, the bottle of pills seems to stand out, like there's a spotlight on it. If the pills are what's making me so confused, what's creating these crazy dreams, I don't want to take them anymore. I don't want to keep wondering what's real and what isn't. There's too much uncertainty: Weirdness with Nick. The nightmares. Wisps of another world.

Enough of this.

I grab the painkiller bottle and go downstairs to the dining room, where my father is eating a sandwich. I tell him that I want to go see the doctor.

"What's wrong, Callie May? Is the pain getting worse?"

"No," I say, placing the pills on the table in front of him. "I need to get off the meds."

"It's too soon," Dad says immediately, not even considering my request. "Your body's been through a great deal of trauma."

I knew he'd object.

"I want my mind to be clear." I hold on to the edge of a wooden dining room chair, my grip tight with determination.

"Clear of what?"

"I've been seeing more of those visions," I say. And it's not a lie. I have. I tried to talk to a bird yesterday, for goodness' sake. Not to mention today's radio and laptop incidents. And after last night, I'm more worried about why I'm so confused about Nick—and why I'm sniffing my sheets for a whiff of a boy who isn't real. While the phantom pains I feel when I don't take my pill on time are unpleasant, the phantom brain activity is worse.

"I see," he says. "Are you still seeing a cloudy world filled with other souls?"

I nod, cringing inwardly at the description that I'd given him of the Prism, this world that lives and breathes in my head. It was more than that, though—it was glistening and calm and quiet, really wonderful at times. And if that place were the only thing that plagued my mind, I could deal with it. What I haven't told my father is that it's the person, the one who echoes inside me somehow. . . .

Thatcher. When my mind lets his name fully form, it's like I feel him pressing against me somehow, holding me close to him and keeping me safe. I feel a flush of warmth so intense I have to sit down.

As I ease myself into a hard-backed chair, my father looks at me, concerned.

"You have to give yourself time to heal," he says, his voice soft and strong all at once. And I know I'm not going to win this fight.

"I feel stronger," I say, still trying. "I do."

"There may be a lot of pain if you go off the pills."

"I know," I say. "I'm tough."

"Yes, you are," he says. "But I'm afraid the answer is still no. We need to work on the doctors' time line—not yours."

I frown at him as I offer a stiff nod. It's useless to argue with a dad who gives orders for a living. Still, I need to show him I'm capable, so I shove the pills into my pocket and stand up to clear his plate.

"Leave it. Carla's coming later," says my father, who hasn't put away a dish in . . . well, ever, as far as I know.

"I can manage," I tell him with a grin. "Let Carla do the harder stuff—like laundry."

"You're getting better day by day, Callie," Dad says, not trying to stop me from moving around for once. He unfolds the newspaper at the same time that he meets my gaze. "Don't think I don't notice."

I put the dishes in the sink and raise my eyebrows at him expectantly.

"But you still need the medication," he says, turning to the front page. "Just a little longer."

I sigh and load the dishwasher, bending over carefully and

assessing my physical state. My legs are pale and a little anemic-looking, marked with lots of small scars and one big one. I wore pants for a week or so, but then Carson convinced me that my scars are badges of honor, "and pretty badass, too."

My arms are starting to feel sturdy again—I've worked with weights in physical therapy, and my final appointment is later today.

While I'm definitely still weaker than usual, and these small prickles of pain do hit at unexpected times, I think I'm doing really well for someone who was lying flat on her back for almost two months.

I shake the pill bottle and pour myself a glass of water, the one I'm supposed to use to wash down my next dose right about now. Dad looks up at me, and I open the bottle slowly. Then I mime sticking a pill under my tongue and swallowing it, like a dutiful daughter.

His smile makes me feel guilty as I drop the pill into the drain and flush it with the remaining water in my glass. My father isn't the only headstrong McPhee in this house.

I walk outside onto the porch. The book I was reading yesterday still rests on the yellow-and-white striped pillows in the swing.

I've been reading a lot since I've been home, partly to avoid going online. The local newspapers have all run stories about my miraculous awakening, despite the fact that I refuse to give them interviews about my accident. Um, no thanks. Mostly they've quoted doctors who didn't treat me talking about comas in general, and a couple of pastors have shared stories of what it might be like to be between life and death. I've read a few, but none of their descriptions have sounded right to me.

Standing at the porch railing, I look out over the lawn. It's vibrating with buzzing bees in the clover and ladybugs crawling on the wild strawberry leaves. There's so much life all around me, and I want to grab it and hold it in my hands, feeling its movement, its pulse, its energy.

Your reverence for life is so beautiful.

I hear the voice. It's not my own, but it's clear as crystal. It's his.

I spin around toward the house. No one's there.

"Who said that?" I whisper.

No response. But he is here. It's not a knowing, or even a feeling. It's more . . . an impression. That's the word. His soul is impressed into my space, and I can tell it's near. Is it the trace of the last pill I took making me feel this way, or is it . . .

"Thatcher, if you're real, you have to show me," I whisper into the air. Maybe when I get further from my last pill, in a few hours, this will be over, these imaginings will be gone, and I'll be back to normal. And that's what I want, right? To be done with this dream-world that makes me feel split in two?

Nick will have the old Callie back, someone who's undistracted and uncomplicated—and fully in love with him. Dad will know my good sense has returned. I'm not a wacko who thinks there's a ghost boy out there trying to reach me. I'll stop whispering to myself, stop smelling sheets and being frightened by radio static and talking to birds.

But just in case . . . just in case he's real, I want to give him a chance to reveal himself.

I wait for a moment, but all I hear is the soft hum of the hot summer day.

And I'm grateful and disappointed all at once.

I read for a little while, but eventually I head upstairs with a plan to stream the newest episodes of my favorite show. From the den, Dad calls, "Get some more rest, Callie. If you expect to go off the pills soon, you need to save your energy."

I pause for a moment in my open door, and then I click it shut and lean against it, frozen.

Save your energy. I've heard that before. From *him*.

A chill works its way up my spine, and although I don't feel pain, I do feel something. The hairs on my arm prick up, and I have that sense again of being . . . not alone. I cast a glance around the four corners of my room. Not an item out of place, not a shadow that moves. And still . . . something, or someone, is here.

Bzzzt.

My phone lights up with a text from a number I don't recognize.

Callie, call me.

My breath quickens as I wonder if it's possible; if he were able to contact me this way . . . would he?

My fingers are hitting Call before my brain catches up to them, and it's ringing, ringing . . . *click.*

"Thatcher?"

"Um, no." A man clears his throat. "Callie, this is Pete Green from the *Post and Courier*. Your friend Carson said that you might be open to talking about—"

"I'm sorry, Mr. Green," I say, cutting him off. "But I've already told someone at your paper that I'm not interested in doing a story."

"But if we could just—" he tries again.

"I'm afraid I can't talk," I tell him. "Please don't contact me again. Good-bye."

I end the call abruptly and throw the phone down on my bed. *Carson!*

I head to the bathroom. I'm so angry with my best friend that I could scream. How can she think I'm ready to talk to the media about any of this? I can't even get my own head straight.

And there's another reason that I was so rude to the reporter on the phone. I thought the text might have been from Thatcher, and I'm shaking with anxiety.

I turn on the hot water, deciding that a shower will clear my head. As the room fills with steam, I look into the mirror. My eyes are watery and threatening to spill over with tears. The mirror is fogging up slowly, masking my sad face.

Suddenly, as if someone is holding a finger up to the glass, a message begins to appear.

N . . . o . . . m . . . o . . . r . . . e . . . p . . . i . . . l . . . l . . . s.

"No more pills," I whisper aloud. And something inside me, some tuning fork in my soul, knows that Thatcher is here, right now, writing these words with his own hand. He's using energy to connect, like he taught me. But ghosts aren't supposed to communicate with the living this way. He's breaking the rules for me.

I feel a surge of happiness inside—he's *here*.

As the message continues, I put my own hand up to the mirror, trying to feel the energy from his soul. I trace each letter as it's spelled out, hoping I can touch something, some part of him.

```
I . . . n . . . e . . e . . . d . . . y . . .
o . . . u . . .
```

I gasp. But then the letters continue.

```
t . . . o . . . b . . . e . . . a . . . w . . .
a . . . r . . . e.
```

I need you to be aware.

"Thatcher?" I whisper.

And then, without hesitation, comes the next word:

```
Y . . . e . . . s.
```

An audible gasp escapes my lips and I lean on the edge of the sink to keep my balance.

"Where are you? Can I see you?"

I'm filled with questions but now that the message has been received, there are no more answers from the other side. He doesn't write another letter. I take a few deep breaths and close my eyes. When I open them, his words are still readable. Who am I to ignore them?

I grab the bottle of pills and pour them all into the toilet, flushing it before I can think twice.

I turn off the shower and step back into my room, where it's as if everything is under water. I shake my head, trying to knock loose the memory I have of this room—this very room—in another universe. It was my sanctuary, my resting place, my haven, and a space where I was safe from . . . from what? I open my eyes quickly, suddenly afraid of what I'll see. I haven't had a pill since last night, and now the visions are coming faster and faster.

This is what I remember: Misty surroundings, quiet awe, a need for peace and order. Thatcher's stormy blue eyes looking at me intensely, questioning my strong emotions as I came to terms with my presumed death, as I tried to understand all the things he told me in his soothing voice. It was soothing, wasn't it? Even though at first it was . . . distant. Thatcher was my Guide, tasked with teaching me to haunt my loved ones and help them move on from my "death" through a connection that transcended both our worlds. He was patient with me, closed off at first but opening up little by little, until . . .

A rush of heat hits my face as I remember a kiss. *The* kiss. The one that did more than take my breath away—it took my soul somewhere.

Tears brim in my eyes. I lost him. I lost Thatcher when I came back to life. And all that time I was in the Prism, all that time he knew . . .

I wasn't really dead. I was alive. I *am* alive.

I grab my phone and take a photo of the nearly faded message on the bathroom mirror, and then I spray the glass with Windex and wipe it clean with a towel so Dad won't see. "Thatcher, help me remember," I whisper into the stillness of my room. But there's no response, and talking to him out loud makes me feel crazy.

I think of something my first grade teacher told me after Mama died, a technique she taught. "If you can't speak it, write it down." I drew picture after picture of Mama, wrote simple words to her about my sadness, about missing her. It did help, a little. Maybe I can use that now.

I take my journal out of its spot in my nightstand, and I curl up on my bed with a green pen, scribbling furiously.

Thatcher,

I'm trying to remember things. The way you were teaching me to haunt. The way you were gentle with me, patient. And also how I could be stubborn, how you could be too. Sometimes you were quiet, other times you were stern. There was so much to you, so many layers for me to peel back. You were a challenge. I am, too. Is that why we were drawn to each other?

I'm afraid. I'm afraid that it was only me, that I wanted to be close to you and that you were just doing your job. But that isn't true, is it?

Because I also remember your face when you looked at me, really looked at me. It was full of emotion—it glowed. Was it just reflecting my own feelings back at me, like a mirror, or did you feel it too? You must have felt it. Because I also remember how I burned when you touched me, like there was a light inside me that had never been switched on until you came.

My pen stills. Am I saying too much? I lean back in my bed, suddenly exhausted by the emotions that are coursing through me.

I'm alive again; I've got a second chance. But living my life means letting go of a world that was starting to become my new everything. Now that my system is getting free of the pills, I'm uncovering the truth: The Prism is real. *Thatcher* is real. And I think I'm in love with him.

Four

TONIGHT, ALL I WANT to do is stay at home and try to connect with Thatcher again. But instead I'm at the movies with Nick. It's our first out-of-the-house date since the coma, and while we should both be excited to kill brain cells at the multiplex, like we used to do every Friday in the very beginning, it feels like our minds are anywhere but here.

My eyes keep darting around as we walk into the theater, looking for things that seem out of place, things that could be messages from Thatcher. Nick is kind of quiet and keeps texting on his phone, turning away from me slightly, like he's worried I might catch a glimpse of what he's writing—and to whom. It's only when we reach the ticket booth that we engage in real conversation.

"So what'll it be? Bloody raw horror? Sappy romantic comedy? Formulaic action movie?" Nick says, gesturing to the list of movie titles appearing on the electronic screen.

I actually have this weird pang of sadness right now. As I read the list, I have no idea what any of the titles mean. It's like I've been missing for a year or something.

"You pick," I tell Nick, forcing a smile. "I'm up for anything."

"*Personal Invasions* is about a guy who finds out that his girl-friend's body has an alien inside it. Hunter said it was good."

I shrug. "Sure."

When we get inside, Nick starts to order our usual Number 3 combo—large popcorn with two medium drinks and a large candy, all for the bargain price of eighteen dollars. But I stop him. "I think I just want a small soda," I say. "I ate a big lunch."

"Oh, okay." He doesn't order anything for himself, which is a little strange. Nick has a gigantic appetite and usually I have to fight him for my share of the snacks. I know I'm not exactly acting like myself, given what happened earlier today, but I can't help but wonder if something happened to Nick too. Something to make his behavior toward me shift a bit.

And then comes the seating situation. In the auditorium, we always sit in the back so we can make out if the mood strikes, but today Nick walks ahead of me and chooses seats right in the middle.

"The best view," he says.

I nod, but I'm tempted to ask him if anything is wrong.

Nick takes out his phone again and stares at it before texting more. I look at him and start replaying the other night in my head. When he said things "didn't feel right," I kind of suspected he meant more than just hooking up. The feeling gets so much stronger as the lights go down and the previews start. Nick and I usually hold hands as we comment on which movies we'd like to see, and make fun of each other for our different tastes—I like action flicks while he prefers quirky ensemble indie stuff. But tonight, we silently stare straight ahead at the screen, our hands folded in our laps.

Two hours later, the end credits begin to roll and I barely know what I watched. While my body was slouched in this chair next to Nick, my mind was churning with fragments of memories from the Prism and visions of Thatcher that made my skin prickle with heat. I'm anxious to get home, and from the way Nick is glued to his phone once the lights come back up, it seems like he can't wait to leave either.

In the lobby, we see a bunch of people from school waiting to get into the nine o'clock show. Nick fist-bumps with a buddy of his, Eli Winston, grinning like he's happy to be blending in with a crowd. I can't help but feel a little relieved that we suddenly have a distraction from the tension that's between us.

Then I hear a girl's voice call out.

"Hey, Nick."

I turn to see Holly Whitman waving at him, and try to ignore the hopeful, almost giddy tone in her voice. I'm used to girls sort of flirting with my boyfriend a little, but what surprises me is the sad look in her blue eyes when her gaze drifts toward me. Moments later, she leans toward one of her friends and whispers something, and the other girl starts staring at me too. It makes me so uncomfortable that I duck away to the bathroom for a while.

I guess I'm nervous that I'm going to get that reaction from everyone on the first day of school—pity for the girl who was in the coma, and gossip about everything that's happened to me. As we walk out of the theater and toward Nick's car, we're both stealing awkward glimpses of each other and fidgeting with our hands.

"Tired?" asks Nick when I cover my mouth to hide a yawn. I think it's the first word he's said to me since the movie started.

"A little bit."

"Rough day?" He opens the car door for me.

"Yeah. I had my last physical therapy appointment," I say, sliding into the passenger seat.

Nick walks around and gets behind the wheel. "I bet you're glad to be done with those."

"I am. It kind of makes me feel like things can go back to normal now. Know what I mean?"

I look up at his sweet, gentle face, and we stare at each other, like we're not sure what comes next.

Or if what I just said is actually possible.

He leans in quickly, like he wants to show us both that everything is fine, normal, and just as it was before. But when his lips meet mine, it feels forced, like he's trying too hard. We both are.

I pull back first, and I can't help but notice that his cheeks flush. Not with heat and excited energy, but with . . . regret, I think.

"Want me to come over tonight?" he asks, shifting around in his seat and turning the car on.

"Nah," I say. "I should probably get some rest."

"Callie McPhee back to almost full strength and . . . resting?" He glances at me and raises an eyebrow. "You're not gonna go do something crazy like go cliff diving or anything, are you?"

I shake my head with a smile. "That's the old Callie," I tell him. "I don't think I need to do that stuff anymore."

"You've changed," he says, and he sounds wistful somehow, though he never really approved of my daredevil ways in the past.

"Yeah." I have. "Is that bad?"

"No," he says quietly. "Well, I have to work tomorrow anyway so I should get to bed too."

Nick's been volunteering all year for Habitat for Humanity, building houses for people in need. I used to love to go to the sites and watch him—all broad shoulders and muscled chest, hammering away in the blazing sun. I'm still attracted to Nick, I realize, looking into his caring brown eyes, but it's so much different from the way I feel about Thatcher. Now that I've stopped taking the pills, my emotions seem stronger, and less like echoes and hints of things I used to know.

I tuck a loose strand of hair behind his ear. "You're such a good guy. You know that, right?"

He gives me a skeptical look, but before I can say more, he pulls out of the parking lot and we drive home, silence overtaking us again.

When I get back to my room, I sit down at my desk and reach for my phone, pulling up the photo I took this afternoon. The ivory tiles of my bathroom are reflected in the foggy mirror with traces of his fingers on it.

No more pills. I need you to be aware.

And then, the answer to my question: *Yes.*

The image calms me. It's there. It's real.

I unplug my laptop and bring it into bed with me. Then I type "Thatcher" into the search box . . . but I don't know his last name. Did I once? I close my eyes and try to recall google-able details, but all I see are full lips and stormy blue eyes, a light stubble on his sharp jawline, and the way his shoulders stood—alert and strong, always.

Larson.

His last name enters my mind without warning, and my fingers type it in and hit Enter. The first result is an obituary.

Thatcher Larson, 18, died on Saturday, November 30, the result of a boating accident on the upper Wando River.

Thatcher was a lifelong Charleston resident and a cornerback for the West Ashley Wildcats. He was a lover of nature and animals, a friend to all he met. He was a member of the National Honor Society and president of the Outdoor Club. He spent time volunteering with the library's Never Too Old to Start Reading literacy program.

Thatcher is survived by his mother and father, Lauren and Joseph Larson; his sister, Wendy Larson; paternal

grandmother, Rosie Larson; maternal
grandmother, Emma Phanor; and numerous
aunts, uncles, and cousins.

After that there are notes about his memorial service, logistics. Seeing it spelled out in black and white is part comforting, part devastating. He's not a boy I invented in my head, a figment of my imagination that developed after my accident. He's real. Or he was, once.

I pause for a moment, thinking about a little boy who grew up loving animals, playing ball, helping people learn to read. My eyes fill with tears, but I wipe them away because I don't want to get caught up in the emotion. I'm on a quest for information.

My fingers fly across the keys as I try to find out who he was, and why I feel like I know him so intimately, so completely.

He died ten years ago. He doesn't have an online profile the way everyone today does, but I click on links that appear lower and lower on the search page, and I piece together that he was a decent cornerback, but not the full-scholarship kind; he was a Boy Scout for about two years; and he once had a photo in a local art show. I click on another link and see a picture of a black Lab, tongue lolling and eyes full of mischief. I smile, and a memory washes over me.

Thatcher is telling me that he once had a dog named Griz. The dog in the photo. We were walking through White Point Gardens; we shared moments as if we were alive. But he was dead. And I was . . . well, I'm not sure what I was.

I stare at the picture of Griz, imagining Thatcher on the other side of the camera. Photography feels right for him. He was always watching me as if through a lens, removed in one sense but also more intense and up close than the way normal people look at you. Like he saw the details. My details.

I swallow, and I remember something else about the Prism—I couldn't feel any physical parts of myself. No sunshine on my face, no ground under my feet, no breath in my lungs. But though those things were missing, there was also a deeper aspect to the Prism—the kinetic connection of Thatcher's being with mine. The way I felt when he was near.

When I let myself click on a link about the accident, the night he died, two other names appear. And though they're not really in bold, they leap out from my screen.

Reena Bell
Leo Cutler

A small ache begins at the base of my skull as the names connect with the voices I heard in my dream the other night—and the tight pressure I felt around my neck before I woke up. The more I let their names float in my mind, the colder I feel, so I refocus on reading the news articles attached to the link.

TRAGIC ACCIDENT CLAIMS THREE YOUNG CHARLESTONIANS

DEADLY TEEN BOATING INCIDENT INVOLVED ALCOHOL

HOMECOMING NIGHTMARE: TRIO DROWNS IN UPPER WANDO

The three of them all died together after a homecoming dance, drowning when their rowboat tipped over in the upper Wando River. How terrifying that must have been. Another girl who was with them, Hayley Krzysiek, survived. Thatcher told me this story, as we got closer. I remember listening patiently, quietly, as he struggled to tell me everything that happened.

I check out another article and it mentions that there's a memorial bench in the downtown cemetery where Thatcher is buried that honors the three of them. I email the location to myself before I move on with my research.

Now I look up each of their names, one at a time. The calm stillness of the night feels almost reverent as I click the keyboard.

Reena Bell, a star cheerleader for West Ashley, beloved daughter of Lydia Bell and Sergeant Harris Bell, older sister to Trenton Bell.

An army kid. I think I knew that.

Even in the black-and-white newspaper photo that's online, you can tell that Reena was beautiful—glossy raven-colored hair, smooth dark skin, doll-like brown eyes. Her smile almost pulses with joy. In the recesses of my mind, I think I can hear her laugh, and it's tinged with this sarcastic edge that seems both harmless and menacing all at the same time.

She said we were friends. But if that were true, why does my stomach churn when I look at that crack in my window?

When I turn to links about Leo Cutler, I find a ton of local news coverage about his football career. Apparently he was a defensive tackle for West Ashley, the kind of athlete who goes on to play in college. His photo, too, shows a buoyant, infectious grin, and his eyes hint at mischief—the good kind. But there's something about the planes of his face, his deep-set eyes, and close-cropped white-blond hair that gives me the chills.

By the time I've learned that Reena was a member of the 4-H Club and Leo used to assistant-coach a peewee football team, my eyes are glossing over. It's close to two in the morning. I need to sleep. I click one last link on a search of Thatcher's name, and I find a small, personal page run on one of those easy-blog sites. It has a few photos from his memorial and it lists the program: a reading by an uncle, donations to United Way of South Carolina in lieu of flowers, and a link to "When You Say Nothing at All" by Alison Krauss, "a song for Thatcher."

I make a mental note to look up this song, and then I let my head fall back onto the pillow, my eyes starting to close, weighed down with the heaviness of the brutal reality.

The more I learn about Thatcher, the more alive he seems.

When I wake up in the morning, I feel two things: energetic and annoyed. I realize that in order to do what I need to do today, I have to text Carson. I'm still mad about her giving my number to that reporter, but the anger will have to wait.

Me: Pick me up?
Cars: Where are we going?
Me: Adventure. 10 mins.

Five

THATCHER LARSON, AGE EIGHTEEN, is buried in a small cemetery in northern Charleston.

This knowledge stirs within me as the breeze musses my hair. Carson's got the top down on her convertible VW Bug, and she's following my navigation instructions excitedly.

"Are we going to see Nick at his Habitat site?"

"No."

"Too bad. You know how I love sweaty, shirtless boys."

Carson's trying to make me smile, but I keep my mouth still, eyes on the road. She's undeterred by my silence. "Are we driving across town to check out the new J.Crew? I hear it's *huge*."

"No."

"Oh." Her shoulders slump. "Wait. Are we really going grocery shopping for my mom like you told your dad?"

"Stop guessing. Please."

At a red light, I feel my best friend turn to look at me. "Are you mad at me?"

"No."

"You *are*," she says, surprised. "What did I do?"

"Nothing," I say, almost wishing I'd called for a taxi this morning. I couldn't very well ask my father to take me to a cemetery without an explanation, but I need some time to absorb what I've learned in the past twelve hours.

"Seriously, Callie, you're mad," she says, turning back to the road as the light turns green. "I can tell, and I don't know what I did but I wish you'd just say it."

"Remember when we were little and we used to play the trust game?" I ask her.

It was this thing we did where one of us would blindfold the other and then lead her to a secret location, usually under a tree in Carson's backyard or by the riverbank in mine. Then the blindfolded person had to touch, taste, and smell something and try to guess what it was. Often it was a cattail or a magnolia—harmless. But it's surprisingly hard to guess what something is when sight is taken out of the equation. And we had to trust that we wouldn't lead each other somewhere dangerous, or make each other taste something really gross.

"Of course," says Carson.

"Well, this is like that," I tell her. "No questions, Cars, please. Just give me a ride, okay?"

She nods, always up for anything she can think of as a game.

I sit back, relieved, as I direct her to turn in to the cemetery gates.

Carson raises her eyebrows, but doesn't say a word. The trust game is in effect.

The website for the cemetery actually had a feature called "find a grave," which is creepy but helpful, so I have instructions on how to walk directly to Thatcher's spot. The memorial bench is supposed to be near it, too. I guess it was his family who sponsored it.

Carson follows behind me, uncharacteristically silent. Partly because of the game and partly because of our hallowed location, I'm guessing.

We take a left turn past military headstones dotted with small American flags and I notice a sad stone lamb marker overgrown with moss. We climb up a steep hill in the early morning sunlight, and my walking slows—and not just because of the incline. Carson slows, too, looking at me questioningly, but I turn away from her and keep walking. My legs are holding up; the pain I've been fearing since I've stopped the pills hasn't come. Still, my pace begins to slow, because I'm wondering: What do I hope to see?

As we trudge up to the blinking blue dot on my phone, my rational self is thinking, *He's in a grave. That's where I'll find him.* But now that I'm about to face the place where his physical body rests, my heart begins to ache. Thatcher's body is here, but I know that his soul isn't.

Where is he? He was in my bathroom yesterday afternoon. That I know. Is he here now? I try to sense him but I don't feel his presence. Can I trust my own instincts?

As slowly as we're walking, we do eventually reach the top of the hill, where Thatcher's grave should be. There are a dozen stones, all lined up in a row like straight-backed soldiers. I take a deep breath and begin to finger the amber heart around my neck, working it up and down its chain.

Carson coughs from behind me, and I jump—I'd almost forgotten she was here.

"Can you wait?" I ask her, and she nods and stops walking as I move up one more row.

When I position myself to read the names, it's the first one I see, almost as if my eyes were drawn to it by magnetic force.

Thatcher Larson.

My body stills, my face frozen as my eyes scan the words.

Beloved son and brother.

Ashes to ashes, dust to dust.

I let go of the pendant, reaching out my hand to trace the engraved lettering. As I press my fingers into the indentations, sliding over each letter one by one, I feel my lip quivering. I know he's dead, but seeing his name spelled out here in gray stone still seems so shocking to me. Not too long ago, I kissed Thatcher, and I don't think I've ever felt that alive in my life.

I remember a field trip to a Civil War cemetery back in second grade. We made art projects from the graves by placing thin paper on the tombstones and rubbing a piece of black chalk over it so that the words showed up on the paper. But those were people from the past . . . not people I know. Knew. *Know.*

I drop my head to the ground as a tear slips down my cheek.

Thatcher's body, or at least what remains of it, is six feet underneath me now. Has been for more than ten years . . . since the night he died.

I look back at the grave.

I won't let you go. I say it aloud then, in a quiet whisper, though I can't feel his presence right now. Still, maybe he can hear it: "Thatcher, I'm not letting you leave me."

Instead of turning my face down to the ground, I lie on my back, over the grass that covers his coffin, and look up into the sky. What if I had really let go of this world? I'd be with him now, with Thatcher in the Prism. My heart pricks at the thought of it—at the horrifying wish I almost have. A wish to have died.

The relentless South Carolina sun is strong even this early in the morning, and it beats down on me. I feel a trickle of sweat make its way from my forehead to the crook of my neck. But I don't close my eyes. I look right into the bright blue.

Carson's shadow breaks my trance.

I sit up, feeling nervous, not ready to explain myself or what's happening, not sure what to say.

She reaches her hand out to help me up, and I take it. She doesn't ask any questions, just glances at the grave and then moves to sit down on a bench under a tree nearby. She pats the space next to her.

We're quiet for a few minutes, but I can feel my best friend getting restless.

Finally, she breaks the silence. "Okay, so I know we're playing the trust game, but does that mean I'm not allowed to talk?"

I feel my anger at her soften. "No, it's okay."

"Phew, because that was hard." She looks at me now, her eyes serious. "Does this cemetery have something to do with what you saw on the other side?"

I try to keep my face still, but I realize I can't hide much from Carson when she says, "Callie, I've believed in this stuff my whole life. I've read books about hauntings and theories about good ghosts and bad ghosts and Heaven and Hell. Not that I think you'd know anything about Hell—of course you'd have gotten more close to Heaven—and you probably didn't encounter any demons or deal with scary things like poltergeists or whatever but . . ."

She pauses and looks at me as my mouth drops open.

Poltergeists. The word makes my heart jump in fear when she says it, opening my mind to a rush of memories I'm not ready for. Images of Reena and Leo . . . and them using me for some kind of sick, twisted game. I take a deep breath. I have to play this off— Carson is sharp and I don't want to give her any reason to keep pressing me when there's so much I have to piece together yet.

"I can't believe you're rambling like this," I tell her.

"Callie, stop holding out on me! You must have seen something, you must remember what you saw while you were in the coma. What was it like? Please tell me."

"Why? So you can give a quote to Pete Green from the *Post and Courier*?"

Carson's face looks like I've slapped her, and instantly I regret my harsh tone. But I'm not letting her off the hook.

"You gave him my number." It's a fact. An accusation.

"I did," she admits. "But only because he's a friend of my mom's from high school so I know he's a decent person—he could tell your story, Callie; he'd be fair to you."

"There *is* no story," I say.

"Oh yeah? Well then why are we here, at the grave of someone who died ten years ago, with you acting more emotional than I've seen since . . . well, ever!"

I look down at the bright green grass under our feet.

"I'm not emotional," I say defensively.

"More emo than Nick at a Bon Iver show," she says, and I stifle a smile.

"I don't think so."

"Okay, not that emo," she says. "But pretty close. I just want to know why."

Her dark-brown eyes are shining with curiosity, and I realize that this is my best friend in front of me, and she's asking me legitimate, natural questions. I'm just not sure how to answer them. So I tell her the truth. Some of it.

"I don't know," I say. "I'm not sure what happened when I was in the coma. A few things I remember in detail, I think." I pause, a flash of Thatcher's achingly kind, frustratingly distant eyes in my head.

"There's the emo look!" says Carson.

I glance at the ground and wipe thoughts of him from my mind before I continue. "Other stuff is more hazy. Think about all the painkillers I've been on."

Carson nods. "I know it can't be easy."

"I haven't taken a pill since yesterday," I confide in her. "My dad thinks I'm still on them, but I want to stop feeling so foggy-brained."

No more pills. Clear your mind.

"Do you feel okay?" asks Carson. "Are you in pain?"

"Not really," I tell her. "I need to get my head straight, even if it means I hurt a little. But Cars, you can't talk to the press. Please. What happened to me isn't even certain enough for me to tell you about it, and it's definitely not something I want to hash out with reporters. Don't you get that?"

She nods, and then her eyes meet mine. There's an apology there—I can see it plain as day.

"I just think it's such a blessing," she says. "You almost crossing over and then coming back to life. It's a miracle. People want to know what it was like. *I* want to know what it was like."

"I know," I tell her. "And I will share as much as I remember with you, once I figure out what was real and what wasn't."

"Promise?"

"Promise."

Carson moves forward to give me a hug and I lean into her, relishing this affectionate touch. And I remember how in the Prism we moved around each other, with space between us. Touching was dangerous, touching was . . .

My eyes flash open as I recall the energy pulls I felt when I was touched in the Prism. When I shared my energy.

Suddenly, a wave of sensation starts to tingle in my toes, washing up through my body in a whoosh, a swell of energy. It starts out as a buzz, but then it escalates into an uncomfortable electricity that's shocking in its intensity. I let go of Carson and stumble off the bench, sinking to my knees as I close my eyes and let my hands feel the soft, mossy earth.

"Callie? Are you okay?"

Carson is bending by my side but her voice sounds far away. All I can feel is the sparking and burning that's happening inside my body. I open my eyes, forcing my mind to stop tricking me, letting my eyes and ears show me what's real, what's solid. My hands grip the ground until my fingernails hit dirt, and then the crackling pulses that undulate in every fiber of my physical body start to ebb.

I lean back against the leg of the bench with a long breath.

"I'm fine," I tell Carson.

"Maybe you need to rethink the meds," she says. "Just for another few days until your body's healed some more."

I shake my head no. I try to tell myself that the jolt of pain I just felt is normal after what my body has been through. It's because of the accident, whatever's left in my system of the pills, the physical trauma I've experienced.

But a part of me wonders if it was something else. Something more ominous.

I look up to ground myself in the world around me before my mind gets carried away. And that's when I come face-to-face with the plaque on the center of the bench.

Of course, the memorial bench.

Three names:

Thatcher Larson

Leo Cutler

Reena Bell

"Callie, what is it?"

Carson catches me staring at the names, and I realize that she knows me too well to be kept in the dark.

"Those people," I tell her, gesturing at the plaque. "I met them . . . on the other side."

"You did?" Her eyes light up.

I look up at the branches of the tree above us, and I remember a moment in a cemetery like this one, where Leo and a friend were shaking branches and frightening people on a ghost tour.

"Reena and Leo, they were the types of ghosts who liked to mess with the Living."

"Like moaning and slamming doors?" asks Carson. I can tell she's letting her mind run wild with the ghost stories she's heard.

"Something like that," I say. And then I start to tell her what I'm remembering as it comes to me. Because maybe sharing it out loud will help everything come together inside my brain. "I spent time with Leo and Reena, walking on the beach, going to a café, almost pretending we were alive. They made me laugh; I had fun with them at first."

"That sounds cool!" Carson smiles at me. "But why do you look so sad?"

"They weren't really my friends," I say, and as I talk to Carson my memories are becoming clearer. "The way Reena taught me to move objects, the way she asked me about my life and shared her friends with me, it was nice. But something wasn't right."

"What wasn't right?"

The word *poltergeists* reenters my mind, and now the underside of Reena, Leo, and their friends is coming into full view. When their smiles faded, I saw that they were angry and bitter, hatching some kind of insane plan to live again. Reena was just using me. I had a special kind of energy in the Prism, and she drew on it because she knew it might get her what she wanted. All the poltergeists did. Thatcher tried to protect me from them as much as he could but . . .

Now that I'm alive, back on Earth, am I safe from them?

"Callie, what is it? What's wrong?"

I've gone silent, because it's getting harder and harder to fill up my lungs with air.

The further away I get from my last pain pill, the crisper my otherworldly memories become. And suddenly, nothing makes sense and the world seems mad. At first I thought it was the meds that were bringing on these visions, these phantom voices. The truth is, they were dulling them, erasing my memory of what happened during the time I was in that coma.

Because one thing is for sure: My body may have been in that hospital bed, but my soul sure as hell wasn't.

I stand up shakily.

"Let's go," I say to Carson. "I'm not feeling great."

"Of course." She hurries to hold my elbow and I keep an eye on the memorial bench as we make the descent down the hill to Carson's car, as if something might arise from beneath the grave to pursue us.

Six

"THE FILET MIGNON FOR Callie May; I'll have the rib eye."

My dad orders for me at our favorite restaurant downtown, where the staff all know us. Soft candlelight flickers on the clean, white-tiled walls, casting shadows in the antique mirrors and on the industrial-steel tables and chairs. This place is a mix of old and new, the past and the present coming together in a modern southern steakhouse. I love it here.

We're having a celebratory father-daughter dinner—it's the first time we've been out since the accident. Dad smiles at me as he tucks his napkin into his collar, a country-boy habit Mama never could break him of. I grin back and smooth the white linen napkin over my lap.

"How are you feeling?" he asks me.

"Good," I say, nodding as if to affirm it. "Really good."

Dad clears his throat. "I'm glad," he says.

The waiter brings over a basket of bread, still warm, with soft butter on the side. I lean forward to take a roll.

"I want us to be honest with each other," says my father. My knife freezes midbutter.

"Me, too, Daddy," I say, not meeting his eyes.

He reaches into his pocket and pulls out an empty pill bottle. "Carla found this in the trash when she was cleaning your bathroom." He sets it down on the table between us, next to the still-steaming bread basket. There is supposed to be at least half of the prescription in there, but now there's nothing left. "Do you have an explanation for this?"

My mouth opens as I start to lie, but I can't do it.

"I flushed them," I say softly.

As soon as I acknowledge it, though, I'm relieved. I hated miming the afternoon pill swallow in front of my dad, hated hiding my own strength from him.

"We talked about this," he says. "I thought we agreed that following doctor's orders was what was best."

"I know. But I'm feeling much better, I swear."

His eyes are questioning and doubtful, so I try to be a little less cavalier. "Okay, I have a few aches, but no real pain," I tell him, dismissing the sharp crackle I felt at the cemetery with Carson. That was a one-time thing—it hasn't happened again. "And my mind isn't as foggy. I feel like I'm thinking clearly, for the first time in forever."

"So you're back to your old self already, huh?"

"I guess so," I say. Inside, though, I feel very different. "I'm strong like you," I tell him, taking a bite of warm bread.

He laughs. "You sure are strong. But not like me. Like your mama."

I stop chewing for a moment, surprised that he mentioned her so casually. Usually any thought of Mama comes with a tortured look in his eyes and a glass of whiskey to chase her away. He misses her too much to think of her.

"You know," Dad continues, his voice quieting, "she hung on as long as she could in this life."

"I know, Daddy." A lump forms in my throat. I remember when she got sick, how she grew weak but kept a smile on her face for me, always lighting up when I came into the room. Even at the end, under the harsh hospital lights. For me, she glowed with love.

"She waited for you," he says.

"What?"

"She was ready to die, but she waited for you to get there. She wanted you to be the one who let her go."

His words hit me in the chest. They remind me of what Thatcher told me, that my mother was able to move on to Solus, the final stage after the Prism, only after I got over her death. My eyes cloud with tears and I take a sip of water, hoping that I won't cry at the table.

"I'm sorry, Callie—I'm upsetting you."

"No." I shake my head. "It's okay. I like hearing about her."

"Well, I just thank the Lord that he let you stay here with me," says Dad. "I talked to him all the time while you were in the hospital. I begged him not to take my other girl, and he listened. We should be grateful for every day we have together, Callie."

I look at him sideways. My father's not much for God talk, especially out in public and surrounded by strangers. Still he makes a good point about being grateful for being together, because I'm beginning to learn just how painful it is to be separated from someone you have an unbreakable bond with.

When our steaks arrive, Dad bows his head in prayer, and I instinctively mimic him, though we don't usually say grace in restaurants. I guess this is a new thing, and it feels kind of comforting.

"We thank you, Father, for the food we are about to receive. Tonight we celebrate the miracle of Callie's life, and the special gifts you've bestowed upon her."

I open one eye to peer at him. What gifts is he talking about? Does he know about the Prism? About my connection with Thatcher?

No . . . he can't.

I close my eyes again and wait for the *Amen.*

On the ride home, I'm a bit shell-shocked by our conversation. That dinner was more intense than I expected. Usually Dad chews his steak and we talk about sports or a documentary he just saw or something. I wasn't prepared for him to talk to me about the day Mama died—or how he begged God not to take me away from him. I'm not sure where any of it came from, or if I was quite ready to hear any of it.

"Look," says my father, slowing down at a red light behind a big green truck. There's a bumper sticker that reads FUBAR, and he says, "Remember when you asked me what *FUBAR* stood for?"

I let out a snort. "Fully and Utterly Bad and Wrong!"

"I had to think of a clean version on the fly," he replies, smiling.

"Well, I guess you conveyed the general meaning."

We both laugh until our eyes fill up with joy tears, and a small spot of happiness settles into my heart. I can't remember the last time being with him was this easy. And it shouldn't be, considering that he knows I've been lying to him about the pills. The father I knew six months ago would have given me a stern lecture and probably even grounded me for "not following orders."

But maybe being grateful for every day we have together means not letting things come between us and keep us at arm's length. Maybe it means giving each other more room to be who we are and loving each other in spite of the fact we might not see everything eye to eye.

My feelings bubble over as we step out of the car, and I rush up to him for a hug.

"Whoa, what's all this?" he asks, squeezing me back.

"I just . . . ," I start. "I really love you, Daddy."

He kisses the top of my head. "Me too."

When I get up to my room, I shut the door and sit down at my desk to open my laptop. My search history shows their names: Thatcher Larson, Reena Bell, Leo Cutler. It would be so easy to go down this rabbit hole again, trying to find clues to trigger all of my memories and a way to call out to Thatcher. I close my eyes and turn inward, concentrating, and I can feel his presence, like a gentle hand on my back, an impression on my skin.

He's here with me. But I can't see him, I can't talk to him.

My computer dings with an iTunes update. I click to cancel it, and that's when I remember the song. The one they played at Thatcher's memorial. I download it and press Play.

It's amazing how you can speak right to my heart.

Without saying a word, you can light up the dark.

The first verses send my pulse racing as a montage of images runs through my mind. Thatcher, greeting me in the mist of the Prism right after my crash, guiding me on Earth and teaching me patience and restraint in my haunting, standing always out of reach until his walls came down and we . . . what did we do? Fall in love? Me and a ghost?

A laugh-cry escapes my lips, and I cover my hand with my mouth. Music always does this to me—sends my mind traveling over memories or wishes for what may come. Always reaching into my soul. Just like he did.

I press Play again when the song is over and I set it on repeat before I go to my bed to lie down. In the hazy place between sleep and waking, where emotions fill your body and dreams seem possible, I call to him. "Thatcher . . . Thatcher."

"Callie."

It's a whisper, a notion . . . but I hear it. His voice is like velvet—smooth and soft, draping a curtain over my reality. I can't tell if my eyes are open or closed when I see the outline of his shape, shimmering in front of me. I sit up and search for him with my hands, but they don't connect with anything. The air feels thicker where he is, but he's not solid. I lean back against my pillow on the bed. "Are you real?"

"I'm here." His voice is enough. For now.

"Thatcher—" I start.

"My mother loved this song," he says, and now I know that he *is* here, in my room and sensing everything around us. Even the music in the background. "It was playing—"

"At your memorial." I finish his sentence.

"Yes."

I feel a plane of warmth around me, like I'm pressed up against a brick wall that's been baked in the sun. I have so much to say to him, but I have no idea where to begin. My breath quickens as I try to figure it out, but then I remember something else I learned in the Prism that instantly relaxes me.

All the thoughts and feelings that I'm having—Thatcher is already aware of them. The sense of intuition and perception that spirit guides have is incredible. So in a way, the pressure of saying the perfect thing to him is totally off. And oddly enough, I've never had that with anyone in my life. Not even Nick.

With that last thought, my body tenses up. I wonder if Thatcher has been witness to everything since I awoke from the coma, including private moments that Nick and I shared in this very room.

"Are you with me all the time now?" I ask him.

"No. I'm here often, to see how you're doing, but I have to return to the Prism when my energy gets low. And there's also . . . other business to attend to."

"Right." I sigh, a little relieved, yet still feeling a bit foolish for ever thinking he would devote all of his time to me.

"I've felt your knowing."

"What?"

"You can sense when I'm here, Callie, can't you?"

There have been times when I think I've felt him near me, as well as a strange coldness that makes it seem like he's far away, but I wasn't sure if my impression of him was real or not.

Until now.

"Yes, I think I can."

"The way we're connected, it's . . . unique," he says. And I think his voice sounds almost loving, but I'm afraid I'm wishing for that more than hearing it.

I'm about to ask him why this connection of ours is different from what he has with anyone else. But all of a sudden, something in the room changes. It's an invisible shift, as if someone opened a door on a bright winter day, letting in a chilling wind.

Although I can't see Thatcher's face clearly or his remarkably blue eyes, I sense his gaze turning serious, like he's holding back his feelings so that he can tell me something important.

"Are you off the pain meds completely?" he asks.

"Yes."

"Good. Thank you."

"I got your message," I say.

"That took a lot of energy. I had to go back to the Prism for a while after that."

"It was a bold move," I tell him. Thatcher, the consummate rule follower, surely wasn't supposed to scrawl something on a mirror for a living person to see. It's a breach of worlds.

I hear the conflict in his voice when he responds. "I had to do it."

"Why?"

He doesn't answer right away, but then he says, "Unclouded thinking is always best."

Thatcher sounds exactly like he did when we were in the Prism together, teaching me about things that I didn't even know mattered, changing me forever.

"It's strange. My mind is getting clearer, but what I'm remembering sometimes seems so unreal that I don't trust myself."

"You should. You've had good instincts from the beginning. You were more aware and alert than anyone else I'd ever worked with."

I feel a big twinge of insecurity when he says that, like we were just business partners or something, but that fades away when my thoughts wander back to the words I wrote in my journal, the ones I thought came from Thatcher: *I'll find them. I'll protect you.*

I remember the fear I felt in the cemetery, and I have to ask him: "Thatcher, am I in danger?"

"You're alive, and that means you're safe."

"But what about the polt—" I start.

"Callie, you shouldn't worry about anything that happened before. It's best if you move forward, live today's life."

Move forward. Does that mean he wants me to forget him?

"I can't." It's a whisper, soft and pleading, because the truth is that I don't want to let go of him or our time together. I don't want him to ask that of me.

"You *can*," he says. "That's what I came here to tell you. I know you've been through a lot, more than anyone could ever imagine. But you have a real second chance, and I want you to embrace it and really *live*." He pauses for a moment, and I can feel how reluctant he is to say what's coming next. "Which is why you have to turn your back on everything you experienced while you were in a coma. Thinking about the Prism or me or anything else from that time is just going to interfere."

"I don't understand. You told me to stop taking the pills and it made me remember more," I say. "If you wanted me to forget, why did you—"

"I wanted you to know that you weren't crazy. That you didn't hallucinate or imagine any of the things you saw. I didn't think you'd be able to be true to yourself if you believed your mind was playing tricks on you."

I curl my legs into my chest and breathe in deeply, letting the sweet air fill my lungs. I missed that when I was nearly dead, I realize. That feeling of my chest expanding and releasing a soothing sigh.

"You have no idea how remarkable you are." Even though his shape is barely visible, Thatcher's voice fills the corners of my room, nestling into the crevices of my bookshelf, enveloping the window seat and the bed, covering me like a blanket. "No one else has ever been to the Prism and returned to Earth like you did. Coma victims usually don't come to the Prism—they linger on Earth until they die or wake. But you . . . you've seen both sides."

"I have. So how can I forget what I saw? What I felt?"

"What you felt?"

He's going to make me say it—make me tell him that I love him. "Yes," I say. "What I felt."

The room goes quiet, and for a moment I'm afraid he's vanished. But then Thatcher speaks again. "You're back with your family and friends," he says. "You have your whole life in front of you. Anything you might have felt in the Prism doesn't matter now."

"Doesn't matter?"

"Callie, don't make this harder on us," he says.

And the sound of those two letters—*us*—lets me know that he felt it, too, that he remembers we did much more than "work" together. His voice deepened in that last moment, and I feel a strange tingling sensation near my ear and running down along my chin, like Thatcher is trying to caress my face.

"The people you really care about are all here—your father, Carson . . ." He pauses, and then he says, "Nick."

As soon as he says Nick's name, the tingling is gone.

"He truly adores you," Thatcher says, like he's trying to remind himself not to cross a line with me.

"I know," I mumble. I want to say that I adore Nick, too, but our relationship doesn't come close to the completeness that I feel right now, at merely the sound of Thatcher's voice. I can't even see him, and yet at the same time he's all I need.

And then he lets an admission slip: "I wish I could . . . be there for you in that way."

My throat tightens as I swallow down a lump of sadness that threatens to rise up and spill into tears.

Thatcher laughs, a small, rueful sound. "I'm almost jealous."

"There's nothing to be jealous of," I tell him, and as I say it, I know it's true. What I have with Nick isn't what I have with Thatcher.

But what Thatcher said is true, too. He's not a part of the physical world, the way Nick is. And as hard as it is for me to acknowledge right now, Thatcher can't give me a future of togetherness. All he could offer me is a life of separation and him haunting me from a place I'll never see again . . . until I die.

"Oh, but there is," says Thatcher. And then I feel a whisper of a touch on my forehead, like he's kissing me good night. I lift my face, hoping that I'll feel the same light pressure on my lips, but then suddenly the temperature drops in the room, causing me to shake.

He's gone. And when I wake up the next morning, I only have a vague sense that Thatcher was with me.

Like it was all a dream.

Seven

"CALLIE, YOU HAVE *GOT* to pay attention!" Carson snaps her fingers in front of my face and I blink.

"Sorry," I say. "What was the question?"

"Classic navy striped dress with ballet flats, or cooler eyelet lace mini with cut-out ankle boots?"

She's holding two potential first-day-of-school outfits in front of me as I lie on my stomach across her fluffy rose-dotted comforter. I'm sleeping over at her house for the first time since I've been out of the hospital—Dad's been reassured by how well I've done off the meds, and the doctor cleared me to start school with everyone else on Monday.

"Both are cute," I say, rolling over onto my back with a sigh.

"Okay, you could not care less," says Carson. "I know that. Indulge your best friend."

I close my eyes and reach out, grabbing one of the outfits. "This one!" I say.

"Callie, this is *serious*," says Carson, throwing the clothes and their hangers onto the chair in the corner.

"It's really not," I tell her. But I sit up with a grin.

"Fine," she says. "I'll decide tomorrow. But I do want to finish our conversation from the other day."

"What conversation?"

"In the cemetery," she says, her eyes shining with anticipation. "Remember, you said you knew those people whose names were on the plaque, and that you were friends with them but that something wasn't right?"

I look down. Now that I've seen Thatcher, I have the feeling he wouldn't want me talking about the Prism. But I've already told Carson something about that world, and my best friend is not someone who lets these things go.

"Can I take a rain check on that conversation?" I ask her. "I'm sorry . . . I'm just not up for it right now."

She looks disappointed, but I can tell she doesn't want to push me too much.

"Why don't you tell me more about the gossip that happened while I was in the coma," I say. "I want to be caught up for school on Monday. What'd I miss? Who's fighting? Who's in love? Who got drunk and hooked up?"

It's a lame attempt to change the subject because Carson knows I don't really care about stuff like that, but she reacts strangely. She freezes for a moment, and her face looks stricken. Then she moves slowly to a spot on the bed next to me, her eyes glistening with tears.

"Cars, what is it?"

She averts her gaze. "I wanted to tell you sooner, but . . ."

The pause is excruciating. "*What?*" I ask finally.

Her face crumples. "Um, it's about Nick."

"What about Nick?"

Another pause. "Two things." I can tell the tears are about to come streaming down her round cheeks. "I've been holding this in and I don't think I can do it anymore and I have to tell you because if I don't I'm going to go crazy and—"

"Geez, Carson! What is it?"

"IthinkIkissedhimwhenIwasdrunk."

She says it in such a gush—"I think I kissed him when I was drunk"—that if I didn't already know about this, deep down, I'd probably have to ask her to repeat it. Carson covers her face with her hands, peeking out through her fingers to see my reaction.

I close my eyes, though, because I'm picturing a moment in my mind, a vision that's been triggered: Reena using my energy to take control of Carson's body during a party at Tim McCann's house.

Carson's lips curving up in triumph. Carson straddling Nick and pressing her lips to his. Her hair falling over her neck as she leans down to . . .

I shake my head to try to stop the memory as it comes. I *saw* Reena enter Carson's body; I saw her *possess* my best friend and kiss Nick in that moment, right after he said . . . that he was planning on breaking up with me.

How did I forget that? Those words came out of his mouth—he even told Carson. But the real Carson wasn't there. She was already possessed. Thinking about it makes my skin crawl and my stomach ache, but I know it wasn't Carson who betrayed me—it was Reena.

As I open my eyes to stare at Carson now, I worriedly search for aftereffects of the possession in my best friend, scared that she might be physically weaker or somehow mentally changed. But thankfully I see nothing different about her at all—Carson is Carson. The possession doesn't seem to have hurt her.

Once that fear has worn off—temporarily, at least—I'm aware that it wasn't her fault . . . and yet, as she looks at me nervously, I feel an arch in my back, a heaviness in my chest. My Nick. She kissed him. I'm surprised at myself. Maybe . . . maybe the boy who's alive has more of a hold on me than I thought.

She drops her hands and grabs mine. "Oh, Callie, I'm so sorry. I don't what came over me. I would *never, ever* do something like that to you! But I know it happened and I'm just . . . I hope you can forgive me."

"It's okay. Grief can do strange things to people," I say to her. It's something Thatcher said to me in the Prism, and it's true. So true that I can't help but wonder if my little fit of jealousy over Nick just now wasn't a piece of me grieving what is clearly the slow fizzling-out of our relationship.

"You don't hate me?"

"No. I don't think I could hate you if I tried."

"Is that because you have a newfound appreciation for life and love and some kind of wisdom that makes you not get mad at your best friend who kissed your boyfriend? Because, goodness gracious, Callie, that is generous of you!"

I want to tell her that I'm not being generous, and another vision of what Reena did to her comes tumbling back to me. Part of me wonders if I should tell Carson, but I should talk to Thatcher first. He said I wasn't in danger anymore, and I want to believe that means Carson is safe too. Even though I trust him, it's hard not to worry, now that I've fully remembered how powerful Reena and her "friends" really are.

I swallow hard and attempt a smile. "Carson, a lot of weird things happened while I was in that coma. Let's add this one to the list."

She hugs me tightly.

"Thank you for telling me," I whisper into her hair.

She pulls back and grins. "I had to. The guilt was eating me alive."

"So. You said there were two things . . . ?"

"Right." She smoothes the comforter under her hands.

"Well, what is it?" I'm truly afraid if the second thing is harder to say than the first.

"I didn't want to mention it, because Nick was in a really bad place and even drinking a lot during the summer but he's stopped that and it seems like things are good with you guys now and I just—"

"Carson!" My patience for her rambling is just about gone.

"Nick was talking to Holly Whitman a lot while you were . . . away."

"Holly Whitman? Seriously?"

She nods, eyes wide, afraid of my reaction.

Nick and Holly. That's what I heard in her voice at the movie theater—it wasn't pity for me; it was sadness that she wasn't standing in my place. For all I know, she was the person he was texting the whole night, too.

I feel my jaw clench. Another visceral reaction to someone else being with *my boyfriend*. But this is different. It's not about Holly wanting Nick. It's about Nick wanting to be with Holly. And even though I've just remembered that he'd wanted to end things with me before my accident, I think about how supportive, sweet, and kind he's been to me since I've woken up, and now all of our time together seems a bit false and forced. Like it was between us the other night.

I finger the amber pendant that I haven't taken off since Nick fastened the clasp for me last week, and I take a deep breath in. I remind myself that when I was in the coma, I was falling for someone else too. I was discovering a whole new part of myself that I didn't know existed and somehow Thatcher knew was always there. Maybe that's what Nick was going through with Holly, and if it was, I have no reason to judge him.

I open my eyes again. "Are they still . . . you know, interested in each other?"

"I don't think so," says Carson. "I haven't seen them together or anything since you woke up. . . ."

I've always known Nick to be a Good Person, and him keeping his distance from Holly is even more evidence of that. Which is why

I should let Nick go, let him be with her or whomever else he might want, even though he's still one of the most important people in the world to me. But as much as I hate to admit this, there's a part of my heart that's acting out of selfishness.

The person I've been longing for is a ghost, someone I can never be with. Having Nick near me, even if what we are to each other is changing, makes that feeling of loneliness somewhat bearable.

When I search my soul and try to sense Thatcher's presence, nothing is there and a tear trickles down one cheek. I wipe at it angrily, feeling like I'm a terrible person.

"Are you okay?" Carson hands me a tissue.

"I'm fine!" I snap at her, but when I see her hurt expression, I soften.

"It's not your fault, Cars," I say. "Things are just...complicated."

She reaches over to give me a squeeze, and I accept it, feeling a little less horrible about myself, thanks to her hug. "You know what might help?" she asks.

"Please not a *Hallowed Hauntings* marathon." I groan.

"I wouldn't do that to you!" says Carson, even though that's her favorite show.

"*Roman Holiday*?"

I smile. "Yes."

I want things to be like this, simple. Like before. So I try to push away my memories of the Prism for tonight, just like Thatcher wants.

We change into pajamas and tuck under Carson's covers, side by side on her bed as she streams our favorite sleepover movie.

When Gregory Peck comes on the screen, his cheekbones remind me a little of Thatcher . . . and my mind leaves Carson's room once again, floating into a wish where he comes back to me for more than just a speech about moving forward.

I fall into a fitful sleep before the scooter scene, and when I wake up in the morning, Carson is already dressed and sitting on the end of the bed, looking at me intently.

"Whoa, stalker," I say. "Why the crazy stare?" I push a wavy mass of my dirty-blond hair out of my eyes. Then I yawn and meet her gaze. Her lips are pursed in anticipation.

"What?" I ask again.

"You were talking in your sleep."

I try to play it cool. "And?"

"Just one question: Who's Thatcher?"

Eight

OUT ON THE PORCH, over a breakfast of bacon, eggs, and biscuits and gravy cooked by Carson's mother, aka the best cook this side of the Mississippi, I finally decide to spill it. The Prism, the Guides, Thatcher, my mission to heal my loved ones—Carson included—by haunting them in a subtle way, a soulful way.

I don't tell her how I felt, how I feel, about Thatcher. I can't put that into words yet—it's too painful. And I'm not sure now is the right time to talk about Reena's possession, and what she and Leo and the rest of the poltergeists were up to. I don't know how Carson would handle it. She has always believed in an afterlife but not necessarily one where people here could be actually threatened by those who have left the physical world.

"I was looking for signs from you *everywhere*," says Carson, her eyes glowing with excitement. "I knew you weren't trapped in that hospital. I could feel it."

I smile at her. I'm a little afraid to be sharing all of this, but it is so nice to be able to tell someone. And she takes everything I say as absolute truth, which is a relief since some of it sounds downright cuckoo.

"Were you hanging around with me a lot?" she asks. "Even when I went to the bathroom and when I was reading that romance novel I have tucked under my mattress? Oh! Were you with me when I googled my face crossed with Ryan Gosling's to see what our baby would look like?"

I laugh and throw my balled-up greasy napkin at her. "Of course not! I didn't have time to watch your every move. I would just visit you . . . sometimes."

Like Thatcher does with me now.

"Let me think," she says, and I know she's trying to recall the moments when she felt my presence.

"When I went on the ghost tour . . . And the radio station changed without me touching it . . ."

I nod. "I was there. But that wasn't the way I was supposed to haunt. Another ghost did that for me, changed the station, and Thatcher got really mad."

I think back to that night, to Leo interrupting Thatcher's teaching and stealing my energy to connect with Carson. In that moment I thought Leo's way was more fun and exciting. But I came to realize how wrong I was.

The poltergeists lure people with their charm, but all of it was just an act to reel me in and then use me for what they'd never have again.

A life force.

"Wait, why did Thatcher get mad?" asks Carson.

"Because there are Guides, and Thatcher's one of them. They teach you about real haunting—the kind that helps people truly move on from someone's death. It's soul to soul; it isn't physical."

Carson nods like she understands. "That night made me so sad," she says. "I thought you were there, but maybe trapped in some dimension and trying to escape or something. I didn't know what to do or how to help."

"That's just what Thatcher taught me—that kind of haunting can do more harm than good," I say. "It doesn't ease the Living; it makes them more anxious about your passing."

"The Living." Carson says it with a shiver. "But you were alive that whole time."

"I didn't know. I thought I was dead."

Carson reaches out across the table and touches my hand. "You should talk more about this—think of how many grieving people you could help. You could tell them that their loved ones want them to be okay. You've seen how it works!"

I pull my hand away quickly. "Don't start this again. It's private. I mean it. You have to promise me you'll keep all this to yourself."

She looks down at the table, but I see her nod.

"Seriously," I say.

"I promise. But I still think you should let people know what you saw."

"Your opinion is noted." I shove a forkful of grits into my mouth.

Carson looks back up at me. "The stuff about the haunting to help people move on is really beautiful. It makes perfect sense to me."

I nod as I chew, wanting to change the subject, now that she's pressed me more about making my story public.

"Your mom did that," she says.

I look up at her sharply.

"She haunted me," says Carson, not backing down.

Carson always told me how my mother would come see her when we were little, after she died. She said she felt Mama's presence, that Mama wanted me to know that she was okay. But we were little girls, just six years old, and no one would listen to Carson. Not even me.

Maybe deep down I believed her, but I was jealous. I guess I still am.

"Why didn't my mom haunt me that way?" I ask her.

"I don't know. Maybe she tried but you weren't open to it so she had to have me give you the message."

Carson says this gently, sweetly.

I take another bite of breakfast, and Carson asks, "So what kind of powers do you have now?"

I nearly spit out my eggs. "Powers?"

"Yeah, like can you still move things without touching them? Are you still . . . telekinetically inclined?"

I roll my eyes. "No," I say. "I don't think so."

"You haven't *tried*?" Carson shrieks in disbelief.

Her mom comes over to bring us more warm butter and we quiet down for a minute until she walks back to the kitchen.

"Go on, make that butter tray move," whispers Carson.

"That isn't how things work." I realize that I sound like Thatcher responding to me when I wanted him to teach me energy tricks in the Prism. How ironic is that? "Besides, I'm back in my body now. I don't think I can tap into energy the same way."

"I bet you can." She grabs my arm and closes her eyes, starting a deep hum.

"What are you doing?" I move away quickly.

"I'm trying to use your energy to connect with something!" She laughs lightheartedly, but I don't join in. What she just did reminds me too much of the way Leo and Reena and the poltergeists drew on my energy and started targeting people on Earth I cared about, hoping to take over their bodies and eventually their lives.

My stomach churns a little, the urge to tell her about the possession she experienced getting stronger every second, but something inside keeps telling me to wait and talk to Thatcher first.

Only I have no idea when that will be. I haven't felt the warmth of his presence since yesterday morning.

"Okay, fine, we can try to move something later," says Carson, still smiling. "So what happens after you haunt everyone and help them grieve? Do you go to Heaven then?"

"Sort of. There's a place called Solus that the Guides say is like Heaven. They call it *merging*, and it's what every ghost is striving for." Well, almost every ghost.

"How long does it take to get there?"

"I think it's different for everyone. Thatcher can't merge, because his little sister never got over his death."

I look over at Carson and her face falls. "Wow, that's so sad." Then she perks up and I see her *I have an idea* face. "If his sister—what's her name?"

"Wendy . . . Wendy Larson."

"If Wendy accepted Thatcher's death, then he'd be able to . . . what was it called?"

"Merging."

"Right. So if his sister got over his death, then he could merge into the Heaven place?"

"Solus." I pronounce it like *solace*.

"Solus," Carson echoes. "He could go there if Wendy moved on?"

"I think so." Carson's interest in this is starting to make me nervous.

"Why don't we help then?"

"Carson . . . no."

"Why not? If we can talk to her and tell her that Thatcher needs her to *get over it*—I mean we'll say it more nicely than that—she'll understand! She'll let go of him, and he can merge with Solus!"

Her face is shining—she's so excited to find that there's some truth to an afterlife, something she's always suspected existed. But I can't let her meddle—not with Thatcher.

"We can't," I say to her. "It's none of our business."

She looks at me sideways. "You don't want him to merge."

What? "Shut up. Of course I do!"

Her eyes light up with knowing. "You don't want him to leave you. You're in love with him," she says. "That's why you aren't crazy mad about Nick and Holly, why your head is always somewhere else. You're thinking of him. Maybe even talking to him! Oh my gosh, were you talking to him in your dreams last night? This is incredible. When you first met him, was it like you'd known him for a thousand years?"

Carson's smile is huge—it's like we're discussing a new crush. But that's not what this is. And I don't appreciate it.

"Stop mocking me."

"It *was* insta-love!" she says, missing my tone and clapping her hands together. "I guess that happens when you're in some crazy world. *I want to visit the Prism!*"

I stand up quickly and my empty orange juice glass falls to the ground and shatters.

We both stare at the shards of glass that glitter across the wide wooden planks of her porch, and I take a deep breath in. "This isn't a movie, Cars. This is my life, okay?"

She's quiet for a minute, and then her eyes leave the mess and meet my gaze.

"You haven't seen him since you woke up . . . ," she says, the notion dawning on her as she gapes at me.

I can't keep a flash of pain from working its way across my face.

"Only in a dream," I say. "I think."

"You've got to try to reach him again! Oh, Callie, if you help him haunt his sister it would be the ultimate act of love."

"I said stop!" I whisper harshly as I step away from the table, piling our plates and taking them inside so Carson won't be able to keep talking and try to convince me otherwise.

"Hi, Mrs. Jenkins." I smile brightly as I walk into the kitchen. I don't want her to know I'm upset.

"Callie, let me have those," says Carson's mom, taking the plates from my hands.

"I broke a glass out there; sorry." I walk to the pantry, where I know they keep the broom and the dustpan. When I turn back around to head outside, Carson is standing in front of me. She grabs the broom.

"If you love him," she whispers, so low that her mom won't hear, "you'll want to help him. You'll want to help his sister."

She places two small cloudy white crystals on the counter. "Here," she says. "Use these."

"What are they?"

"Selenite crystals—they're good for connecting with spirits, and for dream recall."

"This kind of thing doesn't work," I tell her. "It's just silly kids' stuff."

"Like the sage you wouldn't let me burn in your car that might have saved you from your accident?"

"Bad luck wasn't what made that truck hit me. I was on my phone. I was going ninety miles per hour."

"Still," she says, picking up the selenite and pressing it into my hand. "Just keep it with you. It might help—you never know."

I pocket the rocks so she'll stop talking.

"And one more thing." Carson puts her phone faceup on the counter and walks back outside.

I sigh and look at the screen, where Carson has found a listing for Wendy Larson. She's a junior at USC-Beaufort. She lives just over an hour away.

Nine

THE NEXT DAY IS the first day of school. At the last minute, I pick up the selenite crystals from where I left them on my nightstand. I don't know why I'm holding on to them—maybe because Carson has been more on point than I used to give her credit for, maybe because I'm a little afraid of facing the new year. For whatever reason, they're in my pocket.

I never noticed that my school has this *smell* to it. Not good, not awful, just . . . schooly. And the way people's feet fall on the linoleum, it makes a soft pattering noise, especially when there are dozens of us here all at once. The lights make everyone look slightly peaked, like they've just gotten over the flu, but at least we're on even ground in that respect.

And the energy at school—the *energy*. Last year I barely noticed anything beyond my own routine. But today I can almost feel the excitement, angst, nervousness, confidence, fear, hope . . . it's like the hallways are pulsing with emotion.

Nick is waiting by my locker with a single daisy. I smile and stick it behind my ear.

"Thanks," I say sincerely, trying to ignore the sadness that rises in my chest.

"Nervous?"

"No, why?"

"I don't know, coming back to school after a pretty traumatic summer . . . it could make even the steel-nerved Callie McPhee a little shaky." He grins his nice-guy grin, and I try to meet it with one of my own, but it feels so fake.

"I'm good," I tell him.

When Nick texted me last night to see if I wanted him to come over, I told him no. He didn't ask why; he just didn't come. I haven't seen him since the night we went to the movies. And in his absence, I've been closing my eyes before sleep and thinking about Thatcher. I've thought about the way we were in the Prism—how at first he kept his distance both physically and emotionally. He withdrew whenever I got close to him, but as we spent more time together, as we talked, it was like we were being drawn together by a force that neither one of us could understand.

Now he's telling me to turn away from the past, to forget him. And I wonder if he'll ever truly acknowledge what I think we both felt, for a moment, in the Prism.

When I think that, I feel a warm wave of air wrap around me, and I know that he's here. Not like he was the other night in my room, not up close, but nearby.

Thatcher.

I wish there was some way that I could acknowledge that he's here. Actually, I wish he really *were* here. Walking the halls with his friends, living the life that he never really got a chance to live. I feel an intense shot of guilt when I think about how much I have ahead of me, all the things I have to look forward to now that I'm back in my own skin again. This is what the poltergeists were fighting so hard to get—the feeling of being here and whole—and while Thatcher might be too noble to admit it, he has to miss some of this, doesn't he?

"Shall we?" Nick says, offering to walk me to my homeroom by taking my hand in his. And then I feel a cold breeze, though no windows are open here, and I know that he's gone. Thatcher left. Was it because Nick held my hand? I tell myself that Thatcher wouldn't be that petty. He has other people to watch over, other spirits to teach.

But as I suspected, there have to be things that he misses and wishes he could do.

Things that he's jealous of.

"Hey, Callie," says a girl I don't recognize, bringing me back to the present.

"Hey," I say back with a smile that I hope looks genuine. And then I notice that all up and down the hall there are people trying to catch my eye, say hi, smile. I guess I don't blame them—I'm the girl who was almost dead and then came back to life. I'd stare at me, too.

I take a deep breath in, remembering that when I was in the Prism and trying to connect with people on Earth, I would have done *anything* to be seen. And now I'm here, I'm alive, I'm walking through my high school hallway.

This is my second chance, like Thatcher said. And everyone around me knows it.

Pressure much?

As we walk by the main office, I feel a particularly intense gaze and I lock eyes with a slight boy with black hair and dark-framed glasses. His hands are folded across his chest, and while people swirl around him, making their way to class, he's staring at me full on, like I'm a specimen in a lab.

I look away quickly, glad to be turning a corner. I'm no more than a few doors down from homeroom when I feel Nick let go of my hand sort of abruptly. He says, "See you at lunch," and waves quickly before heading off down the hall, not giving me a chance to look him in the eye.

When I see Holly Whitman standing just a couple feet away from me, watching him walk away, it's pretty clear why.

The first day of school is always a throwaway work-wise, and today my mind wanders even more than usual. I can't possibly be expected to live this life of Advanced Algebra problems and World History reading. Not after what I've seen and felt, both in the Prism and since I've been back here. I have to fight the urge to look inward to the space where I can feel Thatcher's presence, and it's a struggle to stay in this world, mentally speaking.

My mind keeps drifting to Wendy Larson. Carson found her. How would Thatcher feel if I went to see her?

Carson meets me by my locker before lunch. As we walk to the cafeteria together, I see her wave across the hallway, and when I follow her eyes, there's the boy again—the one with thick-rimmed glasses and dark hair—grinning back at her.

"Who's that?" I ask her.

"Just a new guy," she says, without meeting my eyes. "He's an underclassman."

"Oh." I'm about to ask his name, but Carson barrels ahead.

"Have you decided what to do about Nick?" she asks.

"What do you mean? Did he say something to you?"

"No, but we have English together, and he just looked . . . unhappy."

"I know . . . things are pretty weird between us right now."

I want to tell her about what happened with Holly earlier, but I'm afraid that what Carson said about me not wanting to let go of Thatcher is also true about Nick—what if in my heart I want to hold on to both of them, so I won't have to choose between this life and the life I know is waiting for me once I truly am ready to leave this one? I can't imagine I'd be that selfish, but . . .

"At some point, you'll need to explain things to him," Carson says gently.

"Explain what?" I ask, lowering my voice to a whisper. "That I was in a world full of ghosts and I was trying to haunt him and I saw him self-destructing? That I know he was planning to break up with me?"

"He was?" asks Carson, looking surprised. "Why didn't you tell me that?"

"Sorry," I tell her. "I'm just starting to get things clear in my head, what I saw while I was . . . Anyway, that was his plan. Before the accident, I mean. I heard him talking about it. . . ." I pause, trying to remember what he'd said that night. When someone bumps into me from behind, I get self-conscious about people listening to us and we start walking again.

"Do you think he's still planning to—"

"I don't know." We step out of the main building and into the sunlight. The humid air hits my face and I take in a breath of the sweet honeysuckle vines growing along the brick wall as I finger the amber pendant around my neck. The one that Nick gave to me as a gift that meant he understood how much I missed my mom. It meant that he understood *me*.

"You love someone else, though. Maybe it's for the best."

"Yeah, but how is loving someone I can't ever be with for the best?"

"That's not what I mean," Carson says. "Maybe you need to let go of that someone else before you can love Nick—or anyone—again."

I give Carson side eyes. "This is not school-appropriate conversation."

She smiles. "I just think there's a clear path here," she says, pulling her phone out of her pocket.

She clicks to find Wendy's address again and makes me look at the screen.

I shake my head, nervous and wondering if Thatcher is aware that we've found Wendy.

Is that why he disappeared this morning? Because he knew what Carson had been bugging me to do?

"This doesn't feel right to me; I'm sorry, Cars."

We're about to walk into the cafeteria, but she pulls me to the side of the doors and around the corner toward the faculty parking lot. Then she gives me a Carson speech, complete with gestures and pacing and voice inflections that make her case:

"Okay, Thatcher isn't, like, constantly with you, declaring his love, so he obviously wants you to move on, as anyone who truly loved you would, because you have a chance to live a life—an *alive* life—again. But he's stuck in this in-between world where he can't merge with the beating heart of the universe or whatever because his little sister hasn't gotten over his death. And we have her address right here, plus all these updates for her about him and how he's okay and how it'll make him happy if she can move on. PS, it'll make her happy, too, because she won't be wallowing in grief. *And* it'll make your life easier because lover boy will have a happy ending."

"But—"

"I know it's not a Disney ending," says Carson, running over my protestation. "You and he won't get to walk into the sunset. But that's not possible in any world, so we have to go for second best here, right?"

I want to be as excited as she is; I do. It's all so black-and-white in Carson's mind, and she makes it sound easy. She believes in the good, all the beautiful things about haunting and the Prism and

Solus—and I love that she appreciates that side. But there are things she doesn't know—about the energy pull I felt, about the possessions that happened when I was still in the Prism, about the poltergeists and what they were capable of.

Just then, Nick peeks his head around the corner.

"Are we going to lunch?" he asks with a grin.

"Yes!" I say, glad to be able to exit this discussion.

We round the corner and I notice Holly waiting by the entrance for us. She's always been a peripheral member of our group of friends, but for some reason, I never noticed the longing in her eyes when she looked at Nick, which is hard to miss right now. Maybe it was never there before I had my accident, or maybe it was and I was just blind to it. I look at Nick and see his face light up for her. He tries to hide it by focusing on me again, but I saw it. He really does like her. When we sit down at our regular table she's far enough away that I can ignore her, but I watch her stealing more lingering glances at Nick.

It's really strange and awkward, being here and knowing something was happening between them, something that I apparently interrupted when I recovered. I feel sort of invisible and lost, and suddenly I realize this is what it must be like for Thatcher when he's hovering over me and watching me with Nick.

Thankfully, some of Nick's soccer teammates are sitting at the other end of our table, being loud and carrying on. It's a nice distraction to have. I haven't felt the need to say hi to them since I sat down, because they're so preoccupied with each other, but then Eli Winston says my name, and my ears prick up.

"Callie hasn't heard about it!"

"Yeah, but the rest of us have heard it a hundred times," says Hunter Black, whose blond hair is shaved into a fauxhawk this year for some reason. I wonder briefly if it was a soccer team dare.

"Hey, Callie!" Eli calls to me, and I meet his dark-brown eyes. "Want me to tell you about my incredible train dodge?"

I have the urge to tell him I already know about his "dodge," and that I saved his ass, in fact.

But instead I say, "Sure, Eli."

It's hard to listen as Eli recounts the hours after Tim McCann's summer party, when he was down by Lyndon's Crossing, drinking with a bunch of people. What he remembers is that he stood on the tracks and jumped out of the way of the train just in time—"literally, like, a split second before the train hit me," he says. "Not even a split, like half a split second."

But here's what I remember:

I was hiding across the way while the poltergeists—Leo and Reena, and their friends Norris and Delia—gathered around the Living, waiting for a chance to mess with them. When Eli stepped on the tracks, Leo shadowed him, moving slowly into his body and pulling energy from me against my will until possession was achieved. Eli couldn't move—Leo stood his ground, having fully taken over Eli's body. And the train might have hit him—hit *them*—if I hadn't come out of my hiding spot and rushed at Eli with the speed of a bullet from a gun and thrown him to safety, forcing Leo out of his body.

No one here knows that version of the story, and I have to fight off chills when I think of it as Eli tells his own tall tale. Thatcher says I'm not in danger and that being fully alive makes me safe from the poltergeists.

But what if Leo, Reena, and the others are stronger than he realizes? The more I think about what they could do with my energy, the more I worry about what they might do to access it again, even though my being out of the Prism would make it really difficult. *What if they find a way to possess Eli again? What if they're able to get inside Carson's head?*

I force myself to smile and nod as Eli winds up the story. "Impressive," I say.

One thing's for sure: Having been possessed by Leo hasn't changed Eli one bit. He's still a bragging fool.

By the time I'm sitting in last period, I cannot possibly listen to another "introduction to my class" speech. I'm considering using my "sick" status to leave early, but I decide to save that card because the afternoon is almost done. I tune in and out as Mr. Hawes, who's been a physics teacher for close to one hundred years as far as I can tell, is talking about mathematical models and abstractions, but when he says we're going to study "high energy theory," I perk up. If I'm getting more nervous thinking about the poltergeists, maybe I should try to figure out if I still have high levels of energy—some way to protect myself, and my friends, in case Reena and Leo ever come back.

I frown at my brand-new physics textbook and let my eyes go fuzzy at the glowing purple fiber-optic-looking image on the cover. If there's one thing Thatcher would not approve of, it would be me trying to tap into the abilities I had in the Prism now that I'm back in my regular life. I can almost hear him inside my mind. *Callie, I want you to live now, as normally as you can.*

I shake my head. That's impossible.

As Mr. Hawes continues to talk, I turn my focus inward, almost like I'm meditating or something, trying to call on enough energy to make something in this room *move*.

Ping. I feel someone tap the back of my head with a pencil.

"Ouch!" When I turn around, Morgan Jackson points her eraser toward Mr. Hawes, who's looking at me expectantly.

"I'm sorry," I say, biting my lip to look contrite. "I must have zoned out."

"I was just saying that we might benefit from having you in our class, Callie," says Mr. Hawes. "After your experience this summer, you must know more about energy at rest than most of us."

I nod dumbly, still unsure what the context of this attention is and embarrassed that the class may have seen me trying to call on energy—so weird. My nod seems to satisfy Mr. Hawes, though, and he returns to the board to write down the page numbers we are supposed to read tonight in our gigantic book.

Mercifully, the bell rings a minute later. I walk out into the hall and head toward my locker to meet my best friend, feeling uneasy. I see a display across the way from my classroom, a glass case filled with sports trophies from years past and ribbons from state math tournaments. In the center is a photo of a girl from my class, Ella Hartley. She died last spring. . . .

And then, I'm hit by a rush of heat—a powerful surge coursing through my body. I double over, dropping my physics book and putting my hands on my knees.

There is a hammer pounding each and every inch of my veins into long, flat strands of agony. The pain slices through every nerve, every bit of skin, every cell—from my fingertips to the inner point of my gut. *Throbbing, beating, pummeling, thrashing.* It's the kind of pain that makes you black out, and when I start to lose my vision, I think that I might.

It's the kind of pain that makes you wish you were dead.

It is that horrible and all-consuming.

As the details of my surroundings start to fade away behind a veil of black, a pair of glowing eyes appears, floating right in front of me. Within seconds, there are hundreds more, piercing through me along with this unrelenting searing pain. A collection of voices seeps into my ears, singing to me sweetly, as though trying to comfort me.

We're coming for you, we're coming for you.

In an instant, they all merge together, forming a devilish roar that sends me to my knees.

And then it's over.

Ten

I HEAR HIS VOICE before I open my eyes, and when I do, the room is dark. I try to get my bearings, but I just see plain gray walls around me. And then he speaks again.

"Callie."

"Thatcher?"

I look around, letting my eyes adjust in the small, square room but I don't see him. And yet he's here. He came to see me. For a moment I think I died—for real this time. I don't feel devastated. I feel almost . . . hopeful. I'm in the morgue, on a slab.

But then I sit up and my hands touch the fabric underneath me. Slabs don't have sheets.

"What's wrong? What are you doing in the nurse's office?" His voice is a whisper, a dream.

That's when I notice the small window with slits of sunlight poking through the drawn shades. *The nurse's office.* I flex my fingers and toes, then my arms and legs. I wrap myself in a hug, trying to see how my body feels, expecting to be sore all over from the incredible anguish I felt in the hallway. But there's nothing. I feel fine. Did the nurse give me a painkiller or something?

"When did you get here?" I ask quietly, and I can't tell if I hear his answers out loud or in my head.

"Just now. I didn't plan to linger, but you seemed hurt."

"It happened in the hallway," I say. And then I tell him about the searing, ripping, earth-shattering pain that I felt.

"Did you see or hear anything? Or anyone?"

The hairs on my arms stand up as I recognize fear in his tone.

"No," I say. "I couldn't. Not until just now with you. There was only this terrible . . . it felt like every part of me was being crushed."

"I'm so sorry," he says. "I should have been closer. I might have been able to—"

"It's not your fault," I tell him. "I went off the meds on my own and I knew there was a possibility that the pain might overwhelm me at first. I—"

"I don't think this has anything to do with your past injuries."

"Then what was it? What caused the pain?"

"Not what. *Who.*"

"Who?"

I hear the regret in his voice, and I can almost picture his solemn face when he says, "Reena and Leo."

"Oh no," I say, my heart beginning to race.

I close my eyes, which helps me block out this bland room and imagine that Thatcher and I are talking together in a better setting. One where the mist moves around us and the air sparkles with an ethereal glow. I picture us in the Prism, where we met. Where we . . . connected.

"You remember them, don't you? And the rest of the poltergeists?"

"Yes," I say. "Everything has been coming back to me slowly."

As I tell him about what I heard in my room, what I felt in the cemetery, and the memories that have been flooding back, a deep chord of dread starts to sound within me.

"Thatcher? Can they still use my energy?"

"The other Guides and I, we think they're still trying," he says. "But now that you're back on Earth, alive, we don't believe there's any way they can draw the level of energy they'd need for another possession or anything close to that."

"Then what just happened to me?"

"I'm not sure. All we know is that they're desperate to gather energy—they'll do almost anything, and you're an obvious target. You were the one they hoped to use all along."

"And you can't stop them?" I say, my voice trembling a bit.

"No, we will, Callie," he says. "It's just that . . . we haven't been able to find them."

"*I'll find them,*" I whisper, remembering what I scrawled in my journal, in a dream state.

"I've been searching since they disappeared, but I will track them down," says Thatcher, sounding more angry than sure. It's amazing what I can hear in his voice when I can't see his face. "It's just that they haven't been back to the Prism since—" He stops.

"Since what?"

"Maybe, in dreams, you've seen what happened?" I open my eyes again, and I notice a ripple in the air, his hand casting about this barren little room. "How your prism was destroyed."

I flash to the double exposure I keep seeing in my own bedroom—the window smashed, the bed torn apart, my things lying broken on the floor. *It's not my actual room I'm seeing in that nightmare . . . it's my prism room.*

"I've seen a vision in my sleep," I whisper.

"Yes."

"I thought it was a nightmare."

"No. It's real, what they've done to your prism."

"How did they do it?"

"You invited them in."

In the Prism, Thatcher told me never to let anyone into my private room, but I was tired of his unexplained rules and there was a moment when I thought Reena was my friend. I'd invited her in. . . . I'd invited them all in.

I feel a rush of shame.

"But when could they have done it?"

"Just before you woke up from the coma."

I think back to that moment, the one right before my eyes opened. When Thatcher drove my soul into my body. I remember his face— tortured, regretful, full of hurt. Despite his own pain, he chose my life. He said it was the only way to save me; he said the poltergeists would keep trying to use me to claim the lives of others as their own.

But he never said what I wanted to hear most. What I still want to hear. He never said that he loved me.

I shake my head and look around the nurse's office, hating the gray walls and sterile paper sheets, and for a minute, myself, for suddenly making this all about me. Yes, I want to know, more than anything, what I really mean to Thatcher.

But doesn't the fact that he's here with me now show that? Sure, there's a bigger crisis at hand here, but couldn't he have sent another Guide to contact me? Now that I'm aware the Prism is real and I'm off the meds, I would have been able to get the message.

He came here himself. He came here to be with me.

"We think the poltergeists have extra energy; that's what they took from your personal prism and why they haven't returned from Earth to regain strength. They can stay here. But not forever. Still, we can't track them until they come back to the Prism."

"How long?" I ask.

"We're not sure, but it's a matter of days—a week at most," he says.

"They'll try to take bodies again." *Carson, Eli.*

"Yes," he says. "In a way, they just did. But they failed."

When he says the word *failed*, I suddenly remember the rule of three—Carson has already been possessed once, and if it happens twice more, Reena will take her over completely. Everything that makes my best friend—her beautiful, wacky soul—would cease to exist and Reena would have what she's always wanted.

The chance to be alive again.

"Carson. Is she safe?" I ask Thatcher, swallowing hard.

"We think so," says Thatcher. "As far as we know, ghosts can't draw enough energy from living bodies for a possession. They won't be able to get to her. It's you I'm worried about—they can still mess with you and drain your energy."

"But if they can't achieve possession, then what's the point?"

He doesn't answer for a moment, but then his voice comes, quiet and hurried. "Maybe there's a reason they believe it's possible. And they have limited time—they're getting more desperate, so they'll try anything, even if it's a one-in-a-million shot. I'm going to do my best to stay near, to be with you more than I have been."

"But you can't be here all the time."

"No," he says. "Like I said, it's not good for you to be linked to anything from the Prism. Including me. I just wish there were some way for you to let me know if you sense them. . . ."

Thatcher goes quiet, and I reach into my pocket, taking out the selenite crystals and opening my palm up into the air with a smile. "Maybe I can use these to summon you when I'm in trouble?"

I'm trying to crack a joke, make things feel lighter, but Thatcher responds enthusiastically. "Good idea!"

"Wait, what? Are you telling me these things actually work?"

He laughs. He actually *laughs*, and the vibration makes my skin warm.

"No," he says. "You can't call me with those rocks."

"I'll have you know that they're selenite crystals! Carson gave them to me."

"Of course she did," he says, and I can hear a tender smile in his voice. "You'll have to tell her that, sadly, those crystals are just pretty rocks."

"So why'd you get so excited just now?"

I can almost see his back straighten up as he says, "I need you to find Wendy, my sister."

My eyes widen in surprise.

"She has something of mine," he continues, "a talisman. It's an old class ring that our grandfather gave to me. I know it sounds strange, but it has a pull over me. If she's ever holding it and thinking of me, I know it. I can feel it, even from the Prism."

"You want me to find your sister and ask her to give me your grandfather's class ring?"

"Yes," he says. "You need to have it. It's clear that the poltergeists are getting close to you, and if they're near, the Guides and I should be able to take their energy and overpower them, which would force their return to the Prism. Wendy doesn't seem aware of what the ring does, and it's the only way you'll be able to call to me if I'm not with you when they approach—I want you to be able to do that."

"I want that, too."

"It's for emergencies only, Callie," he says, his voice turning stern. "I mean it. The ring is only to be used if you feel you're truly in danger."

"Got it," I say. "Don't use the ring because I want to tell you how my day went, but if Reena and Leo corner me in a back alley, it's fair game."

But Thatcher doesn't appreciate my attempt to lift the mood, which has grown solemn again.

"It's not a joke."

"I know," I say. "But how will I get Wendy to give it to me? I can hardly just walk up to her and tell her I know her brother who died ten years ago."

"You're right," he murmurs. "She won't give it to you. She'll probably . . ." He pauses, like he's thinking very deeply. Then he says, "Try first. Try with the truth of how we met in the Prism. Call it the afterlife—that's what the Living are comfortable with. Maybe by now she'll . . ." He stops talking again, and I hear the contemplation in his silence. "If she turns away, or gets angry . . . then tell her . . . tell her, 'The treasure is in the tree.'"

"What?"

"If she won't listen to you, tell her, 'The treasure is in the tree,'" he repeats. "I'm sorry, Callie, I have to end this dream."

"Dream?"

"Yes. Forgive me. I need you to remember this interaction clearly—I'm going to push you now."

Suddenly, I'm falling, falling fast. There's no ground under me and I'm flailing, moving through time and space and nothingness, without him.

I awake with a *jolt*, sitting up on the stiff bed in the nurse's office. I'm panting, the selenite still in my hand, clutched to my chest. It was one of those cliff-drop moments, where you wake up sweating and panting. I've had them before, but never like this.

"Lie back, dear," says Nurse K. Her warm hand presses gently on my shoulder and I look up into her kind hazel eyes. She's been our school nurse for years, and we all love her—she's young but it seems like she has an old soul.

"I'm all right," I tell her. "Really."

"I'm just going to call your father. You had quite a spell."

"I feel better," I say, putting my feet on the floor and standing up to head for the door.

Nurse K tries to hold my arm, but I turn and flash her a grin. "Really," I say, "I'm okay."

She calls out the door after me, "Callie, I still have to call your father!"

But I keep moving. I have to get out of here—I have to find Carson. Because I remember every word Thatcher said to me, and I *need* that ring.

Eleven

NOW MORE THAN EVER, my mind has to be clear.

The last thing I need is to be put back in bed by a bunch of doctors and given more pills to take. So yesterday I told Carson my fainting spell in the hallway was because I didn't eat enough at lunch, not because Reena and the poltergeists were stalking me at school. When I came home to my father pacing around in the kitchen, upset by the concerned voicemail he'd received from Nurse K, I gave him the same story too.

Thankfully, they believed me. Of course, I felt bad for lying, but not bad enough to stop myself from turning on the charm and convincing them that whatever happened to me was just a random, freakish thing. However, late last night I just couldn't hold back from Carson anymore. I called her and told her that Thatcher had contacted me and asked me to reach out to Wendy.

Immediately, she got carried away in some fairy tale version of my life, which she still seems to think is some kind of perfectly tragic made-for-TV movie.

"Oh God, that is so romantic! All the sacrifices and secrets and longing for what can never be!" she gushed.

I wanted to interrupt her and share the whole truth—about the danger I'm in, that she could be at risk, too. But I just couldn't bring myself to do it. I've been telling myself that I should keep the darker side of the Prism from Carson because she's such a believer in the good side of things, the Solus side, the heavenly side. She's the person who wants me to help Thatcher's sister finally cope with his death so he can merge into peace and light, and I didn't want to take that away from her.

But now that it's the next morning, and we're skipping school so we can drive to USC-Beaufort in her VW Bug, I think the reason I can't tell Carson there's evil and hate and betrayal in the next world is because telling her would make it all terrifyingly real. I'd have to admit to her everything that Thatcher said to me, and none of it was particularly reassuring. I'd have to tell her that I'm not sure how strong Reena is or what her powers could do to us. I'd have to tell her that I don't have any clue how we might protect ourselves, or whether there would be anyone else, like the Guides, to keep us safe either.

The only hope we have, really, is in an old class ring. Which I have to get from a total stranger. Maybe then, I'll be able to say the words out loud to her:

The poltergeists are coming for me.

"I can't believe we're doing this, Cal," Carson says as she backs the car out of her driveway. "I thought you'd given up on your wild, crazy ways."

"Me, too." I glance down at the plastic bag on the floor of the passenger side and nudge it with my foot. "What's all this?"

"Stakeout provisions," says Carson, her smile stretching wide across her face. "I got something for every kind of craving. Salty, sweet, sour. You name it."

I smile and take in a deep breath. The fresh air that hits my face when we pull out of our neighborhood feels good. I almost forget for a second or two that I haven't been able to sense Thatcher with me since the last dream I had, and haven't responded to the few texts Nick has sent me. I can almost see the waves of late August heat as we merge onto the highway—it makes the road's white lines look wavy and shaky, like we're underwater. I remember how everything looked *almost* real in the Prism, and I wonder about people like my dad, who always need things to be tangible, solid. I know that life isn't always that way, though.

"I wonder what Thatcher's merging ceremony is going to be like," Carson says, her eyes flicking to the rearview mirror as she makes a turn. "Maybe there'll be harps or something."

"I saw one actually."

"You did? Tell me!"

And this is easy to share, because it's the good part.

"It was Ella Hartley's."

Now Carson is truly rapt. She and I danced with Ella Hartley when we were little and everyone took ballet class, but Ella stuck with it and was actually really good, I heard . . . until she got sick.

"Ella was super skilled at haunting," I say.

"How did she do it?" asks Carson. "Did she do things like changing radio stations or did she do that other kind—the soul kind of haunting that Thatcher wanted you to do?"

"She did things the right way. She spent time around her family—I even saw them walking at the harbor one day. She'd been out on their sailboat with them, and the whole scene was really peaceful."

I pick up the cloth Carson keeps on her dashboard, feeling its velvety softness between my fingers. I take off my sunglasses and clean them with it before I continue.

"Her merging ceremony was like nothing I've ever experienced," I tell Carson. "It happened in a warm, lush place, like a rain forest. There was soft music playing, and all the ghosts gathered to watch, like it was a performance. Ella walked a path surrounded by white stones, up to a central platform where she lifted her face to the sky."

As I say that, I do it. I close my eyes and raise my face into the sun, basking in its warmth in the way only the Living can do. It's a pleasure that feels even sweeter because I couldn't feel it—this earthly sensation—when I was almost dead. I let the rays soak into my skin, and run my hands through my hair. Carson's silent, still transfixed as she keeps her eyes on the road and her mind on my story. And I continue.

"There was a shining light, and thousands of sparkles dancing around Ella, enveloping her. The spirits were playing mbiras, these instruments that mimic a rainfall and usher the dead into the next world."

Remembering it all, reliving it in my mind, makes me long for that world as well, for that feeling of complete rest. Life and the After, both so rich and vivid, tug at my insides. "It was like magic," I say. "I felt a tranquility, a peace I'd never known. It actually made me cry."

"Wow, Callie. That sounds beautiful. I mean, angels-singing, gates-of-Heaven beautiful. But better."

"It was."

"So that's what all the ghosts do, eventually?" she asks. "They merge in this ceremony and then . . . what comes next? What's Solus?"

"It's a leap of faith." I'm quoting Thatcher again, and for a moment it's like he's sitting in the backseat, happily going on this weird road trip with us. "Solus is the heart of the universe—it's where we all belong."

"And that's where Thatcher will be, once we talk to Wendy."

I feel a pang of guilt at not being straight with Carson, not telling her the real reason we need to see Wendy. But I tell myself I'm going to come clean soon, when we know more about what we're really up against.

"Hopefully." I turn the radio up, not wanting to dwell on the thought of Thatcher merging. Maybe after the poltergeists are gone, maybe then, I can think about how to help him, and Wendy. But it would mean saying a true, final good-bye. And I'm not ready yet.

"You okay?" asks Carson.

I nod, just as my phone sounds—I silence my father's ring.

"Your dad?" asks Carson.

"Yup." I glance at the clock: 8:04 and I'm not in homeroom. The school probably called him.

"Better to beg forgiveness than to ask permission," says my usually good-girl best friend.

"Carson Jenkins, you're becoming a badass."

She smiles and raises her sunglasses, batting her eyes at me. "In the name of love? I'll do anything."

Carson pulls up in front of a brick building with enormous old windows and a pretty garden out front. "This is Wendy's dorm," she says.

I look around and the campus is flecked with palmettos, the South Carolina state tree, and the grass is trim and bright, welcoming students back to campus with a lush green spirit. The brick buildings give off a stately air, each entrance announced with regal white columns. There are some boys to our left throwing a football out on the quad and two girls in retro-style bikinis are applying more sunscreen on our right. I look out at the buzz of the campus, and a surge of gratitude washes over me—I will do this. I will go to college, and live my life. I feel sad for all of those who won't. For Thatcher, of course, but also Reena and Leo and everyone I met who died young.

It just isn't fair.

"It's so beautiful," I whisper.

"Hand me the Fritos," says Carson. She's not quite in the same appreciate-all-the-little-parts-of-life zone that I'm in.

I reach down and snag her a bag. She tears into it and starts crunching. Then she presses the button to put up the top on the convertible so we won't burn in this strong sun.

"What do we do now?" I ask her.

"We wait."

"Until . . . ?"

"Until you see Wendy come out of the dorm," says Carson, as if this is such a *duh* question.

"How will I know it's her?" We looked Wendy up online, but it's not like I'm *sure* I'll recognize her. There are a lot of girls with blond hair walking around.

"You'll know," says Carson confidently. "You'll feel it inside."

When I give her a skeptical glance, she adds, "She'll remind you of Thatcher."

Carson saying that makes my heart thump louder, and I sit still, watching her finish a fun-size bag of Fritos.

After one more bag of Fritos, three MoonPies, one apple (Carson: "Yes, I *did* bring healthy stuff, too") and one Coke each, I'm about to doze off. But then there's a sharp rap on the driver's-side door.

"Y'all can't park here," says a college guy outside as Carson rolls down her window.

"Oh, sorry, sir!" says Carson in her sweet-as-honey voice. "We're visitors. We're trying to find Wendy Larson and she didn't tell us where to park."

"Just because you're pretty doesn't mean you can break the

rules," says the guy, who has close-cropped brown hair and a sunny smile that's beaming toward my best friend. "You need to go to South Lot. It's around the other side of campus."

"Aw, thank you!" says Carson. "We're just going to wait for a couple more minutes but we'll head right over to that lot as quick as we can."

She rolls her window back up and rolls her eyes at the same time.

"Cars, that guy was totally cute, and totally hitting on you," I say.

"No he wasn't," she says. "He was like a college safety monitor . . . telling me I can't park here. Why not?"

I point to the bright-red hydrant near her front bumper.

"Well, I'll *move* if there's a fire, obviously," she says.

"Whatever." I pull down the visor mirror and smooth out my eyebrows. "You should have talked to him more. He's a *college guy.*"

Carson waves her hand. "I don't need the hassle."

"What do you mean?" I ask her. "You never think of romance as a hassle." I study my face in the mirror, wondering if Wendy will think I look like a crazy person when I tell her I met her long-dead brother this summer.

I realize Carson's gone quiet and I'm about to press her further about the cute parking guy when, reflected in the mirror, I see her. I see Wendy.

She's walking out of the dorm, carrying a single book and a blanket and striding toward the grassy quad.

Carson was right. I just *know.* It's the way she's walking, confident and purposeful. It's the way her eyes stare straight ahead, like no one will deter her from her path, and her lips, they form the softest of smiles. I can see it from here. It's almost like I'm seeing . . . him.

"Stay here," I say to Carson.

"But I—"

"Stay." My eyes must convey what I'm feeling. *I need to do this alone.* Carson shuts her mouth and nods.

Then I bolt out of the VW Bug and rush up to Wendy, but when I get right next to her we almost collide, and she steps to the side.

"Whoa, watch it," she says. Her light hair is shaved on one side and her eyes are lined with thick black kohl. She has a bunch of piercings—all up her earlobes and one in her lower lip.

But when I look at her eyes, swirling oceans of blue, and the shape of her lips—soft and full with a perfect inverted arch at the top—my knees go weak and my mouth opens dumbly.

She frowns. "Do I know you?"

I nod slightly, but I can't seem to make my body do anything else. This girl is wearing all black, full of metal, and yet at the same time, she looks so much like Thatcher that it makes my heart melt into a pool in my chest.

My silence is getting weird, and I watch her eyes cloud over.

"Watch where you're going next time," she says.

And then she's moving again, walking away.

"Wendy, wait!"

She freezes and turns around slowly. "Are you in my Shakespeare class? Are you the girl who's always late?"

"No. I'm . . . I'm . . ." *Why can't I talk?* Maybe it's because of her hair—it's the exact color of Thatcher's: blond with copper tones threaded through it, a slight wave at the ends. Her cheekbones are high and sharp, her nose long and thin. There's a smattering of freckles across her face, and even the way she tilts her head at me, like she's trying to figure out who I am . . . it's just like he would do it. She could be his alterna-twin.

"What's going on?" Wendy's voice is clipped. I won't have her attention for long.

"I'm Callie McPhee," I say. "I'm a friend of your brother's."

She sneers at me. "You look really young to have been a friend of my brother's," she says. "Did he babysit you when you were in kindergarten or something?"

I shake my head no.

"I met him this summer."

Wendy narrows her eyes at me sharply, and I know I've made a misstep.

"What I meant to say is, I knew him a long time ago . . . and then this summer I thought maybe I should come find you and tell you a little bit about what I remember about him," I stammer, trying to save this moment.

"Why?"

"Can we go somewhere and sit?" I don't want to do this without some ground underneath me. I'm weakening just looking into Wendy's ocean-blue eyes.

Wendy studies my face.

"I don't think so." She folds her arms across her chest, holding her blanket like a shield.

The wind starts to blow and her face is shadowed for a moment in the rippling shade of a palmetto tree.

I can tell that she's about to leave. I have to do this. I don't want to lie to her. I realize that I want to tell her the truth, like Thatcher said to. So I do.

"I was in a car accident at the beginning of the summer," I begin. Then I lean down to roll up the leg of my linen pants and show her the biggest scar. I want to prove things to her, show her the tangible parts of my story, because I know what I'm about to say is going to be hard for her to believe.

She winces at the pinkish puckering slash on my calf.

"It's okay," I say. "I mean, I'm okay. Now. But I was in a coma for a few weeks."

"Oh!" Wendy's face softens slightly. "That's why you look familiar. I read about you in the the *Post and Courier.*"

She's warming a little now, and I remember something Thatcher told me about her: that she was always wanting to take care of people, always looking for the happy endings. She had cancer as a child, and she beat it, but she never lost her faith in life and joy and miracles . . . until he died.

I nod, rolling down my pants and standing up again.

"I'm glad you're okay," she says, her frown returning. "But what does this have to do with my brother?"

She reaches up and lowers her sunglasses so I can't see her eyes anymore. And I'm partly glad, because they look exactly like his eyes, and they make me feel untethered.

I take a deep breath. "While I was in the coma, I found myself in a world that's somewhere in between Earth and Heaven, an afterlife. And that's when I met Thatcher."

"Is this some kind of stupid prank?" She glances over her shoulders at the other students on the quad.

"No—" I start.

"Did Bella Cryer put you up to this?" Her voice is angry now. "Because it's NOT FUNNY!" Wendy shouts that last part, and I reach out to put my hand on her arm, but she pulls away quickly, like I've got a contagious disease.

She starts to turn from me, but I can't let her go. "I know he was drinking at Homecoming, at the upper Wando River," I tell her. "I know he was with Reena and Leo, and someone named . . . Hayley. She lived, but—"

"That was all in the newspaper," she snaps, turning back to me. "Everyone can read those details online."

"He talked to me about your cancer," I say, and as she looks at me, her lip and its metal ring start to quiver. "You were four years old and spending most of your time in a hospital."

"Anyone could have told you that," she says. "I don't know why you would go to such lengths to play a cruel joke on me, but that's obviously what you're doing."

"Wait, Wendy," I say. "I'm telling you the truth. I do know Thatcher, from another dimension." I pause for a moment, realizing how insane I sound. But she's standing there, staring at me, so I start again. "We were friends . . . he sent me to find you, he sent me to get a ring, your grandfather's class ring."

She tilts her head. "You want me to give you my grandfather's ring?" she asks, her voice full of wonder at my audacity.

I'm doing this all wrong. I'm losing her.

"I don't know who you are or who told you to do this to me, but I want you to leave. *Now.* And take your crazy-ass friend with you." She points to the curb in front of her dorm, where Carson is leaning out of the window of the Bug watching us with a rabid intensity. I'm surprised she doesn't have binoculars.

Wendy turns and starts walking away, quickly. My heart speeds up. I'm not going to get the ring. *I need the ring.*

"Wendy!" I shout. "Thatcher says, 'The treasure is in the tree!'"

She stops in her tracks, turning so I see her profile, which is so like her brother's that it takes my breath away. "What did you say?"

I'm quieter now, realizing we're attracting attention.

"Thatcher said to tell you, 'The treasure is in the tree.' Please . . . you have to get the ring for me."

Wendy spins on her black boots and marches back, coming to stand as close as she can without touching me. Her face is filled with fury. "I don't have to do anything!" she whispers, her teeth showing as her lips curl back in anger. "And if you did see Thatcher in some afterlife, you should know that he hates me enough to want me dead, too."

My face must register shock because she smiles triumphantly.

"That's right," she says, backing away. "If you know so much about my brother, you should know that he blames me for his death. He told me so himself, when I was just twelve years old. So you tell me how I'm supposed to let go of *that*."

Twelve

"DO YOU THINK SHE'S crazy?" asks Carson.

Seeing Wendy didn't take as long as we thought it would, and Carson and I stop at the Dixie Diner on the way home. In the car, I told Carson about what Wendy said last—about Thatcher blaming her for his death. Now, in front of a tuna melt (Carson) and a grilled cheese (me), we try to figure out what she meant.

"No," I say. "I think she's grieving. It's kind of insane that it's still so raw after ten years, but I think she believes what she said."

"Thatcher hates her?"

"No," I say. "He talked about her with so much love. She must remember wrong. But she thinks he blames her for his death. I just don't understand why."

"Well, we have to ask him," says Carson, scooping a big lump of tuna fish out of her sandwich and putting it on the side of her plate as she, who ate two bags of Fritos and two MoonPies earlier, mumbles about portion control.

"Ask who?"

"Thatcher," she says, biting into her sandwich.

I tilt my head sideways at her.

She grins, her mouth full, and chews rapidly before wiping her lips with a napkin.

"I get that he probably wants to stay in the shadows or whatever. I know he wants you to move on," says Carson. "It's noble. Blah, blah, blah. But this Wendy thing? There's something going on there. He should want her to heal; he should do whatever he can to make that happen. And what he can do right now is help her, through you."

She looks up at the ceiling of the diner, at the lamps of red-and-blue glass and the silver fans, circling slowly. "Do you hear me, Thatcher?" she says in full voice, drawing stares from other diners. "You need to help us do this."

"Sh!" I quiet her down.

"Well, if you won't talk to him, I will," she says, taking another big bite of tuna melt.

I love Carson for her big heart, for her willingness to help me, but she's not on the same mission I'm on. She doesn't know about the ring, or the poltergeists.

Not yet.

When we get outside, Carson stretches and yawns in front of her car. "I'm sleepy. You wanna drive?"

I hesitate. I haven't driven since the accident.

Carson smiles at me, reading my mind. "You have to start sometime." She hands me her keys.

When we're back on the highway, it feels good to be behind the wheel. Carson fiddles with the radio.

"Why the slow lane?" she asks.

"I'm not in as much of a hurry as I used to be."

"That's probably a good thing." She leans her seat back and relaxes in the passenger seat, starting to doze off.

I drive steadily for forty minutes, letting everyone pass me on the left, including a few 18-wheelers. I feel good—not shaky, not nervous like I thought I would. I smile at the blue sky. Driving is such a pure pleasure. I'm glad to have it back.

When we get to our exit I slowly veer to the right and turn left at the stop sign, heading back to our neighborhood. I'm crossing under the overpass, stopped at a red light, when suddenly I feel a crackle of pain in my leg. Before I can think, my right foot presses down on the gas and we take off, blowing through the last seconds of the red light as the car increases speed.

Carson starts awake. "Callie! What are you doing? Slow down! There's another red light ahead!"

I'm panicking—my foot is tingling like mad, like it's surging with blood, and I have no control over its movement. It's pressed to the floor as if there's a cement block on top of it. I watch our speed climbing: 20 mph . . . 30 . . . 40.

"Callie!" Carson's scream rings out over the rev of the engine as she grabs the wheel and steers us around the car waiting at the red light in front of us. A van to our right skids to a stop and spins out to avoid hitting us. "I can't lift my foot!" I shout, and I see Carson's face flash with fear.

And then, as quickly as it happened, I'm free. My knee flies up under the pressure I've been exerting to lift it, and I immediately slam down the brake, tires screeching in protest as we skid to a stop just before we reach the next intersection. Carson and I are thrown forward by the sudden move—I feel my seat belt tighten around me, digging into my shoulder sharply.

My breath is coming in rapid bursts, and I look over at my best friend. Her face is white.

"Carson." I reach out my hand to her.

"Let's pull over," she says, taking it and squeezing. "I'm okay. I'll drive."

I carefully get us into the closest strip mall parking lot and we pull up in front of a floral shop. I look at the display of hydrangeas and peonies, all blue and pink and white in the window.

We open our doors and switch seats, shaking as we walk.

Once Carson's behind the wheel, she starts the car. But then she cuts off the engine and turns to me, her eyes watering a little.

"What the hell was that?" shouts my best friend, who never swears.

"I don't know," I say, but a half second later I realize that of course I do.

This is it. The moment when Carson finds out, and it all becomes real.

"I haven't told you everything," I say.

She frowns. "Okay, so tell me now."

"It was the poltergeists." When I say the *p* word, I know she understands what I mean: evil ghosts.

"They exist too," she says, nodding like it makes sense.

"Yes. And I've really pissed them off."

She looks at me, trying to read my face in the way she's done since we were little. As usual, she's good at it. "Why didn't you tell me you were in danger?"

"I guess I didn't want to freak you out," I tell her. "You're so into the afterlife and there's so much that's beautiful about it. I just didn't want you to see the dark side."

"You thought I couldn't handle it," she says, looking away.

"That's not it," I say to her, putting my hand on her arm and making her turn back to me. "I wanted to protect you from it. As long as I could."

"Well, the whole speeding-through-stoplights thing has got me involved now," she says. "So tell me what's going on."

"I'm not entirely sure," I tell her. "But I do know that just now they were here; they were using energy to somehow hold my foot down on the accelerator. I felt it."

"Ghosts can *do* things like that?"

"Not ghosts," I say. "Poltergeists. Carson, you don't know what they're capable of." I bite my lip and stare out the windshield. Sunlight reflects off the glass of the flower shop and I lower my sunglasses to avoid the glare. I sit back against my seat and tell her all about my relationship with Reena and Leo, how they tried to lure me into their group and turn me against Thatcher. It was all part of their plan. "When I was in the Prism, they . . . they tried to use possession as a way to live again."

"Possession?"

"Taking bodies. They get inside a body and force out the soul that was there—"

"I know what it means," she says, a bit flustered. "But how do they take the bodies?"

"Through me." I explain that my energy was unique in the Prism, that I had extra to spare and it was so much that when other ghosts shared it they obtained powers beyond the normal realm. "I think it was because I was in the coma, caught between two worlds."

"But you're not anymore . . . ," says Carson.

"It doesn't matter; they're still after me for some reason," I tell her.

"So that thing in the hallway yesterday?"

"It was them," I admit. "Look, I'm not safe, and it's pretty clear neither is anyone around me. So maybe you should stay away—"

"Callie, if you think I'm going to ditch you just because some poltergeists are messing with you, you're wrong," says Carson defiantly. She smiles. "But I'll drive from now on."

I try to smile back. I appreciate her bravado. But there's more I have to tell her.

"Oh no, what else?" she asks, reading my face again.

"You've been taken," I say, my voice wavering a little. I lock eyes with my best friend. It hurts so much to tell her this, but at the same time it's also a little bit of a relief, being totally honest with her finally. "Reena targeted you."

Her mouth opens slightly in surprise, but I see the wheels turning in her head, trying to figure out when and where.

"It was at Tim McCann's party this summer," I say.

Carson's face goes blank for a moment, but then realization dawns in her eyes. "That was the night I—" She stops, looking at me to see if I know.

"The night you kissed Nick," I say, filling in the blank so we can move past this awkward point.

"I—" Carson starts.

"It was Reena." I say it loudly and clearly. "I know that."

Carson's face blanches anyway, but I barrel ahead. "The point is that you're vulnerable—you've been possessed once already, and Reena only has to take you two more times in order to get permanent control over you."

The car goes silent as this information sinks in. I can hear the bang of someone shutting a car door near us and the echo of someone's footsteps in the parking lot.

"So you're telling me Reena was *inside* my body," says Carson, whose face color is returning to normal. She seems way more rational than I thought she'd be right now.

I nod.

"Where was I?"

"In the peach room," I say, remembering Tim's parents' prettily decorated guest quarters.

"I know *that!*" she says. "I mean where did my soul go? And what happened while I was gone . . . I mean besides . . ."

She grins sheepishly.

"I don't know," I tell her.

"But there's not, like, a piece of me missing?" asks Carson.

"I don't think so. But another possession could be more severe. And a third . . ." I try to finish this horrifying sentence but I can't. Actually, I don't have to.

Carson's eyes widen. "The rule of three."

"How do you know about that?" I ask.

"It's always three on *Hallowed Hauntings*," she says, like that's so obvious. "Three is a mystical number."

"Well, you're right." I'm amazed that there is something real on that "reality" show. And I clarify how if a poltergeist can possess a body three times, it will own the body and extinguish the soul that was there before.

She's silent again, staring down at her hands like she's inspecting them for flaws.

"Thatcher says they shouldn't be able to use me for possession anymore," I tell her, trying to ease her worries. "They can screw with my energy but they shouldn't have the ability to . . . take you. They haven't been back to the Prism and that means they should have less and less power as time goes on."

"That's a lot of *should*s." Carson looks up. "He's not entirely sure what's going on, is he?"

My stomach clenches. She's right, he isn't entirely sure. Again, I find myself struggling to find words, but Carson doesn't miss a beat.

"Okay, so what do we do now?" she asks. "I've got a ton of sage at home. That might protect us for a little while at least."

"Actually, there might be something better than that," I say.

"What is it?"

And that's when I tell her about the ring.

Facing my father when we get home is not fun. As I walk toward our house, I see him rocking back and forth on the porch swing in a raging silence. Even from far away, I can see by the line of his mouth that I'm in for it.

I head slowly up our driveway—Carson went straight to her house because she has her own parents to deal with—and when I sit next to my father on the swing, when I look at his eyes up close, I notice that it's not quite anger. Maybe it's hurt.

"Daddy, I—"

He silences me with a hand in the air. "Lord, give me strength," he whispers. Then he turns to look at me. "I shouldn't have let you go back to school so soon after the accident." His voice is quiet, thoughtful. "Perhaps you need some more time to handle the pressures of an academic day."

I shake my head no. "That's not it, Daddy. There was just . . . something I had to do."

He puts his arm over my side of the swing. "Anything you have to do, you need to tell me about. It's only fair, Callie May. I don't even know where you were today. Can you imagine how scary that was?"

"I'm so sorry." And I am. I see now that I've frightened him, that I've hurt my military-tough father.

"I can't risk losing you again," he says. I notice his shoulders are slumped, his face more lined than I remember, and it makes me tear up a little.

"You won't lose me."

He stands and leans against the porch rail, facing me. "Where were you?"

I can't tell him anything near the truth. My father was reluctant for me to go off my meds; if I give him any reason to think I'm unstable, I might be back in the doctor's office, undergoing treatment that would prevent me from helping Thatcher and keeping the poltergeists at bay. I can't let that happen.

"Daddy, did you see the blue of the heavens today?" I gesture toward the open sky, where the blazing sun shines through a few perfectly cottony clouds.

"Callie, I don't know what the sky has to do with—"

" 'This is the day that the Lord hath made!' " I'm quoting a song we used to sing in Sunday school. " 'Let us rejoice and be glad in it.' "

My father looks confused.

"I'm so happy to be alive," I say to him. "I felt that so strongly this morning. I just couldn't be cooped up inside a classroom. I felt called to spend the day outside. It was me who convinced Carson. She and I . . . we took a drive. We sat out in the sun, ate snacks. I just needed a day to be grateful for my life."

It may be a sin to lie about this and use my father's renewed faith in God against him, but I can see it working. And I need it to work—for both our sakes.

He can't lose me again, so I have to fight the poltergeists with all I have.

His face softens. "That's what Saturdays are for," he says. And then: "Don't do it again."

"I won't. I'm sorry."

He walks inside, and I marvel at the fact that I got off easy. But later that night, at dinner, he tells me I'm grounded for three days. I'm to go straight to school and come straight home. No Carson, no Nick—which shouldn't be too much of a problem, given the fact that he and I haven't seen or heard from each other in while.

I nod and head up to bed. I understand that Dad's doing what he needs to do. I just hope he understands that I have to do the same.

Carson had no issues with her parents because I told her it was okay to play the "Callie needed me and she's having a hard time" card. The next day at school, she tells me she was up all night trying to find a phone number for Wendy, but she only got a school email address. We sneak away at lunch and craft a message to send:

Wendy,
Please call me. I can explain everything, and we need to talk.
Thanks,
Callie

"Short and sweet so she can't misinterpret things," says Carson. We leave my cell number in the PS and cross our fingers. Then I try to act normal for the rest of the week, which isn't easy when I'm looking over my shoulder all the time, either waiting for another attack or hoping that I'll feel Thatcher near me. When I don't sense anything—like a threat of searing pain or his warm, inviting comfort—there's a part of me that's frightened that he's found the poltergeists and they've discovered a way to capture and hurt him somehow.

But on Saturday night, the fear subsides. My dreams come again, hazy and muted, like they're happening underwater. I hear Thatcher's voice, but it's muffled and unclear. What is he trying to tell me? Then my world sharpens, and I'm in more of a memory than a dream. It's the night we left the Prism and stood on the edge of the water, next to a carnival, watching fireworks pop in the distance.

And he's there, gazing at me. I take in the breadth of his shoulders, the strength of his stance, and I try to memorize every detail down to the arch of his top lip.

I smile, so happy he's okay.

The fireworks night was a gift, a small transgression. And even though I can sense that he came to me in this dream state because he knew I was worried about him, there's something in his eyes that lets me know he's here for himself too. Which is very much against the Guides' ethics.

But maybe, hopefully, true to his heart.

"I've done a lot of rule breaking since I met you," he says.

My hands want to reach out to Thatcher, to hold him. But as always, he's out of reach—a whisper, a shadow.

"Sorry," I say.

"Don't," he replies. "Don't ever be sorry."

I want to ask him what that means. If he's giving me absolution for the whole spirit world falling apart, or if he doesn't want me to have any regrets about us.

Ding-ding!

My eyes open with a start and I see a glow coming from my nightstand as my phone lights up with a text message.

The clock reads 3:19 a.m., and the text is from a number I don't know.

It says, "I'm outside."

Thatcher.

I race to the window and open it, staring out into the tree and down at the grass below, but finding no one. I pad gently downstairs, careful not to wake my father. In the entryway, I can see someone trying to peer in through the glass that frames the front door. When I open it, I'm face-to-face with Thatcher's lips, his blue eyes, his strong gaze . . . and lots of piercings. My heart thuds.

Wendy.

"Hi," she says, as if it isn't three in the morning. As if she's here for afternoon tea and cookies. "Can I come in?"

She perches cautiously on the arm of my mother's overstuffed floral chair in the corner of our formal living room, which is on the opposite end of the house from Dad's bedroom—he shouldn't wake up. I offered Wendy juice or water, but she shook her head and went straight to the chair. Her boots are up on the fabric, but I'm afraid to ask her to put them on the floor. She makes me nervous.

I sit across the coffee table from her, on our stiff-backed blue sofa.

"Sorry if I was rude before," she says.

"It's okay."

Leaning forward so I can see her eyes, which have remained downcast, I ask her, "How did you find my house?"

"How many Callie McPhees in Charleston do you think there are? It wasn't hard."

"But why?" I ask her. "What made you believe?"

She reaches into the pocket of her cargo shorts and brings out a small green figurine, one of those little toy soldiers that kids play with. He's holding a big gun over his head, like he's wading through water. She fingers it carefully.

"'The treasure is in the tree,'" says Wendy. "I know Thatcher told you that."

It's almost like she enters a trance when she explains how they used to play a game, she and Thatcher. He had his favorite army guy, this one, and when she was a toddler she used to think it was funny to hide it from him. Eventually, that became their game, finding it and hiding it, finding it and hiding it. "We called it 'the treasure' so our parents wouldn't know what we were talking about," Wendy says. "When Thatcher died, I looked for it for weeks. I was desperate, sure I'd never find the last place where Thatcher put it. But I did. A few years later, I remembered a knot in one of the trees out back, and I stuck my hand inside. There it was: the treasure."

Her eyes fill up with tears, but no wetness falls on her cheeks. They just create pools that her pupils seem to swim in when she says, "No one in the world would know that except for me. Us."

Us. It's such a little word, just two letters, but the way Wendy says it is so filled with such pain and loss. I understand. Completely.

"I don't know if—" I start.

"Wait." Wendy puts her hand forward to stop me. "I have more to say."

I sit back against the sofa.

"This week has been strange," she says, furrowing her brow. "I've been having weird dreams, which is your fault." She narrows her eyes at me. "And today, I had this urge to drive home, to hold the treasure in my hand again." Her fingers move over the toy. "When I did, I felt a sense of calm, of peace almost. It was like . . . my brother was near."

Of course. Thatcher has been spending time with Wendy, trying to help her see that I was telling the truth.

"He *is* near," I say to her, and as I do, I see a ripple in the curtains by the front window. I wonder if Wendy does too.

She frowns. "I know you know that when I was little, I was sick," she says. "Having a little sister with cancer wasn't easy for Thatcher, but he was patient and loyal. He never complained about our parents missing his football games, never mentioned the fact that I got twice as many gifts at Christmas for a while."

She smiles, her face shedding some of its tired angst, and I see even more of Thatcher in her now. "He was the perfect big brother."

"That's not hard to imagine," I say.

"What do you mean?"

"In the afterlife . . ." I pause, wondering if she's really understood what I've told her about how Thatcher and I know each other. It sounds so strange, so unbelievable. But she nods with acceptance, and so I continue. "He was a guide for me, always taking care of me and never thinking about himself or his own needs.

He protected me, too." As I tell her this, I realize it's true. I was like a petulant child who chafed under what I thought of as his rules, but really he was guiding me toward Solus, the closest thing to Heaven there is.

"He was always that way," she says. "When the doctors told us my cancer was in remission, Thatcher was the first person there to hug me and hold my hand. He had tears streaming down his face. An eleven-year-old boy with so much love for his sister that he cried in front of the whole hospital staff."

She wipes away a tear herself, and it leaves a trail of black on her cheek, where her eyeliner runs. I take a deep breath in, almost choking on the emotion that's rising in my throat.

"After that, things were great for a few years," says Wendy. "The cancer never came back, and our family felt normal again. Mom and Dad always went to Thatcher's games, I got into photography with a camera Thatcher bought me for my ninth birthday . . . everything was normal."

I stay still, sensing that the story is about to drop off a cliff.

"About a week before Thatcher's senior homecoming dance, I started to feel sick again. It was just a bug, I was sure, but he got worried. He was doting on me, treating me like a little kid with cancer. I was twelve then, and I didn't like it. I snapped at him, said mean things. . . ." She grimaces at the memory. "I said I wanted him to get out of my face.

"On the night of the dance, I heard Thatcher tell my mom he didn't want to go, that he didn't want to leave me alone while I was sick. Looking back, I know he was only expressing concern, and I should have just reassured him. But at the time, I felt this deep sadness and guilt. I'd made him miss so much of his life already—he couldn't miss homecoming because of me, too!

"I told him that he was making me feel sicker by being around me. I told him he had to go. So he did. And then he died."

She grows quiet, like she's done talking.

"Wendy," I start, leaning forward, "what did you mean the other day, when you said that he blamed you?"

"He wasn't a drinker," she says, her eyes holding mine. "I know he left the house upset—I saw his face as he closed the door behind him; he looked so hurt. And I made him feel that way. He wouldn't have had that much to drink if he wasn't trying to block out what I said. Even at twelve years old, I knew that instantly when we heard how he died."

"But you can't possibly think—" I try again, but Wendy's steely gaze halts my words.

"After Thatcher passed, it was like everything in our house was soaked in grief. And it was weird, because I think my parents had come to terms with the possibility that I might die, in a way, but they didn't even think about losing him. The shock nearly killed my mother. She got really thin. My dad started working late, not coming home. And me? I went a little crazy. Because on the first day after his death that I felt happy again, he came to see me—to show me how much he blamed me."

"What do you mean, he came to see you?" I ask.

"Thatcher visited me in the spring after he died. I was at the beach and he gave me a message."

"A message?"

She smiles, but it's not the good kind of smile. It's that cracked, crazy kind that makes people feel really uncomfortable.

Crash! My mother's Tiffany lamp, the one on the corner table across the room, topples over and smashes on the floor.

Wendy and I lock eyes.

"I guess someone doesn't want you to hear the rest of what I have to say," she says, her tone accusing.

"Callie?" I hear my dad coming out of his bedroom.

"Hide!" I whisper to Wendy, and she ducks behind the long blue curtain against the wall.

When my father walks in, I'm picking up jagged pieces of stained glass.

"I couldn't sleep," I say. "I was going to read a little and I must have knocked into the lamp when I went to turn it on."

"Be careful, you could get cut," he says, coming over to help me.

"I'm sorry."

"It's only a lamp," he says. Then he gets the broom and sweeps up the mess. The toes of Wendy's black combat boots peek out under the curtain, but Dad never looks in her direction. I breathe a sigh of relief when we're done.

"Back to bed," says my father.

I give him a salute. "Just one more chapter."

He nods wearily and heads to his room.

"All clear," I whisper to Wendy when I hear his door close behind him.

She steps out from behind the curtain with her keys in her hand. I can tell she's not in the mood to finish her story now—her eyes are dark and angry.

"Wendy, can we just—" I start, but she stalks toward the front door.

I follow her, mad at Thatcher for interrupting us and disappointed in Wendy for letting him get in the way. But then she reaches into her shirt. "Here," she says, pulling out the chain that was resting under her black cotton tee. There's a ring on the end of it, heavy and gold. "This is what I really came to do."

Their grandfather's ring.

I look up at her in surprise.

"You said you needed it," she says. "Maybe it's better to get rid of this piece of him and try to forget."

My eyes fill up. "No," I say quietly, but she shushes me as she unclasps the necklace and slides the ring down the chain until it drops into my open, waiting palm. I grip it immediately, feeling its coolness, wondering at the power Thatcher says that it holds.

I stare at it for a moment, and then I open the front door. When she steps into the warm, humid darkness, I call after her. "Wendy?"

She turns, and in the soft glow of our porch light her features are softened, her harsh makeup faded, and she looks almost angelic, like a fragile, lovely ghost herself.

"Promise me one thing," I say. "Promise that when you do find peace—and you *will*—that you'll accept it. It's real. And it's coming from Thatcher."

She tilts her head like she doesn't quite understand. And that makes sense, because what I've said is so New Agey and vague that I hardly understand it myself. But it has to do with what I know about haunting the right way. All of which her brother taught me.

"No thanks," she says, and then she looks around the entryway, almost like she's talking to someone else. "I'm done expecting anything from the brother who tried to kill me."

And then she's gone, back into the night.

Thirteen

WHEN I WAKE UP in the morning, I open one eye and reach for the ring. I kept it under my pillow last night, and I tossed and turned, hardly sleeping. Wendy's parting words shook me. I know she was angry, and I'm sure she was lashing out because she felt her brother was trying to stop her from telling me the whole story. She really believes that Thatcher blames her for his death. Maybe he did blame her, at first. It isn't easy to be in the Prism, if you remember what life was like. But what she said . . . that Thatcher tried to kill her.

It can't be true.

But what if it is? What if that's why he interrupted our conversation with the stupid lamp shattering?

I shake my head—no. I know him. He isn't capable of that.

I turn the ring over in my hand, watching it shine in the early sunlight, wondering how it works, if it'll heat up or glow or something if I use it to call to Thatcher. I squeeze the ring again, and its energy makes me feel ill at ease. Am I just imagining that?

It's for emergencies only. Thatcher's voice echoes in my head.

I roll over and press my face into the sheets, wondering if Dad will mind if I stay in bed a little longer.

But then I hear my father's voice loud and clear, and inflexible: "Callie May! Church in twenty minutes!"

Among the sanctuary's dark wooden pews and bright stained glass windows, I hear the whispers about me: "Praise be." "Blessing." "Miracle."

When we sit down, my father bows his head and closes his eyes.

Since I've healed enough to get to church, we've been coming here every Sunday. We used to attend services with Mama, but after she died, Daddy lost some of his faith, I think. We only got here on holidays.

But now, today, I watch his open eyes and the way he sits—chest forward, head up, eyes trained on the pulpit. I can feel his faith next to me like it's a living being.

Mr. and Mrs. Yates, an older couple I've known since childhood, come by to say hello, and she takes my hands in hers. "You're a walking wonder, honey, that's what you are," she says. I smile politely at her, and the others who say similar things to me as they pass. I've realized that to them, I'm a beacon of hope, a soul brought back from the brink, proof of . . . of what?

The truth is that I feel uncomfortable in church now, like people can see just by looking at me that I know something they don't about life and death and Heaven and God.

But when I focus on the candles at the front of the church and watch the way their flames flicker, suddenly I feel this overwhelming sense of safety, like nothing bad could ever touch me here.

When Pastor Williams calls us to attention, I reach into the pocket of my skirt, where Thatcher's grandfather's ring meets my hand, solid and true.

This gold band feels more real to me than the words being spoken. More powerful than the "Amens" echoing around me as the service proceeds. Stronger than the voices of the choir that sing the hymns to uplift us all.

I feel guilty, believing in this token more than I do the religion I was brought up with, especially when I look over at my father and I see that his face is changing as the pastor speaks. Where the lines were hard and angles were square, they are softened and eased in this moment. Almost like someone is taking a hurt that is deep inside of him and drawing it out. Almost like something is *healing* him.

Turning back to the stained glass at the front of the church, I exhale. Maybe the specifics of religion don't matter. Maybe it's the feeling, that comfort, that sense of peace, that is true. Because that was a goal of the Prism, too.

When the service lets out, Dad and I are standing on the steps and talking to other parishioners and well-wishers when I see Carson shouting and waving at me from across the parking lot.

"Hey! Callie!"

When I look back at my dad, he's grinning. "Go ahead," he says, ushering me away from the people around us.

"Really?"

"Really. You've done your time this week. But be home for dinner."

I give him a big hug and a kiss on the cheek before bounding off to Carson's VW.

When I get into the warm car and almost burn my legs on the vinyl seats, I smile at the sensation. It's a Sunday in the sun and I'm here in Carson's car and she's turning the radio up and putting the top down and saying, "Let's do something fun today! Celebrate freedom and all that."

This morning while I ran around getting ready for church, I called Carson to tell her that Wendy gave me the ring. She's pretty confident that Reena and Leo won't be visiting us again, and while I feel very secure having it with me, I'm a little less inclined to believe that the poltergeists will just give up. Not when they have so much to lose.

I want to be cautious, like Thatcher would be. I want to be alert and mindful about everything around me. But doing "something fun" and being free is all I longed for when I was in the Prism—I wanted my life back, and now I have it. When I close my eyes and feel the wind rush over my face, my heart is torn.

Why can't I have all of this *life* and Thatcher, too?

My phone buzzes with a text and Carson leans over to look at the screen.

Nick: Upper Wando at noon—picnic! Please come.

"Oh cool," says Carson. "Let's go!"

I've been to a dozen picnics on the upper Wando—there's a perfect little beach with a small dock you can swim out to. Still my heart jumps into my throat. Not because this is the first time that Nick has reached out to me in a few days, but because Thatcher took his dying breath in that water.

Carson turns left toward our neighborhood. "I'll stop to get our bathing suits." When she pulls up to my house, she says, "Why are you being so weird? We have the ring. If something happens, we'll use it, okay? Run in and change. I'll meet you in my driveway in ten minutes. Oh, and can you bring that good face sunscreen you have?"

"Carson, I don't know if we can go," I say.

"Of course we can."

When I don't move or respond, she places her hand on my arm. "Is this about Nick? Do you not want to see him right now? I know things are weird, but maybe facing him and talking it out is what you both need, you know?"

"It's not that." I look into her eyes and bite my lip. "The upper Wando is where Thatcher died. He drowned there."

Carson's mouth falls open in shock and she stares back at me for a moment. But then, to my surprise, her eyes light up and she smiles.

"Callie, this is *it*," she says.

"What?"

"I saw something about this on *Hallowed Hauntings* last year— the death spot is a very powerful place. If you want to really connect with Thatcher, that's where it would be most likely to happen! It's the perfect place to try the ring and see if it's as strong as we think it is."

My pulse quickens. She's right. I know that the location where someone died holds a lot of energy. I feel the weight of the ring between my fingers. "I don't know . . . Thatcher said not to use it unless there was an emergency. And the poltergeists haven't tried anything since that day in the car."

"But you should test it, right? What if you're in a bad situation? It's good to be sure first."

I nod. What she's saying makes sense but . . .

Carson narrows her eyes at me. "Do it for me, okay, Cal? I know I've been acting all brave and everything, but that stoplight thing really freaked me out. I haven't been able to stop thinking about it since. The idea of something bad happening to you again, even knowing what I know about the other side, I just . . . please. Make sure the ring can protect you."

I reach over and hug her tightly, silently asking Thatcher to forgive me in my mind. "All right. I'll do it."

• • •

At the picnic spot, Nick throws a Frisbee back to Eli and jogs over to meet us. "Hey," he says, knocking me on the arm awkwardly.

I look up at him and force a smile. "Hey."

We spread out our towels on the sand and Carson rifles through the cooler that she packed with cold cuts and a pitcher of homemade lemonade that Eli will undoubtedly spike later. "Who wants a sandwich?" she shouts.

All the guys, plus Jessica Furlow and Gina O'Neill—girls we've been hanging out with since preschool, but in a peripheral way— raise their hands and Carson starts getting out the bread and spreading mayonnaise across each piece.

There are four of Nick's soccer teammates here, and six girls total, including Holly Whitman, whom I notice is wearing a really cute retro bikini.

Nick nudges me over on my towel and I let him sit. He brushes his hair out of his eyes and I notice the extra freckles that have formed on his cheeks since I last saw him. He's obviously been spending some time in the sun, and I instinctively glance again at Holly, checking to see if she has a burn or anything else that might connect them together. It's a little petty of me, given that I've been avoiding Nick for the last few days, but I can't help myself.

Even though we're drifting apart, it's still weird to think of him with anyone else.

"It's good to see you," he says, bumping my leg. "Sorry I've been kind of MIA."

"Me, too," I say, remembering the first time Nick and I touched years ago. It was electric then, sparks flying. But now it feels like sweetness, like friendship.

It's hard to admit, but something inside me just aches over it.

Eli trots over, and I'm thankful for the distraction. "Hey, Callie," he says, reaching for the cup of lemonade Carson is pouring. "Good to see you out."

"Thanks." My voice is hesitant, because did Eli Winston just make a sincere statement that wasn't followed by a joke or an insult?

He turns and jogs back to the Frisbee game.

"That was unexpected," I say.

Nick nods. "Eli's misunderstood. He's not a bad guy, you know. He just isn't as in touch with his feelings as, say, I am."

He stretches out his leg and it knocks over my canvas tote, sending Thatcher's ring tumbling out onto the sand. I snatch it up before Nick notices and hold it tightly in my hand.

"My bad." Nick stands my bag upright again. He didn't see the ring.

"It's okay." I finger the smooth gold edges. What would I have done if I lost it in the sand? My chest tightens when I allow my mind to consider it. Then a pang of guilt creeps up on me. I'm sitting here with Nick, holding on to a piece of someone else—no, someone dead—wishing for the impossible.

"Callie?"

"What?" I look up at Nick, and it's clear that he was saying something to me. Something I didn't catch because I was lost in my thoughts.

His eyes look wounded. "I thought a little time apart might

help. But I was wrong, wasn't I?"

"Nick!" It's Holly, her voice high and playful. "You promised you'd show me how to throw better."

I drop my sunglasses down over my eyes and pretend like he didn't just ask me that question. "Go ahead," I say. And I mean it. He shouldn't be sitting with me.

"You sure?" he says, a little surprised.

"Yeah, I'm fine," I say gently. "Go help Holly with her Frisbee toss."

"Do you want to play, too?" he asks. It's kind of him to try to include me. He didn't have to ask me to this picnic. He admitted he was trying to give us some space. It's just in his nature to care, and I'd never want to take advantage of that.

And yet I am a little.

"Nah," I say. "My skills are too advanced for this crowd."

Nick lets out a guffaw that's almost insulting and then he leans toward Carson. "Save me a sandwich."

"If you're lucky," she says.

After he goes back to Frisbee, she whispers, "What was that?"

"Eavesdropper."

"Obviously. I'm right here!"

"I don't know," I say. "I think we're kind of letting go. Or becoming friends. Or something."

Carson sighs as she places a circle of bologna onto the bread in front of her. "You guys are like the sitcom couple who are best friends and everyone kind of wants to be together, but then there's a handsome, mysterious stranger who comes in season two and then everyone wants the girl to be with him."

I swat her arm. "Um, thanks for reducing my life to a bad sit-com, Cars."

"You're right. Not a sitcom. Totally an hour-long paranormal drama with a few funny parts. And your show won't make it to season two if you don't test out that ring and make sure we're safe." She smiles at me. "Now's your chance."

"I will; I just need a minute."

I sit back and fold my knees under my arms as I gaze out over the water. It's a sunny day, the sky is clear and blue, and the trees are the vibrant green of summer, hanging into the river's soft, marshy edge. I hear my friends' laughter across the beach, but suddenly they all sound very far away.

When a cloud covers the sun for a moment, the palette of the day changes. The water . . . it looks black to me. It looks like death.

The story that Thatcher once told is before me. I can almost hear his voice. "It was homecoming night, after the dance, and we went out to the upper Wando River for a bonfire." He was with Reena, his date—actually, his girlfriend—and Leo, and another girl named Hayley. They found a boat, and climbed in. His words echo in my mind again. "We'd had a lot to drink. In the rowboat, Leo and I were standing up and being stupid. It had just rained for three days straight and the river was higher than usual, rougher. We shouldn't have been out on the water."

When the rowboat tipped far out in the river, they were too

drunk to swim to shore. Hayley hung on to the boat—she made it. The rest of them never came back. Three bodies in the water, one girl who escaped.

I shiver, despite the warm sun on my arms, the image of Thatcher's lifeless body filling my thoughts. My breathing is becoming labored, too, like my lungs are filling up with fluid. It's crazy, but it's almost as though I'm in the river, ten years ago, drowning alongside him.

I close my eyes and tell myself it's not a dark night where people are going to die. I tell myself what I'm feeling isn't because Reena or Leo are somehow forcing themselves on me, trying to cause me pain and scare me. It's a bright late-summer day with my friends. I have Thatcher's ring, and that's all I need to feel safe. That's all I need to make the thought of him drowning go away, and then I won't be hyperventilating like this.

I finger the ring again, smooth and powerful. But it's not enough.

I have to get away from this picnic and be with Thatcher.

"I'm going to take a little swim," I tell Carson.

She eyes me carefully. "Want me to come with?"

"No," I say, flashing a smile as I pull off my cotton sundress and stand up, still holding on to the ring. "I'm just gonna cool down for a minute."

I kick off my shoes and walk right in, diving under the water, warm from a summer of the hot Charleston sun. It feels like a relaxing bath, and now that I'm here, up close, I see that it's not black.

It's just the Wando—green and blue and sparkling in the bright day. My breathing is starting to return to normal, my lungs filling with clean air. Maybe I was just working myself up before. Maybe all those physical symptoms were just me channeling genuine empathy and not the evil hand of the poltergeists.

Jessica and Gina are lying on the floating dock and they wave at me as I go past doing the breaststroke. Everything seems to be okay, but still part of me won't accept that.

I swim out farther and farther, trying to still my thoughts and enjoy the feeling of the water moving gently over my skin. I bob my head under and up, under and up.

When I get out far enough, I tread water as I open my hand just above the small waves. The gold class ring is wet and sparkling in my palm. I look back toward the shore. Laughter, lunch, friends, games. Life.

And in my hand? Longing. An impossible love. Death.

I turn to face the stretch of water in front of me, and I close my eyes at the same time that I wrap my fingers around the ring.

Thatcher. I don't call with my voice, but I call with my mind, my heart, and my soul. I feel desire rush over my entire body like the *whoosh* of a sudden kicked-up wind.

Then I hear a small splashing behind me. When I turn, I see Nick. He saw me come out here and followed me.

For a second I'm annoyed, because it seems like he still thinks I need monitoring, but then something in the water changes. It's like there's an energy field connecting us—me and Nick—and as he comes closer, I see his eyes. His brown eyes. But they're blue.

A stormy blue with wind and rain and lightning in them.

He swims right up to me, and I put my feet down to touch the bottom, suddenly feeling weak. My toes just barely reach the soft mud below.

"Callie," he whispers. "There's no danger?"

I shake my head no, but I'm not sorry I called to him.

Thatcher's eyes flash angrily for a second, but just a second.

And then he's kissing me, his arms pulling my bare waist toward his bare torso, his hands running up my back with a fever. I feel a flash of heat tear through my body, and it's painful for a moment—agonizing—but then the hurt is gone and I melt into the kiss. It's like nothing I've ever had with Nick; it's not so much a kiss as a force of nature rushing through me, and I wrap one of my legs around his waist as I tilt my head back for more and put my arms around his neck and close my eyes so that I can see him with my other senses.

His lips taste like sugar, his arms feel strong and sure around me, the sound of his kiss is quiet but insistent, his skin smells like morning rain. He spins me around in the water, lifting my toes off the ground and burying his head in my neck, kissing me gently and breathing in deeply with a sigh that sounds happy and sad all at once.

"I knew it would be like this," he whispers.

In Nick's voice.

When we part, I keep my eyes closed, knowing it's Thatcher I'm with and wanting to feel that truth. But then he speaks again and his voice reminds me that even though what's happening is real, at the same time it's the farthest thing from it.

"I shouldn't be doing this," he says. "I'm so sorry."

I don't know whether he's apologizing to me, or to his fellow Guides, but he's right—he has crossed a line. We both know it's wrong, and I'm feeling guilty, too. But still I put my finger up to his mouth. "Shhhh."

I press my lips to his again, wanting more and more of him, needing to taste the softness of his tongue. It feels like I have no control of my body; I'm overcome, overwhelmed, overspent, and moving automatically to bring him close, closer, as close as we can get. I feel his chest against mine and I run my hands over his shoulders as we kiss, touching him in a way I never could in the Prism.

When I come up for air, I open my eyes. They're blurry from the water dripping off them, and I can almost see him—his blond hair, his angled cheekbones, and his perfectly crooked smile.

"I'm glad we did this . . . ," Thatcher says. "Just once."

He pulls me tighter to him, holding me in the water, and I can feel the energy pulsing around us, through us. This is real. This was meant to be.

"You can use my energy any time," I say to him, half meaning it, but knowing that we can't do this—*he* can't do this.

"I didn't," he says. "That's over—you don't have the same energy anymore."

"But I felt the rush—that crack of energy inside of me."

He grins. "You felt our chemistry," he says. Then he lifts my chin to make me look up at him, at his face, and it's *his face*. Thatcher's. My heart swells.

"The Guides have the power of possession—but we don't use it unless there's a crisis," he explains. "When I heard your call I thought . . . well, I guess I used it as an excuse to justify this."

He looks down at his body, which is not his body, and an even stronger surge of guilt hits me.

"I'm sorry, I . . . ," I start. I'm about to apologize for calling to him, but I'm struck by the desire to reach my hand up to touch the stubble on his cheek. It feels so real. He must be here. He must be alive. This can't be anyone but Thatcher.

"I thought you were in trouble," he says. "But now I have a reason to do this." He leans in again with a soft, slow kiss that seems to touch every inch of my soul.

When he pulls away this time, though, his gaze darkens. "Callie, you can't possibly know how much I've wanted to come to you this way. But the longer I'm here, the more I'm compromising the host."

The host.

He can't bring himself to say Nick's name. And I can't say that I blame him. I lower my eyes, the dreamy part of this moment fading as I start to feel ashamed. Like what we're doing is the most selfish thing in the world, and maybe it is.

"Will he be okay?" I ask.

"Yes. One possession won't hurt him. But another . . . it can't happen again."

"Is there some other way for me to hold you?" I ask him. All my inhibitions, my coy notions, are stripped bare now that he's here with me, in the flesh. Almost.

He shakes his head sadly. "I wish there was. But . . . you have someone else. Someone who cares about you, just as much as I do."

"We're not . . . like that anymore. And besides . . . it's you I love."

His lips crash into mine again and it feels like I'm being carried into the wind, flying up into the sky.

Too soon, our kiss is over, and he backs away.

He turns his head toward the shore, and I can see the green moon glowing on his neck—the symbol that indicates he's on the path to Solus. For the poltergeists, that area is black and charred, a dark mark. The features of Thatcher's face start to ripple and fade. I know he's going to leave me soon.

I straighten up and square off with him, willing myself not to go weak at the sight of him in front of me. I hold the shape of his profile in my mind to burn a memory I'll turn to again and again. After.

After the poltergeist threat is gone.

After Wendy heals.

After I help him merge.

I'll need to do that.

"Thatcher," I say, afraid he's going to disappear before I get to say this. "I know you interrupted Wendy's story last night. Whatever happened, you can tell me. I know she's wrong about you, that she's confused. I can help her . . . let go."

He sighs but doesn't respond.

"You could merge," I say. "Solus . . . it's all you've wanted."

Thatcher turns back to me. He traces my neck, his fingers moving up to my cheek as he cups my face in both hands and looks into my eyes. "It's no longer all I want," he says, and the pain in his voice makes me think of slipping under the water and leaving this world, joining him in the Prism and being with him again.

"Don't *ever* think that," he says, reading my eyes. "Knowing that you'll grow old and live a beautiful life—that will keep me going for an eternity."

I wrap my arms more tightly around his neck, refusing to look anywhere outside of the two of us. But I feel him pulling away.

"No," I whisper, and I look at him.

His eyes flicker for a moment and then his full lips set into a grim line.

"You can't call me again this way," he repeats. "Not unless there's something really wrong."

"I know." I resolve to be strong.

"My energy will be low after this; I'll be away for a little while. Callie, please be careful. Keep the ring close. The Guides . . . we still haven't found them."

Leo and Reena. They're still out there, invisible hate floating around in the atmosphere, waiting to strike.

I nod, my lower lip starting to quiver.

He leans down to my ear and whispers, "I love you." And then, "Always."

"Hey, Fisher, get a room!" Eli's voice hits me like a bomb, and the water around me immediately goes cold. My body feels like it's shed a skin, and I back away from Thatcher. Only it's not Thatcher anymore, it's Nick. He's confused and weakened as he looks at me, his eyes full of questions.

I fight to keep the devastation out of my face. Fight to remember how to breathe and speak.

Eli and Gina swim over. "You guys were getting pretty hot and heavy," teases Eli. He dead-arms Nick, who smiles back at him.

"Making up for lost time," he says, but I can tell he's not sure what happened. I wonder what he remembers, how his body feels. Mine is vibrating with sadness, but I plant myself in the sand at my feet to stop the shaking from showing.

I look at Nick, examining his face. He looks okay. Bewildered, but okay. After we all get back to the shore and dig into the leftover sandwiches, he lies on a blanket and pulls me down beside him.

"We were swimming?" he asks, his voice quiet.

I nod.

"I must have spaced out," he says, but then his eyes flutter shut. "Man, I'm so tired."

"Me, too," says Carson. She's lying a few feet over, her eyes closed as she works on a tan. "The sun is getting strong. I feel like I just ran a marathon."

I sit up and glance at both of them, the same look of drained energy in their faces. At least Nick might believe it was just a long day at the beach, like Carson's feeling. I doubt he'll admit to completely blacking out or not remembering kissing me in the water.

"I'm exhausted, too," I say, reclining in the crook of Nick's shoulder, wondering if I can capture any essence of Thatcher there. It's an act of pure desperation, of me wanting to cling to something that's already disappeared. But when I breathe him in, it's all Nick— Old Spice and wintergreen Tic Tacs. Comforting, familiar, sweet.

But nothing like what I felt in the water.

A tear trickles down my face as I realize what I'll lose as soon as the poltergeists are found and forced back into the Prism.

I'll lose my love, my soul mate, the boy who should be my forever.

Fourteen

I HAVE TROUBLE SLEEPING that night—I toss and turn in my bed until finally I give up and go downstairs, where I fall into uneasy dreams on the couch in front of the TV. I wake up in the early morning and wander back to my room to get dressed for school, but I end up just staring out the window. I'm replaying the kisses, the touches, the holding. All of the magic of a moment I know I'll remember as long as I live, and maybe beyond.

Lost in my thoughts, I barely have time to put on clothes before I hear Carson honk from the driveway. She was so tired last night driving home that she didn't ask any questions, but today she'll want to know what happened out on the water. I take off the amber pendant from Nick that I've been wearing, and I slip the gold class ring onto a chain that I can loop around my neck and into my shirt. Then I run out the door, grabbing a piece of bread for breakfast.

In the car, I tell Carson that we're safe for now, that the ring worked and Thatcher spoke to me when I called. But I play down the full story, because it feels private, like it's just for me and Thatcher. Amazingly, she doesn't push me—she still seems a little zonked from the sun.

I spend the day in something like a trance. At least I can use my "coma all summer" status as a way to avoid too much pressure from my teachers.

Since the water went cold yesterday, I've felt Thatcher's absence more profoundly. A warmth is missing, like when someone has their hand on your back and then they take it away and that spot feels even colder than the rest of you. It makes me ache inside. Only the ring brings me comfort today.

When I walk out of physics at the end of the afternoon, I feel a slight tingle, a pull, inside of me. I look around nervously, and I see that there's someone staring at me from the doorway across the hall. That guy, the one Carson waved to, the one I saw on the first day. His black-framed glasses catch the fluorescent lights and his face looks open, friendly. But the way he's eyeing me—it's so intense. I glance down at myself to see if I have some big ketchup stain from lunch on me or something, and I notice that Thatcher's grandfather's ring is visible outside of my cotton button-down. Is that what he's looking at?

I tuck the ring back underneath my shirt and turn away, walking toward my locker as the humming inside me starts to build. Carson is waiting for me a few feet down the hall. "It's time to wake you up," she says, as everyone else streams by us. "You've been dragging all day. Ice cream?"

I nod and give her a half smile for trying. If anyone can get me through this, it's Carson. We don't even take two steps before she starts in on me. "I've been thinking—we should try to see Wendy again. I think if you let me talk to her, I can—"

Suddenly I'm doubled over, falling to the floor. A lightning bolt of energy tears through me, and my eyes go blurry as I try to hold on to my books. But there's no holding on to them. It feels like I'm being ripped apart by the electricity that surges through my body, and the books fall to the floor as I gasp in pain. All the cells in my body are screaming for relief, like they're being squeezed by a giant hand in a death grip.

Then, as quickly as it hit me, the excruciating instant is gone. My eyes clear and I take a deep breath.

When I look up into the hallway, a few people are gathered around me, wondering if I'm okay . . . again. Mr. Hawes is asking me something, but I can hardly hear him. And I realize I'm in the same place where this happened before—right in front of the display case with sports trophies and Ella Hartley's memorial photo. I stare at her face for a moment, and my eyes refocus. Not on her photo, but on the glass itself. I see a reflection there. Everyone in the hallway is looking at me, except for him. His back is turned, and I can see the image of his face in the case.

Eli Winston.

But his smile . . . something about his smile isn't right. I've known Eli since preschool. He has a cocky, close-mouthed grin. But right now his mouth is cracked open, showing a full row of gleaming white teeth as he marvels at his own reflection. His arms are crossed over his chest, his back straight and puffed up, like he's celebrating a victory.

Oh no. *It's Leo.*

His mouth doesn't move, but still I hear his voice, echoing inside my head: *Don't bother calling for him. He won't be able to save you.*

My mind reels as I comprehend what's happening, but I have no time to wonder why—my body moves on its own, on instinct, and in a split second, I lunge at him, my feet moving faster than they should be able to and my arms shooting out to push him, to propel Leo's spirit from Eli's body.

Like a trained fighter, he turns and is ready for my assault. When I collide sideways with Leo-Eli, we both crash into the glass of the case behind us, and the shattering sound echoes through the hallway, drawing even more of an audience. I see Nurse K rushing over to us, and I realize that there's a piece of glass stuck in my shoulder, shallow but bleeding, I note, as I turn to look at it and pluck it out.

Despite the crowd around me, and even Nurse K trying to hold me back, I am focused as I stare at Eli—trying to see if it's worked, if I've expelled Leo's soul. His legs are taut and ready, his arms open for a fight. I didn't hit him head-on.

Not quite, Callie . . . , his inner voice taunts me. Leo is still possessing Eli.

Nurse K gasps, dropping her hold on me, and I rush at him

again, full speed, and he jumps aside so my body clatters into the lockers. I can feel a bruise blooming on my hip, which took the brunt of the impact. My muscles feel beaten, tired, but my mind is screaming with panic. Leo can't be possessing Eli. He can't! Thatcher said it shouldn't be possible.

I feel the gold ring, heavy and solid around my neck, but before I can reach for it, before I can call for help, I see Eli-Leo coming for me and I move on instinct again, hurling myself at him. This time, I hit him squarely in the chest, pushing him back into the brick wall next to the mangled glass case. I see Eli's limbs jolt up as the back of his head hits the bricks, and then he slides to the floor in a lump.

I back away from him slowly, not sure if I've done it. Not sure if Leo has been expelled. A few moments later, though, Eli shakes his head slowly and looks around. "What happened?" he asks. "Did that freshman cheerleader finally jump my bones like I know she's been dying to?"

And I know it's pure Eli. He has no idea that we fought and he's trying to play off his confusion.

My legs weaken in relief and I drop down beside him.

"I'm sorry." I may have hurt him. I reach around to feel the back of his head when suddenly my other arm is being pulled away.

"We need to get out of here," says Carson. "Don't worry, he's obviously fine."

She grabs my elbow and pulls me through the gathered crowd of students, dodging a couple of shocked teachers who surround Eli. Carson takes me straight into the girls' bathroom and opens the handicapped-stall door, bolting it behind us.

"What on the good green earth was that?" she shout-whispers.

I sink to the floor and Carson notices my injury. "Hold on," she says, rushing to the faucet to wet some paper towels. She comes back and starts to clean up my shoulder.

"It doesn't hurt much," I tell her. Though the bruise on my hip is starting to emit a dull throb.

"So, are you going to explain this to me?"

"Leo just possessed Eli's body." I pause and breathe deeply. "This was the second time he's taken Eli."

"*What?*"

I nod. "It's true. You weren't the only one they took this summer. Eli was the other victim."

"But I thought Thatcher said they couldn't achieve possession anymore, now that your spirit is here."

"He did say that." I look down at my hands. "But he was wrong. I *know* that Leo used me again today. I *felt* him take my energy."

"That's why you stopped short in the hallway," she says, putting it all together.

"Yes."

"But you were able to fight him—you got Leo out of Eli's body."

"It was instinct, something I guess I remember from being in the Prism," I tell her. "But if he achieves possession again, it'll be the third time, and Eli's soul will be lost. I don't know if I can even attempt an expulsion after that."

"Callie, if there's ever an emergency, I think this is it," says Carson.

"You're right." I reach up to finger the ring, but I don't feel it right away, and I look down, undoing the top buttons of my shirt frantically now.

"What is it?" asks Carson.

It's not there. "It's gone!"

We're interrupted by the booming voice of Vice Principal Hutch.

"Miss McPhee, Miss Jenkins, kindly come out of there."

We move quickly, as her tone commands, and when I get out into the hallway I look around, trying to spot the ring—it must have fallen off in the fight. Students are still gathered there, buzzing about what they saw a few minutes ago. Two janitors are shooing everyone away from the broken glass as they sweep up, and I bend down, trying to see what's in their dustpans.

"Miss Jenkins, head home," says Vice Principal Hutch, dismissing Carson. "Miss McPhee, come with me."

I'm still looking—*where is it?* But Vice Principal Hutch's voice reaches me again. "Now."

After getting patched up by Nurse K, who still seems shaken from witnessing the fight, I wait alone on a green couch just inside the main office for a few minutes, trying to formulate an excuse, some sort of story to explain this all away. It must have looked insane. Like I attacked Eli without provocation.

And the ring. *I lost it.*

I'm thinking about trying to sneak out of here, go search the hallway again, but there are teachers by the door. And then I hear the distinct sound of my father's footsteps on the linoleum outside.

His face does not look calm when he walks in, but Vice Principal Hutch is at his side, so he can't start shouting yet.

"Come with me, Captain McPhee, Callie," she says, and she leads us into Principal Faulkland's office, where Eli is sitting next to his mom with an ice pack up to his face.

"Mr. Winston is going to have one heck of a headache for a while thanks to you," says Principal Faulkland.

"He may have a concussion!" Eli's mother chimes in.

"I'm fine," Eli spits out angrily. "There's no way that Callie gave me a freaking concussion."

He glares at me, and I realize that now that he knows what happened, he's embarrassed that he got beat up by a girl. It would amuse me if the vibe weren't so serious in here. I know I'm in big trouble.

"I'm sorry, Eli," I say to him earnestly. Then I turn to Principal Faulkland. "Since the accident, I haven't felt like myself," I tell him. "I don't know what came over me today. I think it was a flashback, because I hardly remember anything."

"Same here," I hear Eli whisper under his breath.

I face my father, whose expression isn't giving anything away.

I turn back to Principal Faulkland. "I can't explain what happened. All I can say is that it won't happen again."

"I'm glad to hear that, Callie," says Principal Faulkland. "But I'm afraid that for the rest of this week, your time here will be spent in ISS."

In-School Suspension.

I nod. This is good. If I'm not near Eli, no one can take my energy and try to possess him. "I understand."

Eli's mother snorts in disapproval. "One week for an unwarranted and vicious attack?" she huffs.

Principal Faulkland looks her in the eye. "Yes. This is a first-time incident from a student who has been through a lot recently. One week will suffice."

Eli stands up. "Can we go?" he whines.

"I really am sorry," I tell him. And then I lean in to whisper, "Eli, I lost a ring. It's important—it's a family thing, it's—"

"Get away from me." He pushes past, walking in front of his mother as they leave.

Some thanks I get for saving his life.

On the way home, my father seems more contemplative than angry. The car ride is silent. And all the while I'm trying to figure out how I can find the ring. Eli must have it and not even know.

When we walk in the door, my father drops his keys in the bowl by the entryway and says, "Callie May, is there something going on that you're not telling me?"

So much.

"No." I kick off my shoes and go into the kitchen, washing my hands and then taking things out of the fridge to busy myself with making dinner so I won't have to look my father in the eyes while I lie to him.

Romaine, red onion, feta, walnuts, apples, and a little vinegar and oil for the dressing. I spread salad ingredients on the cutting board as Dad sighs loudly and sits on one of the stools at our island.

I chop up the walnuts and spread them on a baking sheet to toast in the oven, setting the timer for ten minutes.

"I'm trying hard to be understanding, you know," he says.

I slice into a big red onion. "I know, Daddy. What happened today wasn't . . . it wasn't me. I'm sorry."

"What was it, then? Was it really an unprovoked attack like Eli says? Did he say something that set you off?"

"Not exactly . . ." I pause with the knife in my hand, thinking of all the secrets I have from my father now. It doesn't seem fair, but I know if I tell him, he's going to take me straight to the doctor to get me checked out, and I can't afford what might happen after that.

"Callie, can I ask you something?"

"Sure."

"Did you speak to God?"

"What?"

"When you were in the coma, did you go to Heaven? Did you speak to God?"

"No." I shake my head.

"I did," says my father. "And he was listening." He has the tone he gets when he's absolutely sure of something. "I prayed harder than I have in my entire life, and he heard. I've always known that you're a very special person, from the day you were born to when we lost your mama to when you woke up from that coma."

"Daddy, every father thinks his daughter is special."

"Not like you!" He bangs his fist on the counter, and I jump a little, startled. "I'm sorry, Callie, but it just makes me so upset to see you doing things like skipping school last week and now getting into a fight over something that was surely trivial."

I raise my eyebrows and think, *Not exactly trivial*, but I don't respond, and Dad goes quiet again.

The water runs loudly as I wash the lettuce, but when I turn it off and start to dry the leaves on a paper towel, he says, "You know you were the only one who could release your mama from the pain she was in."

"Daddy, I was six years old," I say, trying to push down the sadness that's rising in me. First our strange conversation at the restaurant and now this. *Why is he bringing up Mama again?* "I didn't release her. She just died. She was sick and she died."

"No," says my father, shaking his head. His face is full of emotion now, and I wonder how we went from making salad and discussing Eli to rehashing my mother's death. "You need to know something so you'll recognize how extraordinary you are. I've wanted to tell you this for a long time. I tried to at dinner the other night, but I—I lost my nerve."

"Tell me what?" I've moved on to the feta, and I'm crumbling it over the salad bowl with sticky fingers.

"She died in your arms."

My sticky fingers freeze.

"Mama died in the hospital," I say slowly.

"Yes," says my father. "In the bed. In your arms."

I dump the rest of the feta in the bowl and reach for a towel to wipe my hands, turning away from my father so he doesn't see the tears that fill my eyes.

"What do you mean?" I whisper to the cabinets.

"On the afternoon she died, I went to get more coffee," he says gently. "The nurse stepped out to check another patient. You were holding your mama's hand, refusing to leave her side. You must have decided to crawl into bed with her."

I clench my eyes shut and I'm back in that hospital room. The blue-gray walls, the harsh lighting, the flimsy cotton gown that my mom wore in those final days. I remember climbing up on the side of the bed, asking her if it was okay. She couldn't speak much toward the end, but I saw the *yes* in her eyes and I lay down next to her, with my face tucked into the crook of her neck like always when we'd cuddle. Her hair was still long and soft on my cheek. Her skin still smelled like honeysuckle. I wrapped one arm across her chest, the other over her head.

"You fell asleep," says my father, standing behind me now. He puts his hand on my arm as I start to cry. "When I came back, you were asleep with your arms around your mama . . . she was gone."

I turn to him quickly so he'll catch my sobs in his chest, and he wraps me up in his arms, big and strong, and holds me tightly as I let out what feels like ten years of tears. I'm lost for a few minutes, and then the timer goes off.

Dad squeezes me closer and he whispers, "Oh, Callie May, you gave your mama such a beautiful gift that afternoon."

I sniffle and back up, turning off the oven before I look into his eyes. I hardly recognize him, this man who's opening up to me so much right now. "A gift?"

"You helped her to let go," he says. "She'd been staying past her time. For me, for you, for everyone who loved her. But she was tired. I didn't realize that I was holding on so tightly that I wasn't giving her permission to leave. But you, my miracle girl, you crawled up to her, you held her close, and you relaxed into sleep. You released her."

I tilt my head, marveling at what my father has just said to me. I think this is the most he's ever spoken about my mother's death, and I wonder how long these words have been in his heart.

"Why didn't I remember that?" I ask.

"I picked you up when I got back to her bedside. I looked to the nurse, and she nodded to confirm that your mama had passed." He pauses, steadying his voice. "In that moment of ultimate pain, I had you in my arms, a heavy bundle of sleeping child whose presence helped soften the most heartbreaking event in my life. I let you rest. I let you have a few more minutes of not knowing she was gone. It seemed only right. When you woke up, well . . . I told you that you and Mama had both had a nap, and Mama wasn't going to wake up anymore. That she was in her eternal sleep."

I lean against my father again to steady myself, tears still falling. "Daddy?"

"Yes, Callie May?"

"Thank you for telling me this. But why now? After all this time?"

"Because I want you to know and understand that you are my very special child. You are God's own wonder. You had the strength at six years old to let your mama leave this earth for Heaven's gates. And now, you've returned from a horrible accident that it would take a miracle to awaken from. That's why you've got to take care of yourself more. I don't know what happened today at school, but you're better than that. You have a higher calling. There's a reason you're on this earth, and it's not so you can fight with people like Eli Winston."

It's the most words my father's said at once in years. He reaches over to the island counter and hands me a tissue. I blow my nose and dry my eyes.

He's right. And I know he's thinking that my higher purpose is something like starting a nonprofit or being a strong female commander. He's always hoped I'd follow his footsteps into the military. But I'm thinking about the poltergeists. How they're here. How they can possess bodies. How they may kill someone soon. And how if the Guides can't find a way to stop them, then I have to.

I'm washing dishes after dinner when the text comes in. It's from a number I don't know, and it says, "I really need to talk to you about what you're experiencing. Please call."

Dammit, Carson. Again? I fire off an angry text to her.

DID YOU GIVE MY NUMBER TO ANOTHER REPORTER?

Two seconds later, my phone rings.

"What are you talking about?"

"I just got a text from someone I'm sure is a reporter. It says, 'I really need to talk to you about what you're experiencing.' Who else would send a text like that?"

"Callie, I haven't talked to anyone in the press since that day you got mad at me. I swear. I—"

There's a pause as she gets a text beep, and then I get one, too. I hold the phone away from my ear to look. Same number, but this time the text says, "I know where the ring is."

I slowly put the phone back to my ear. "Cars, someone just—"

At the same time, Carson's saying, "Dylan has the ring!"

"Wait—I think we just got the same text," I say.

Another beep on my phone, and this time the text reads, "This is Dylan Dixon, btw."

"Carson?" I ask. "Who the hell is Dylan Dixon?"

Fifteen

DYLAN DIXON IS THE guy from the first day, the one who was staring at me in the hallway just this afternoon. Carson seems to know him a little bit, enough to have him in her phone anyway. "I've been to his family's bookstore," she told me. He gave us instructions to meet him on Rainbow Row at midnight, and while I am not in the habit of meeting with strangers late at night, I do need that ring back.

So when I sneak out of my window at 11:45 to go to Carson's down the street, I feel guilty, but not enough to stay home.

"How's your shoulder?" Carson asks when I slip into the VW Bug and close the door softly behind me.

"Fine. Expertly patched by Nurse K."

"Love her."

"Me, too. She seemed more than a little upset by the fight, I have to say."

"She always has that faraway sad feeling about her, right?" says Carson, who's always so in tune with people.

"Yeah, but this was different. She kept talking to herself, mumbling something like, 'It couldn't be him.'"

"Well, it's not every day that a girl-guy fight breaks out on the honors hallway," says Carson. "I'm sure it was shocking for everyone."

"True."

She turns right out of our neighborhood, toward the historic district.

My shoulders tense, and Carson sees it.

"What's wrong?" she asks.

"What if the poltergeists try something again?"

"Hello, that's why I'm driving."

"I don't mean just messing with my energy—I mean possession. I could be putting you in danger just by being near you."

Carson smiles. "Let's just get to Dylan's," she says. "He has that covered."

I look at her sideways. "Okay, I need more information on this Dylan person."

Without hesitation, she launches in. "He moved from Seattle last year, his dad grew up in Charleston, his grandparents still live here. I found his family's bookstore this summer while you were . . ."

"In a coma," I fill in. "You can say it."

"Right, in a coma." She looks at me as we pull up to a red light and stop.

"What?" I ask her.

She sighs. "I don't want you to get all weird."

"About what?"

The light changes to green and she says, "He's really into the other side, too."

"Ghost stuff?"

"Yes," she says. "He knows a ton more than I do even, and he's been fascinated by you since you got back to school."

I frown, and she catches it. "Not in a weird way!" she says. "Callie, he seems cool. And the bookstore is amazing."

I look out the passenger-side window and watch the streetlights cast shadows across the car as we drive slowly down the empty late-night road. Sometimes Carson is too trusting for her own good. Then again, sometimes I'm not trusting enough.

When we pull up to the main tourist strip of Rainbow Row, I start to get antsy. Why here, in one of the most supposedly haunted parts of Charleston? Is this guy just a crazy ghost hunter?

Carson must see the doubt in my eyes because she says, "It'll be fine." And then she opens her door.

We step out of the car and onto the cobblestone street. Our footsteps echo on the empty walk, and it's extra eerie because this area is usually crowded with tourists.

Carson stops in front of two row houses—pink and green. "There," she whispers.

I look to where she's pointing, and I see that there is a tiny, narrow alleyway in between the two homes—one that I've never noticed before.

"I thought they were all row houses," I say. "With no space in between."

"That's what you're supposed to think," she says, and I can hear the glee in her voice at knowing this secret path. "Come on."

We have to go sideways to fit in between the buildings, and my back presses against the pink one. Suddenly, Carson stops.

"What is it?" I ask.

"The gate," she says. I rise up on my tiptoes to see that there is a flash of iron in front of us—a locked sliver of a gate. And Carson has a key. It's an ancient-looking skeleton key that fits smoothly into the old rusted lock.

"What in the world . . . ?" I start, but she shushes me and waves at me to follow her as she opens the gate.

When she does, I breathe easier. The alleyway widens so that there are a few inches on either side of us, and as we get farther away from the street, I see a glowing light behind the houses. There's a small outbuilding here, with two windows and a door. It looks like a fairy-tale cottage that belongs to a fictional character, with flowers in the window boxes and a gingerbread lattice.

"Is this Dylan's *house*?" I ask her, and she puts her finger to her lips again, and then knocks four times in quick succession.

When the door opens, I see Dylan standing there in thick black-rimmed glasses and a black hoodie. He has a little bit of stubble on his chin, but I can tell that there's a baby face behind his specs. He ushers us in and closes the door softly behind us.

"Callie, meet Dylan," says Carson.

"Hey," I say to him.

He pushes his glasses up his nose and waves hello before shoving his hands into his pockets. He's about the same height as me, and wearing skinny jeans that show off his thin legs.

"Callie McPhee," he says, rocking back on his heels. "A pleasure." Then he smiles at Carson, and I swear that even in this dim light I can see his cheeks flush a little bit.

"So anyway, this is Dylan's grandfather's bookstore, and it's kind of become my, um, *haunt* for all things supernatural," says Carson.

Dylan chuckles at her joke, and I notice again that he's really staring hard at my best friend.

"Well, nice to meet you, I guess," I say to Dylan. "Where's the ring?" Not exactly my most gracious moment, but this is a strange situation.

"Callie!" Carson bristles at my forwardness.

"What? He texted about the ring!" I look to Dylan. "Do you have it?"

"No," he says. "But I know who does. Sort of."

"Sort of?"

"Can we talk first?" he asks.

I cross my arms, feeling impatient.

"Listen, I'm not saying we should chat about the weather. Don't worry about niceties, even if we are in historic Charleston." Dylan grins in the face of my frown. He's more talky than Carson, if that's possible. "Besides, there's no need to play a game like those inane icebreakers they do at summer camp. Carson has already told me all about you—the coma, the Prism, your Guide, the possession you're dealing with involving a poltergeist named Leo. I can help, and I'm ready to get to work."

My mouth drops open as he gestures to a table in the center of the room, piled high with thick volumes of dusty old books, some splayed open.

I look at Carson, feeling betrayed.

"I know," she says. "I promised I wouldn't tell anyone. But Dylan isn't anyone—he's been studying the other side for, like, his whole life and he knows everything there is to know, and he already has some ideas for how to help us, and oh, please don't be mad at me, Cal."

"This isn't a game, Carson," I say to her, my anxiety rising.

"'Secrets are things we give to others to keep for us,'" says Dylan.

"Excuse me?" I ask, annoyed.

"Elbert Hubbard," he says. "Late-nineteenth-century author, philosopher—"

"Are we in English class?" I look at Carson.

"Callie, he's just trying to say that he can be trusted . . . that *we* can be trusted." My best friend moves to stand next to Dylan.

I look at him now and he gives me a what-are-you-gonna-do shrug.

"You really trust him?" I ask Carson.

She nods her head vigorously. "I do."

And what choice do I have? I've got to know where that ring is, and this guy already seems as stubborn as Carson. "Okay," I say. "Tell me what you know, Dylan Dixon."

Immediately, he plows into the pile of books.

"This one talks about a realm between Earth and Heaven, a sort of waiting area where souls linger," he says.

I give him a withering stare. "I don't need to rehash what I already know," I say. "I need to know more."

He smiles at me. "Carson said you were serious."

"Dead serious."

Carson laughs nervously then, and I can see how much she wants me and Dylan to get along, how much she hopes he's the answer to all the things that are we're dealing with. But he's just a kid in a bookstore. Still, he does know about the ring.

"Okay!" says Dylan, springing into action again and moving around the table like a jumping bean. "Possession, right? That's the immediate issue we're facing."

"Right," I tell him. It still feels strange to be talking about this stuff openly, but it's a relief, too. "Listen . . . there's something I'm worried about. If the poltergeists are using my energy for possession, they may be able to attempt it at any time. I may be putting both of you in danger by being near you right now. The ring is the only thing that can protect us."

"How?" he asks.

I hesitate slightly. "Well . . . it's a way to call to someone who can help, if we need it."

"A ghost?" Dylan's eyes light up.

"Yes. A ghost." I shoot a glare at Carson and she gives me a nod of encouragement.

"The talisman," Dylan whispers.

"What?" I turn my head sharply back to him. That's the word Thatcher used.

"'Love is the talisman of human weal and woe—the *open sesame* to every human soul.'" He pauses. "Elizabeth Cady Stanton. I've read about this." He takes three strides across the room and reaches up to a high shelf for a slim black book. He flips through the pages quickly and finds what he wants—this kid who loves obscure quotes is faster than Google. He starts to read aloud: "Every soul that remains in limbo has a talisman, an object of some value to their living selves which binds them to Earth and the living world. With this talisman, the ghosts can be summoned by living beings."

He pauses. "Unfortunately, most living beings aren't aware of this fact. They hardly ever recognize the talisman as something of value."

It's just what Thatcher told me. I sit down at the table next to where Carson is standing.

"Okay," I say to Dylan. "I think I'm starting to trust you."

He smiles, like he knew I'd come around.

"And by the way," he says, a confident lilt in his voice. "You don't have to worry about poltergeists taking your energy right now. We're safe here. This store is a no-fly zone for ghosts."

"A no-fly zone?"

Carson jumps in. "It was founded by an old-school believer

back in the seventeen hundreds."

"A great-great-something-uncle of mine who worked on a spell to protect this space," says Dylan, puffing out his chest proudly.

I look around the bookstore, dusty and dim with row upon row of well-worn volumes. It's much larger than it appeared from the outside. "I had no idea it existed," I say. "How big is the store anyway?"

"Bigger than it looks," he says. "It was built in a way that uses tricks of the light—and the darkness—to obscure its location and size."

"How does anyone ever find it?" I ask.

"It finds you," says Carson.

I give her a skeptical look, but her earnest gaze tells me that this is for real—or at least she believes it is.

"This place was founded by someone who understood that the knowledge in these books was worth protecting," says Dylan. "Someone who could talk to the other side . . . like Carson can."

She waves off the compliment, but her lips turn up a little, like she's pleased he's noticed. "I haven't mastered that yet," she says. "But I'm trying."

"You have natural talent," says Dylan. "You just need the right words."

Carson nods. "That's where the books come in." She turns to me. "None of this stuff is online. I know, because when you were in a coma, I—"

She stops, looking sheepish.

"What?" I ask.

"She used an incantation from this book to try to bring you back," says Dylan, holding up a dusty red volume.

I flash back to a séance Carson attempted in her room with Nick. Reena and I were standing on the sidelines watching, and I thought it all looked so silly . . . until my voice locked up and a strong vibration hit my core. I woke up in the Prism later, not knowing what had happened.

I remember the words Carson said that night. I close my eyes and recite them now: "By the light of the moon and the branch of the tree, I call the soul of Callie McPhee back to me. . . ."

When I open my eyes, Carson and Dylan are staring at me, their mouths hanging in parallel Os.

They turn and look at each other. "It was working!" squeals Carson.

"It almost did," I tell her. "I was there. You almost brought me back."

Carson and Dylan grab hands and do what I can only describe as a happy dance. I need to put a lid on this.

"Y'all, I know this is exciting for you," I say. "But there are lives at stake here. Real people's lives." I stare at Carson meaningfully. *Like yours*, I think.

They tamp down their enthusiasm, but it takes some effort. Having me here to confirm what they've been reading about and believing in must be like a little kid meeting the real Santa Claus. Except he doesn't exist. But the ghost world does.

"Anyway," says Dylan, gesturing around the bookstore. "This space is protected."

He looks up at the ceiling—all wooden beams and hanging lightbulbs, no glowing force field or double-reinforced orb of other-worldly safety—and I'm about to ask him more questions, but then Carson says, "Believe for once, Callie."

I think about all the years when I dismissed Carson's ghost stories and her feeling of connection to the other side—to my own mother even. It wasn't fair of me, especially as she stuck by me through my cynicism and scoffing. She never lost her confidence, never wavered, and now I know that she was right all along. So maybe I owe it to her to believe now.

"Okay." I lean in on my elbows and look up at Dylan like he's a teacher. "Continue."

My best friend pulls a chair alongside mine.

Dylan beams at her as he starts to talk.

"Possession," says Dylan, returning to the task at hand. "It's all about energy."

"Right," I say. "I had extra energy in the Prism. And it seems like I still have a lot of it, because I know that Leo used my energy today at school to possess Eli. I felt it happening."

"A blessing and a curse," says Dylan, and suddenly he sounds like Thatcher in Guide mode. "They're using your supply, but it's also what enables you to expel them from a body—that takes huge amounts of energy." He digs through a corner pile on the table and finds a book with a plain brown cover. "This one talks about controlling energy and moving physical objects—telekinesis."

I nod. "I did some of that in the Prism," I tell him. "I was able to move things . . . sometimes."

"It takes a lot of concentration, especially if you don't have a physical body," says Dylan. Then he smiles at Carson. "Imagine trying to pick up a glass of orange juice with your mind!"

"Or blow dandelion seeds into the wind with your thoughts," says Carson.

"Or take out the trash with brain waves!" says Dylan.

"Okay, okay!" I jump in. "I think we all get the idea."

Dylan and Carson laugh together, and I'm almost charmed by how cute they look. But I'm also impatient—I need him to keep going, get to his point or what he thinks he knows, and tell me where the ring is.

"Sorry, sorry," says Dylan, and he straightens his mouth into a line with some effort. "Do you remember how you moved things?"

I think back to Reena's instruction. And it's strange that I'm calling upon the teachings of my enemy in this moment. But at the time, I thought she was my friend.

We took a walk on Folly Beach. She led me to a bonfire, where I met two other poltergeists, Norris and Delia. It was there that she taught me how to blow out a flame using my memories of birthday-cake wishes and scented candles. "You have to feel yourself blowing out the flame before you can actually do it—almost like you're imagining it happening first," she told me.

I nod. "I remember."

"Today your energy worked for you on pure instinct," says Dylan. "I've never seen anyone move as fast as you did, or as furiously."

"You were there. I saw you outside my classroom."

"I have chemistry on that hall last period. It was hard to miss the fight."

"I don't know what I did in that hallway," I tell Dylan honestly. "I didn't think—I just acted."

"Well, it worked," he says. "And we can review what happened if you like."

"What do you mean?"

Dylan holds up his phone. "I caught most of it," he says.

I freeze. "You recorded it?"

He comes over to me and sets the phone down. I stare at the white triangle Play icon for a moment before pressing it and watching myself move like a trained fighter. I review it twice—seeing how quickly I moved and what the final shove looked like, the one where I expelled Leo fully. I'm amazed at myself, at my own strength. Do I actually still have the ability to fight them, even without my extra energy from the Prism?

Or Thatcher's talisman?

Dylan leans in and says, "You were great. But if you learn how to harness that power a little better, you'll be more prepared for next time."

"Next time?"

"You don't think they'll stop now, do you? Not when they're so close."

Dylan's words make me shiver despite the musty heat in here. Reena and Leo are obsessed with living again. They won't stop until they've killed someone to get what they want—a body.

And although Thatcher has told me he's searching high and low for them, maybe it's too late.

Maybe they're untouchable.

Sixteen

OVER THE NEXT HALF hour, something unexpected happens. Carson, Dylan, and I actually start to have fun. Dylan keeps turning back to his books to give me more instruction, more ways of honing my energy.

"Let's use this." Dylan turns and pulls out a silver candelabra from the cabinet behind us.

Carson giggles.

"Are you for real?" I ask him.

"What?" he asks, a smile in his voice. "Too stereotypical ghost?"

At first I think I won't be able to do anything. I tested my energy already in class, and nothing happened. But somehow, right now, I start to feel the power again. I remember what it's like to not have a body, and the body that I have now isn't getting in my way.

While I face a wall covered with old pictures and dusty papers,

I focus on a black-and-white postcard of a fountain that looks like it's somewhere in Europe—Italy, I think. I imagine its scalloped edges on my fingers, its slight weight in my hand. I close my eyes, but inside my mind I can see the postcard clearly; I can smell its musty paper scent, feel the slight ridge on the corner where the stamp is still stuck.

I know I'm moving the postcard before I open my eyes, because I hear both Carson and Dylan take breaths in, like they're seeing a rainbow, or a snowflake, for the first time. It crosses my mind that it's usually only in childhood that people make that sound—that breath intake that signals pure delight. I open my eyes and see the postcard floating across the room toward Carson, and I exhale in absolute wonder.

I am moving an object with my mind.

Carson plucks the card out of the air.

"Ouch!" she says, dropping the card and looking at her fingers.

"Are you okay?" I ask.

"Just a shock."

"Sorry, Cars."

"Are you kidding? Don't be sorry! That was amazing!" My best friend rushes up to me and puts an arm around me, squeezing my shoulders.

"It was," says Dylan, still beaming. "Your energy is really high. That's a good thing." He picks up the postcard and places it back in its spot on the wall.

It is good, I think, amazed. I'm using the imagined touch that I called on in the Prism to interact with earthly objects. I'm not saying it's as easy as snapping my fingers, but it's doable.

"Does it make you tired?" asks Carson.

I shake my head no. "It takes a little concentration, but it's not bad," I say, wondering what Thatcher would think of me playing with powers. I'm sure he feels they are better left forgotten, even with the poltergeists still at large.

"Well . . . I have good news and bad news," says Dylan.

"Bad then good," says Carson. "Always."

Dylan looks at me and I nod in agreement.

"The bad news is that there are only certain locations where you can use this power," he says. "This bookstore, this spot specifically, happens to be an energy vortex. It channels energy from both this world and from the other side, and it's one of only a handful of spots like that in Charleston."

No wonder I couldn't use my energy in physics class. But that means . . .

"So I can only protect myself in certain locations?" I ask. "What if the poltergeists strike somewhere else? Somewhere outside of a vortex?"

"That's the good news," says Dylan, picking up a small yellow book and tapping it with his finger. "According to this text, they can only 'strike,' as you put it, in these particular locations, because that's where your energy is present, and they have to draw on you to achieve possession."

I take in what he's said.

"Is there a list of these . . . what did you call them? Vortexes?" I ask.

Dylan points to the wall, where there's an old map with ragged edges—like something you'd imagine a pirate tucking into his pocket—in a glass frame.

"The areas that are circled in dotted lines represent vortexes," he says.

"They're not very big," I say, staring at the map.

"No, they're just pockets. Maybe the size of a small backyard."

"And what are they exactly?" I try to listen hard, because this is the type of thing I can easily pretend to understand but not really grasp.

"It's like Earth and the Prism are divided by a thin layer of fabric." Dylan gestures as he talks, just like Carson does when she goes on a monologue. Right now he's stretching out an imaginary piece of material between his hands. "The fabric is mostly smooth, but in certain parts, it's bunched up—almost like it's sewn with a tighter weave in those spots. Those are vortexes. The connection is closer between worlds, so the energy is higher."

"What makes the connection closer in those specific spots?" I ask.

Dylan looks to the map on the wall. "The way it's laid out here seems to suggest that the vortexes exist in places where there were mass deaths."

"Mass deaths?" I lean forward.

Pointing to the map, Dylan fingers one spot that looks like it's the harbor. "This was a Civil War battle site," he says. Then he moves his hand to another location. "And there was a horrible hotel fire here in 1902."

"So the places where a lot of people died at once . . . those are now vortexes." I stand up and walk to the map to look with him.

"Right," Dylan says. "And there are a bunch in Charleston."

"Our city has always been a ghost town," says Carson as she comes over to join us.

My eyes travel over the map carefully. The landmarks on it are old and outdated . . . it's hard to know where they are in today's geography.

I point to one spot that has familiar points of reference around it, and Dylan comes up beside me. "This is—" I start.

"School," Dylan finishes. "I know. The hallway where you and Leo fought must be a vortex. And there may be some that aren't on the map . . . it's from 1912, so any multiple deaths since then could have created more."

I scan the map again to see if I can locate the point where the poltergeists took control of my car. We must have passed through a vortex where they were waiting in that moment.

I take a picture of the map with my phone. If Reena and Leo are ready for a fight, I'm going to give it to them.

"Good idea," says Dylan. "You can use the map to help you avoid these places."

I pocket my phone. "That wasn't why I took the picture."

Carson sighs at me. "Callie, don't even think about charging headfirst into these spots. We know how dangerous it is."

"So I'm supposed to run away from the poltergeists?"

"Not run away . . . *avoid*."

I raise my eyebrows. "Yeah, well, they're the ones threatening me."

Dylan looks at me with intense eyes. "We don't know what exactly they can do. And it's not just you they're trying to hurt." His voice quiets and then he says, "'Often the test of courage is not to die, but to live.' Vittorio Alfieri, Italian poet."

I turn away from him, bothered by his silly quoting habit, but also cut by the fact that this line, though he can't know it, has another meaning for me. If I died, I could be with Thatcher. I could fight the poltergeists by his side, and make sure that my friends were safe. Alive, I feel vulnerable, like I have no control over when or how they use me. They're invisible and powerful and lurking in secret.

Maybe Dylan's quote is right, though. Staying safe, staying alive, is the braver choice.

I look at Carson. I'd never forgive myself if something happened to her because I was feeling reckless or mad at Reena. *I'll wait*, I think. *At least until I get the ring back.*

"How will I even know if I'm in a vortex?" I ask. "You said yourself the map isn't really reliable."

"You'll feel it," says Dylan. "When you're in a spot, you may experience a pull or a shock or something—"

The energy pulses, the waves of electricity . . . I know them all too well. "I've felt that," I tell him.

"When you do, you have to leave," warns Dylan. "Those are the spots where you'll be vulnerable and used. Very few people will recognize their potency, but they're places where ghosts and the living mix."

If I had Thatcher's ring, though, I wouldn't have to retreat. I could call on him and we could counterstrike together, like we used to in the Prism. But without it, I think I'm going to have to follow Dylan's advice, as much as it infuriates me.

"Okay," I say. "I understand."

"Do you think the upper Wando is a vortex?" asks Carson. She turns to Dylan. "We were there the other day, and I felt a weird energy thing."

"What do you mean?"

"Well, I remember when we got to the river, and then just before we left . . . but I felt so exhausted by the time we went home, and I don't even remember most of the middle part of the day."

Dylan tilts his head, interested, but I dismiss her.

"Sunstroke," I say, remembering how Nick and Carson and I lay on the shore together during the picnic. Nick was weak and forgetful because Thatcher had taken his body, but Carson was just being dramatic.

"I don't know," says Carson. "Maybe I can feel some of the ghost energy, too!"

There's a chance she's right. Wouldn't it make sense that she's becoming more sensitive to the spirit world, given how much time she's been spending around me?

"I have one more test for you, Callie," says Dylan. "And Carson, you can see if you can feel some of Callie's ghost energy in this one."

She beams and stands up as the faded bluebird clock on the

wall strikes one. It makes a crazy chirping noise and I vow not to stay until two. I don't think I could bear to hear that again.

"Guys, I really need to get home," I say. "And you haven't even told me where the ring is."

Dylan smiles. "I showed you."

He points to his phone, still on the table, and I press Play again.

"Right there," says Dylan, pausing it just as I'm about to slam into Eli-Leo for the third time. It's blurry, but I can see Eli's hand reaching out to take the chain.

Looks like my suspicions are confirmed.

"It was Leo who grabbed for it then," I say.

"Yes. But it's an earthly object, and Eli may actually have it."

"I asked him about it in the office later but he just pushed right past me."

"He may not remember he has it," says Dylan. "Like you said, it was Leo who took it."

"This is getting confusing," says Carson.

"I'll say." I pick up my keys. "I need to go talk to Eli."

Dylan points at the clock. "It's after one in the morning," he says.

"I've got to get that ring back," I tell him.

"We will, I promise," he says, making it clear that together we're all a team. "But first, we should be sure you know what you're doing . . . in case the poltergeists show up again."

I sigh in frustration.

"Your spirit-world instincts kicked in today," says Dylan. "That's good. But it's even better if you truly know what to do and *how* you did it. And we can't be sure until we test you on the movement of living energy."

I look down, impatient.

"Callie, it's important," says Dylan. "I was reading about this and it's very rare—in fact, I can't find proof in any of the books I've read that a person could ever truly move living energy."

I stare at Dylan, trying to read his eyes behind the lenses of his big glasses.

"You don't believe I can do it," I say, sensing his doubt.

"I don't . . . ," he starts. Then he pushes his glasses up his nose again. "There's just no evidence that it's possible."

I give him a patronizing grin. He's like my father in a certain way. He believes in so much, but he needs proof, either in books or in life, to make him sure. Dad didn't even renew his faith in prayer until his own daughter had come back from near-death.

"You want evidence? No problem."

I turn to Carson and focus my energy on her petite frame. She nods, signaling that it's okay to use her as a target. I move toward her slowly, not like I ran at Eli today, but still deliberately—I know what I'm doing.

When I reach out my hands to strike, I focus not on the edges of her physical being—her shoulders, her chest—but instead on the interior layer of energy that lies underneath.

Carson stumbles backward in response to my push.

"Oops," I say. "Sorry."

She smiles and spaces out her feet as she steps back onto her mark. "I'm ready this time."

I try again, with the same results.

"You're not trying to move her physical body," says Dylan.

I let out an annoyed breath. "I *know*," I tell him, thinking that I'm a lot more aware of what's going on than he is.

"Okay; well, if you're already reaching beyond that with your mind, then it's just a speed issue," he says.

"A speed issue?"

"Yeah." He grabs his phone and presses Play. "Let's watch the part again where you rush at Eli. You did this thing where you stopped your body completely from moving just at the point where your hands could reach him . . . there! See how they pushed out like a shot, almost too blurry to register on the recording. Your hands burst out at him at high speed. That must be the trick."

I tilt my head and watch it again. What Dylan's saying makes sense to me. The next time I back up, I make a point to stop myself right in front of Carson and see if my arms automatically do what they're supposed to.

My hands flash through her, almost like she's not there, and Carson's eyes immediately go blank. They lose their light. My best friend slumps over and Dylan reaches forward to catch her. But before she falls, her muscles spring back, like she's one of those wind-sock puppets that advertise used-car sales, and I see the light pop into her eyes again.

Phew.

I turn to Dylan with a smile. "It worked."

"Amazing!" he says. He hovers near Carson to make sure she's okay, but she's laughing already so I know she is.

"That was incredible," says Carson. "Dylan, you better write this down for posterity."

Dylan's still shaking his head in wonder, whispering to himself. "It must be because you've been to both sides . . . you have energy pulled from Earth and the Prism together. Or maybe it has something to do with . . ."

He raises his voice as I gather my things. "Callie?"

"Yes?" I turn to him, ready to get home and be alone with time to think about everything that's happened tonight. I need to figure out how to approach Eli tomorrow, and if there's some way I can get Thatcher to come to me without the ring. He should know everything I learned here tonight, and if this place is a fortress that ghosts can't penetrate, the only way he can find out is through me.

"Have you ever been close to anyone who died?" Dylan asks.

"Um . . . yeah, of course," I say. "Carson didn't tell you about my mother?"

"She did; I'm sorry, by the way," he says. "That's not what I meant though. What I'm trying to say is, have you ever been *physically* close to someone who died?"

I lock eyes with Carson, but then I realize that she doesn't know the details about what really happened on my mother's deathbed, so she can't have told him. I just found out myself that Mama died in my arms.

I don't want to talk about this. Not with someone I just met. I can't.

"No," I say to Dylan.

Seventeen

CARSON AND I SCOOT our way back down the narrow alley and onto the street, now glittering under a full moon that has emerged from the clouds. It rained while we were in the bookstore, and the cobblestones are slick and shiny.

I'm still shaking a little, wondering why Dylan asked about that—whether someone had ever died near me. I probably should confess what my father told me today. . . . Dylan knows a lot and he's helpful. But I just met him. How can I tell him about my mom's last moment, now that I know exactly what it looked like? It's too painful.

"Callie!" Nick's voice breaks the night's silence, and Carson and I both turn, startled.

He's standing twenty feet away from us, car keys jangling in his hand and dressed in the jersey shorts I know he likes to sleep in.

This is a long drive from where he lives.

"Give me a minute," I say to Carson. I walk over to him, leaving her by the VW.

"I went to your house," he says. "I saw you sneaking out with Carson and I followed you here. But then you disappeared. And I didn't see where you went. What the hell are you guys doing out here in the middle of the night?"

We were in the bookstore for over an hour. I look back to where the entrance is, hidden to the eye unless you know it's there. Nick must have been so confused. "You've been waiting all this time?" I ask, not wanting to fully answer his question.

"I had to see you," he says. "You didn't answer my texts, and I had to be sure you were okay after the thing today with Eli. Which I didn't want to believe because it's absolutely crazy, but Hol—" He pauses for a moment, realizing his misstep. "I heard that it was true."

I nod. I owe him an explanation. More than one, really.

I turn back to Carson and wave to her. "Go ahead."

Nick gestures toward a bench, the one we used to sit on while we looked up at the pink house with the five perfect second-floor windows, the house I used to stare at after my mom died, where I imagined someone with a dream life lived. And I realize that the time is now. This is a good place to talk.

"What is going on with you?" asks Nick. "I know for a fact that you'd never attack anyone. Especially Eli. I can barely take that guy."

"I'll tell you, but it's a long story and it's going to sound really weird."

"I've got time," says Nick. "And I'm already freaked out, so . . . go ahead."

I take a deep breath. We stay quiet for a moment in the still of the night. I'm worried about what to say to him. But out here, in the dark, the truth has to come to light. And not just the truth about Eli.

"You were here without me," I say finally, my voice barely a whisper.

"What?"

"Over the summer . . . you sat out here alone."

"Being here reminded me of being with you."

"That day on this bench, you were listening to Bon Iver."

He laughs. "I guess I'm predictable. Either that or you know me really well."

"You put out your hand," I continue. "You whispered to me."

Nick's body stiffens now and he turns to look at my face. I can feel his gaze, but I look straight ahead, at the pink house. It gives me comfort, still.

"I took your hand," I tell him. "Our fingers curled together."

I put my hand out now on the bench, reaching out to him like he did to me that day. But this time, we're both here in body as well as soul.

Nick places his hand over mine and our fingers intertwine— muscle and blood and bone.

"What are you trying to tell me?" he asks.

I can feel something inside him opening, a tiny door in his mind that I've unlocked. Because he does remember that day, and he did feel my presence here, even though I was just a ghost in that moment. It's all I need, and I rush in.

For the next hour, my voice is a soft and steady sound on East Bay Street, laying everything out before him: the Prism, my haunting mission, the poltergeists and the danger they posed and are still posing. I tell him about Eli, how he has a ring that I need to keep us safe. About Dylan, how he and Carson are the only other people on Earth who know about what's happening here in Charleston—the vortexes, the possessions.

The only piece I leave out is Thatcher, because I just can't bring myself to explain to my sort-of boyfriend that I fell for someone else on the other side.

Nick's eyes flicker with doubt, but I keep talking to convince him with details, things I couldn't have known unless my spirit was with him.

"I saw you with the bottle of Jack Daniels in your room. I saw you drinking in the woods before Tim McCann's party. I was with you when you crashed your car in Mr. Dodson's field. And you remember this bench. I know you do—you remember feeling my presence here."

"It's not that I don't want to believe you . . . ," he starts. "Carson knows about some of those things, too, and maybe you're good at guessing the details. Maybe somewhere in your mind you even believe yourself . . . but none of this sounds real. You've been through so much."

"You seriously don't believe me."

"It's a lot to take in, Callie," says Nick.

I'm realizing how Carson must have felt whenever I dismissed her beliefs, about connecting with my mother, about her intuition.

I take my hand away from his. "I know other things, too," I say, ready to get everything out in the open. "I know you were texting Holly Whitman while I was in the coma. I know you were planning to break up with me, Nick."

Nick's face falls. "She told you?"

"She didn't have to. I saw the texts when I was in the coma, hovering over you as a ghost. I saw the texts to 'H' in your phone."

He winces. "You went through my phone?"

"I was a ghost! I saw you texting her!" I rake my hand through my hair in frustration. "I know you don't believe me, but that's the truth."

Nick looks down at his hands and I feel the frustration drain from me as quickly as it came. In its place is sadness. I shake my head. "It doesn't matter," I say softly. "This isn't how I want us to be."

"Me neither," he says.

"Holly is a nice girl," I say. And it actually feels good to admit that to him.

"She is."

I take in a deep breath.

"Things are so different, aren't they?" asks Nick. He looks into my face and I meet his eyes. "Is it because of the coma? What you think you saw?"

I frown. He *still* doesn't believe me.

"No," I say to Nick. "You were over me before I even got into the accident."

"I know," he says. "I just didn't feel the same. . . . I thought we needed to break up." He pauses and I can feel him searching my face. "But afterward it felt like we had a second chance. Didn't it?"

"After . . ." I shake my head. "It did, for a little while."

I think about all the nights he's spent helping me fall asleep, cradling me in the nook of his shoulder and keeping me calm, safe, and warm.

"I wish things were different," I say to him.

"So do I." He drops his head and looks at his hands.

"Callie?" His voice sounds like a prayer in the darkness. "I'm not going to deny that Holly is . . . well, that I like her. But in a way, I'll always love you, you know."

"Nick," I say softly, his name on my tongue like a remembered sweetness. "It's okay to let go of what we were."

He nods, acknowledging what we both know, and when I let a tear fall, Nick wipes it away.

We sit there for a few minutes, the night wholly silent around us. There are three porch lights on, and even from across the street I can hear the bugs smacking into them—it's that quiet.

I stare at the narrow alleyway that leads to the bookstore, and to Dylan. I think about his family, their history here and their connection with the other side. I watch the wind rustle through the palmettos and hear the distant sound of a barking dog. A streetlight flickers on and off down the street. Charleston feels like such a haunted city. I used to think that was all superstition and made-up stories; I hated hearing about the ghost legends. Now I realize that there are advantages to such a spiritual presence—there is otherworldly wisdom here, and it seems like a lot of it lies inside Dixon's Bookstore.

Nick's profile is serious and sad. I wish he'd believe me. I wish he'd help us. He's always been so good with people—he could talk to Eli for me, maybe even get the ring back. And besides, he's been a friend for so long. . . . I don't want him out of my life completely.

I look down at my scuffed flats and scrape them along the sidewalk. When the left one hits the ground, I feel a wash of sensation rush through my body—tingles and sparks and crackles that put me on edge. They're here.

Of course—this bench is a vortex. How else could I have connected with Nick on that day, even before I really knew how to haunt? My energy must be stronger in this spot.

I turn to Nick, suddenly frantic. I don't want to put him in danger. "We have to go."

"I know. It's late and—"

I don't hear the rest of his sentence, because the tingles disappear, and then I realize that it's not the pain of a poltergeist approach that I'm feeling. It's the gentle warmth, the soft comfort, of Thatcher's presence.

He's with us. I'm sure of it. He told me after the Wando that he'd come back as soon as he could. I just never expected it would be in another moment with Nick, given how torn up he was about all the rules he broke that day at the river.

"You're here," I whisper, and my voice is full of surprise and longing.

There's no response. He's hasn't come to interact with me—he intends to stand in the background, to guard and guide me. But that's not enough right now.

Actually, it's never going to be enough.

"Callie?"

I turn suddenly at the sound of Nick's voice, remembering that he's still beside me. "Who are you talking to?"

I bite my lip and look around, trying to pinpoint Thatcher's location, but the feeling of his presence is almost everywhere and nowhere at once. "Can you help me explain to him?" I ask the quiet night sky. "Can you help me make him believe?"

The air is thick with Thatcher's hesitation—I can sense it, a nervous quivering in my stomach.

"Please," I say, standing up and spinning in all directions. "Thatcher, I need Nick by my side in this."

I see a ripple in the air then, and a hint of Thatcher's face. Am I imagining it, or is there a dark web of pain in the dim profile I'm able to catch? Then, in a smooth and deliberate movement, I see the shadow of Thatcher's hand reach out to graze Nick's shoulder.

Nick jumps off the bench and backs away from me. "What the hell was that?"

"That was Thatcher," I say. I don't know how else to describe him right now so I just add, "A good friend of mine. From the Prism." I almost wince when I reduce him to that; what Nick needs to know is that I was close to someone on the other side.

"A ghost? You're telling me that I was just touched by a ghost?"

I have to smile at his words, and at the relief that comes with the promise of Nick believing me. "Yes," I say. "You were."

I don't know if it's the combination of everything I've just told him and Thatcher's little trick, but Nick's eyes light up, and I see some of his doubt disappear. He runs his hand over his mouth as if to rethink what's happened tonight.

"You believe now, don't you?"

He shakes his head. "I . . . I don't know," he says. "Maybe."

"Maybe?"

Nick pulls out his phone. "It's really late. Let's get you home."

I hesitate for a moment, turning my back to Nick as I stand and gaze into the darkness where I think Thatcher must be. I reach out my hand, low, but deliberate. I'm trying to give Thatcher a sign that I have to see him, that we have to talk. As much as he wants me to turn away from the spirit world, there's no way that I can. Then I let my hand fall to my side and follow Nick to his car.

We drive back to my neighborhood in silence and he pulls up quietly a few houses down from mine. He drops me off with a confused half smile. "Get some sleep, okay? We'll talk more tomorrow," he says.

I nod. He needs time.

I climb the tree Nick is famous for scaling and slip into my bedroom window so I don't have to open the front door and worry about making noise inside the house. My body, now almost fully healed, feels strong and able, energized in a way I haven't felt in a long time. I think some of it stems from the fact that I truly let people in tonight. I shared my story, and it didn't make me more vulnerable like I thought it would. Talking about what happened to me, about the truth, is doing the opposite actually. I'm sturdier, more centered even.

But when my head hits the pillow and I drift off to sleep, all of these thoughts fall away.

In my dream, I'm walking down Union Pier in the historic district and the air is cooling a bit. I smile to myself as I remember that our first moment on Earth together was here, mine and Thatcher's.

I'm so grateful he's coming to me this way.

"Did you choose this location, or did I?" My question echoes in the darkness. At first there are only the sounds of the waves and the wind in response, breaking the night's silence.

But then I feel the light breeze swirling around me, and I hear a familiar chuckle. "The setting is all you," he says.

I spin around, looking for Thatcher, and there is his face. His yellow-blond hair, hanging in front of his indigo eyes. The sharp line of his cheekbones. His lovely mouth is inches away. But that's all I can see. His body is completely hidden—invisible except for a faint outline.

Even here I can't seem to have all of him.

"You asked me to turn away, but I can't," I say. "I've tried."

"I know you have. I've tried, too." He moves closer to me and all of a sudden I feel like I'm being wrapped in layers of silk. "But now that I've held and kissed you, I . . ."

His voice falters, like he's getting choked up.

"You what?" I ask, after a moment.

"Sometimes it's just harder to do what's right," he says, and the softness I feel around me quickly turns hard and cool. "Callie, I shouldn't break into your dreams when I can sense you want me to.

Or reveal myself to other people on Earth."

"I'm glad you did though," I say, daring to reach out and stroke his face, if I can. I don't feel his skin on mine; there's only air. But his body begins to come into view more, taking a solid shape that makes him seem more real. "Sometimes I don't feel like me when I can't feel you."

"It's like that for me, too. That's why it's so hard to stay away," he says. "It's just . . . I *feel* everything so much more now that you're gone from the Prism. Happiness. Fear. Guilt. Everything. And the closer I am to you, the more intense it all gets. I don't know, it's like . . ."

"You're alive again," I say in a whisper.

"Something like that."

My throat tightens and the world around us bleeds out into a vast plain of whiteness, like we're stuck inside a blank sheet of paper. Thatcher glances down at my hands and concern floods his eyes.

"Where's the ring, Callie?"

"That's why I wanted to talk to you," I say.

His mouth tenses instantly and then he blows out a deep breath, like he knows what I'm about to say. "What have they done now?"

I start with the car story, knowing that Thatcher was nowhere near me when the poltergeists pressed on the brake pedal. He would have stopped them.

"How the hell are they doing this?" he says, his voice sharp. "They haven't been back to the Prism, and yet they still have enough power to hide on Earth and torture you? What are they trying to prove? What could they possibly have to gain by—"

"Thatcher," I interrupt. "Leo took Eli again, too. At school."

As I tell him about the confrontation in the hallway, how I managed to expel Leo from Eli's body, how I know they were using my energy . . . and how Leo took the ring, Thatcher's face reddens and the bright whiteness around us turns black as ink. "They'll try again, I know they will."

He turns around, his back to me as his shoulders tense. "Damn it," he murmurs into the darkness.

"It's not your fault."

"Are you kidding me? Of course it is!" Thatcher shouts. "The Guides are completely clueless as to how Reena and Leo are evading us. The Prism is in total upheaval over this and there's so much infighting about what to do that we're almost at a stalemate."

Thatcher begins to pace, like he's been waiting to unload all this pressure but hasn't had anyone to confide in. If I were still a part of his world, I know I could be that person, someone he could lean on. Maybe I could still be, even if we're separated. If he would just let me.

"And the Wando River possession. I was recharging my energy in my prism for much longer than I would have if I had just . . . resisted. Don't you see, Callie? I was weak, and because of that, no one was watching over you."

"Don't do that to yourself," I say. "Don't take all the blame. A lot of this is out of your control."

"It's out of your control, too, Callie. You may have fought off Leo this time, but it's clear they have some kind of secret energy source that they're latching on to. It's the only way they could achieve possession now that you're no longer in the Prism."

"Maybe it has something to do with the vortexes."

He lets out an exasperated sigh, which is an all-too-familiar sound. "How did you find out about vortexes?"

"From Dixon's Bookstore."

"Really? You've been to Dixon's?" He sounds impressed.

I nod. "This kid Dylan at school seems to have a crush on Carson. I guess his grandfather is the owner?"

"Charles Dixon," says Thatcher. "He's not a fan of ghosts, you know."

"I do," I say. "I guess now I know where to go if I want to get away from you."

I'm joking to lighten the mood a little, get Thatcher to stop punishing himself for what's happening, but he's not exactly in the mood to play along.

"It's a safe zone, Callie. One of the only places in Charleston that's truly spirit-free."

"So there have been other poltergeists? In the past?"

"Yes. There's a long history of ghosts going rogue, not accepting their deaths," he says. "I don't know it all, but there are a lot of answers in that bookstore. Maybe it's good that you found it."

"Well, could the vortexes be it? Could they be what makes my energy so high?"

Thatcher shakes his head. "Plenty of people walk through vortexes all the time without being used for energy, even former coma victims like you. No, there's something more."

I take a deep breath, thinking about the question that Dylan asked me just before I left the bookstore: "Have you ever been close to anyone who died?" I'm starting to realize what he might have been suggesting, and a ray of sunlight cuts through the darkness, landing right on Thatcher's chest, where his heart would be, if it were still beating.

"Thatcher," I say softly. When he looks up at me, his face brimming with concern, I know that I need to be completely open with him. We're in this together, and anything that might help us understand the poltergeists' movements is essential information. So I tell him, "My mother died in my arms."

He blinks at me, confused. "What?"

"In the hospital bed," I tell him. "I didn't remember it, really. But my father just told me that she took her last breath with my arms wrapped around her, while I was sleeping."

Thatcher's face cracks with emotion—he looks as if he might cry. But somehow I feel incredibly strong in this moment, baring my truth for him. Like with Carson, Dylan, and Nick, it feels good to speak the truth. It feels good to trust.

"Oh, Callie," he says. And I know that if he could, he'd put his arms around me and hold me.

"Is that important?" I ask him.

Thatcher nods, composing himself. Then he looks me straight in the eyes and says, very slowly and very clearly, "Yes. It means that you're a death spot."

Eighteen

THE RAY OF SUNLIGHT becomes a radiant beacon as Thatcher explains that my being a death spot, plus the fact that I was in the Prism while still attached to my living body through the coma, must be the unique combination that makes my energy so strong—and so coveted.

"I've never heard of these situations coming together before," he says. "I've guided souls who were death spots; dying in someone's arms isn't as rare as you might think. EMTs, hospice nurses . . . it happens. But that plus the coma and a living body—it must have sent your energy into the stratosphere."

And that's why the poltergeists can use me. Only me.

"But how did they know I'd still have the high levels of energy?" I ask.

"I'm not sure that they did," says Thatcher. "Maybe they've been testing your energy—in the hallway, and in the car —and they found it strong. Callie, they're experimenting with you whenever you're in a vortex, and somehow it's allowing them enough power to stay hidden from the Guides and to keep possessing people."

"So what now?"

"We can't underestimate their focus. You're their only key to living again, which means you have to be very, *very* careful in the days to come."

Thatcher theorizes that Reena and Leo will go for the bodies they've "broken in"—meaning Eli and Carson—because there's more chance for full success, a three-time possession, with them. Eli especially is in terrible danger, since he's been taken twice.

"Dylan warned me to stay away from vortexes," I say.

"Listen to Dylan."

I smile.

"What?" asks Thatcher.

"I think that's the first time you've ever advised me to listen to someone other than *you*."

He softens. "Callie, if we can wait out the next few days, maybe the poltergeists will rapidly decline and we might finally be able to track them—to keep them from harming you."

"Why won't you let me help you? I can do more than just play it safe. I've tested my powers and instincts; they're still strong."

As soon as those words leave my lips, he and I are back on the pier again. I look out over the edge into the water, which was calm when this dream started, but now it's choppy and rough.

"I know that it must feel like it, but this isn't your fight," he says plainly.

My eyebrows rise. "I can't believe you just said that."

"When you entered the Prism and I was chosen as your Guide, it became my duty to look out for you. I'm the one who should be taking the hits here."

"So you feel obligated to me? Is that what you're saying?" I don't want to argue with him, but he can't possibly think that I'm going to let him get away with making me feel helpless.

"No, it's nothing like that," he reassures me. "You're . . . you're everything to me."

Suddenly I hear a beeping from behind me. I whip around to face Thatcher.

"What's that?"

"It's your alarm."

"No!"

There's so much more that we have to say to each other. I still don't know what really happened with Wendy; I can't wake up now.

"Please, Callie, be careful. I'll stay near you if I can—until you get the ring back."

"Don't go, not yet," I say, reaching out for him, but in a split second he completely vanishes from sight.

And then I feel a sharp shove to my shoulders and I fall off the pier.

My eyes flutter open and I shoot up in bed. It takes a minute to calm my rapidly beating heart. I remember everything about the dream, and I'm still tired, as if I didn't sleep at all. I turn off my phone alarm and look around my bedroom; everything is still neatly in place. I know what Thatcher wants me to do, but I have no choice but to listen to my intuition, which is telling me that waiting this out is a mistake.

And that this is most certainly my fight.

Nineteen

THE IN-SCHOOL SUSPENSION ROOM is down a set of stairs that feel like they lead to a dungeon. The windows in the basement room are tiny and near the ceiling. Still, they let in little rays of sunlight, and I can see the dust particles dancing in them like tiny polka dots. Despite that weird school smell, I take a deep breath and close my eyes for just a moment. Even though I may be in high school, in the ISS room with tiny windows, I have a special energy that the poltergeists are willing to kill for.

Because I'm a survivor of the Prism . . . and a death spot.

I open my eyes with a sigh, and as I stand in the empty space trying to choose a seat, I hear a voice behind me.

"'A punishment to some, to some a gift, and to many a favor.' Lucius Annaeus Seneca, Roman statesman and philosopher."

"Mr. Dixon," I say, turning around with a smile.

"Ms. McPhee."

It turns out there's a reason I haven't seen Dylan much at school—he's nearly always in ISS. And as his latest quotation indicates, he likes it here. I didn't know a person could maintain such a consistent schedule of being suspended without actually, you know, being expelled, but he seems to do it.

"I got ISS the second day I was here for trying to do an incantation during chemistry," he says, sliding into the back corner desk that is, apparently, his regular seat in this dank room. "I was so into it that I zoned out and I let some toxic mixture explode in my beaker. Sonia Bigby got a piece of glass in her arm."

"Yikes," I say, but he waves off my concern.

"She was fine," he says. "Drama queen."

"Do your incantations work?"

"Possibly," he says, scratching his head thoughtfully. "I don't have evidence that they do, but maybe their repercussions are happening in a dimension I can't see."

I smile, impressed by his optimism, and he tells me that he only does positive incantations, because he believes that the good and evil of using energy is all about intention.

"Like with haunting," I say.

"What do you mean?"

"Just that setting an intention of peace for your loved ones is part of the process," I explain. "It's one way to achieve a truly soulful connection."

Dylan stares at me with big eyes. "I wish I could see what you've seen."

I look down, sad, blinking to keep my emotion in check. "No, you don't. I lost people there, in the Prism."

When I glance up he has sympathetic eyes behind his thick-rimmed glasses.

The door opens with a creak and Mr. Dunkle, a slightly balding but fairly young substitute teacher, who seems to weave in and out of classrooms yet always have a stint for the day, walks in. He looks at us and says, "Hi, early birds."

Then he nods at me and the way Dylan and I have our desks turned toward each other since we've been talking. "Recruiting friends, are we, Mr. Dixon?"

"You know me, sir," says Dylan.

"By now I do." Mr. Dunkle puts his feet up on his desk at the front of the room and opens up his newspaper. "As you were. Don't let me interrupt."

"Dunkle's really easy on me," says Dylan, lowering his voice, but only slightly. He explains that he gets his assignments from his classes and basically does them in ISS so he can keep up.

"So for you, this is more like a private learning environment," I say.

Dylan shrugs. "Yeah, I prefer to think of the acronym as standing for *Independent Study Situation*," he says. "I don't really like class. It bores me." He reaches into his backpack and lugs out two gigantic and ancient books. *Tomes*, really, is the word for them. "These are today's work."

"What are they?"

He opens up the first one and blows a layer of dust off its pages.

"They're both about possession," he says. Then he thumps the other one with his hand. "Dig in."

"What am I looking for?"

"I'm not really sure," says Dylan, looking thoughtful. "Something about how to banish poltergeists from the Prism and ensure that they either merge or are kept away from Earth forever?"

"Right. Easy."

"'All good is hard,'" says Dylan, and I can tell he's quoting someone again—his voice changes slightly when he does it. "'All evil is easy. Dying, losing, cheating, and mediocrity is easy. Stay away from easy.'"

"Who said that?" I ask.

"Scott Alexander, film writer and director."

I smile. "He sounds smart."

"I only quote the smart ones." Dylan winks at me. "Let's get going."

I nod. He and I are on the same page.

I start flipping through the smaller book, which still weighs like twenty pounds. There's nothing that jumps out at me right away, but eventually I find a section on the rule of three.

> *If a body has been taken three times, the original inhabitant's soul vanishes, giving fully vested control to the possessing spirit, which can now stay in the body until such time as the body dies.*

A chill creeps up my spine. I should tell Dylan about the danger Carson's in, in case she hasn't. She may be downplaying all of it, like she does with a lot of serious things.

"Dylan?" I whisper tentatively.

Just then, the classroom door opens.

"Ah, Mr. Fisher," says Mr. Dunkle, barely looking up from his paper. "I didn't know you were coming in."

"It was spur-of-the-moment," says Nick, handing Mr. Dunkle a note.

Mr. Dunkle glances at it and nods. "Take a seat; entertain yourself quietly."

I meet Nick's eyes and he looks sheepish as he walks over to us.

"Hey," I say softly.

"Hi," he replies, standing at my desk.

The feeling between us is heavy, but not as off as I expected. Something has shifted within him; at least that's what I'm hoping.

"Why are you here?" I ask.

"Hunter was talking crap this morning," he says with a frown.

I raise an eyebrow.

"He said you must be on steroids to have all that rage, that you must be addicted to painkillers and hallucinating after your coma." Then Nick smiles. "So I laid him out."

"You *hit* him?" I ask.

"I couldn't let him doubt you," he says, grinning. "Not when every word you say is true."

I know he's telling me that he believes me, he believes all that I told him last night. I feel a swell of gratitude as he shows me his bruised knuckles. It isn't like Nick to hit someone, but if it had to happen . . .

Dylan leans over to see Nick's bruises and lets out a low whistle.

"The soccer boys are having a rough week," says Dylan.

Nick sits down at the desk in front of mine, facing us.

"Who's this?" he asks me.

"Dylan Dixon," I say.

"Double D," says Nick.

"Ah, yes," says Dylan, sighing as if the burdens of the world are on his shoulders. "If you must know, it's Dylan Mason Dixon, so let the jokes continue. Great sense of humor my parents have."

I laugh, but Nick doesn't. He's eyeing Dylan.

"So what are you guys up to?" Nick asks, gesturing at our open books, and Dylan instinctively closes his.

"It's okay," I tell him.

"What?" Dylan asks.

"Nick knows," I say. "He may be the only other living person in the world who does, but he knows everything."

"Wait," says Nick. "*This* is the bookstore Dylan who knows about this stuff? I thought you were talking about an adult!"

"He's—" I start.

But Dylan doesn't need me to speak for him. "I happen to be the future owner of one of the premier paranormal bookstores in the entire world, one that you probably don't even know about though it exists under your very nose, and one that is going to provide the information that will solve Callie's dilemma." His whisper is quiet, but authoritative.

"Whoa," says Nick. "Pardon me, Encyclopedia Brown."

Dylan huffs, but I can hear the softening in Nick's voice.

"Guys, I may have found something important," I say, interrupting. I turn back to the page I was on and I read the part about the rule of three to them aloud.

"Right," says Dylan. "A triple possession means an elimination of the original soul. So we need to be really watchful around Eli."

Diiiiiing.

The lunch bell rings, and Mr. Dunkle stands up. "Y'all aren't allowed to head to lunch, so I hope you brought sandwiches. I, however, need to grab a bite. I'll be back in twenty, and Mrs. Harris across the hall in woodshop will be keeping her eye on the door."

We all nod, and Mr. Dunkle chuckles. "What am I saying? Y'all have been reading all morning—you're not going anywhere. ISS is practically a library project today!"

He gives us a wink as if he secretly likes us; he shakes his head as he walks out the door. I exhale. I doubt he's heard anything we've said so far, but what I want to say now is pretty intense.

"Okay, listen up," I say. "It's about Carson."

"What about me?" My best friend pops her head into the doorway and then, seeing no teacher, slinks inside. Dylan beams at her as she sits down next to Nick with a smile.

"What is it, Callie?" Nick's voice is comforting, encouraging. Carson and Dylan both lean in. I look at their three faces—two I've known for years and one brand-new—and I feel a warmth among us, almost like we're connected, like we're supposed to come together in this moment. It sounds hokey but I sense us becoming a team, and it gives me the courage to go on.

"Cars, they should know, too. . . ."

She nods, instantly realizing what I'm about to say. "You're right."

And so I tell Nick and Dylan about how Reena took over Carson's body once this summer.

"It was at Tim McCann's party," I say, and then I look at Nick knowingly, to see if he'll remember.

"That was the night of my car accident," he says. "It was the night she . . ." He pauses.

"Kissed you," I say.

"But I didn't—" Carson starts.

"It was Reena." I say it loudly and clearly for everyone's benefit.

Dylan scowls. I know he's jealous.

"Whoa," says Nick, a sheen of sweat on his forehead.

A boulder's weight of guilt settles on my shoulders. Nick's been possessed, too, by Thatcher. He's not at risk of being taken again—Thatcher would never do that—but I feel weird not telling him. Still I try to put those thoughts out of my mind for now and press on.

"So a third possession is worse than death," I say.

"How can something be worse than dying?" asks Nick.

"Because after the final possession, there's no Prism, no Solus," I tell him. "The soul just blows away like dust. That's what Thatcher said."

Nick looks away at the sound of Thatcher's name, and my stomach knots. He has to know that I haven't told him everything about Thatcher—Nick is quick to pick up on things. But how can I really explain my relationship with him? How to do I tell Nick that Thatcher is everywhere I turn—in the pages of these books, in my thoughts at night, haunting my dreams? How do I admit that I'm in love with a ghost? As soon as that thought enters my mind, I can feel Thatcher's impression in the room. The air feels thicker all of a sudden and its stale smell is replaced by this almost honeysuckle scent. I think I'm the only one noticing, but maybe that's okay.

There's something beautiful in that. In me being the one person who can sense that he's here, watching over us.

I open my eyes and come back to the room, comforted by the thought that there are five of us here, not four. And although Thatcher is probably not pleased that I'm getting more involved in this battle than he thinks I should, the fact that he's not interfering like he did with Wendy sort of signals that he respects my decision, doesn't it?

Well, that's what I'm going to choose to believe in this moment. I have to if we're going to get anywhere.

"Only Eli is more vulnerable than Carson," I continue. "If we're ever together near a vortex, it could be disastrous."

"Okay," says Dylan, standing up like he's making a speech. "'The only thing we have to fear is fear itself.' FDR."

"What does that mean?" asks Nick.

"I don't know." Dylan sinks back into his chair. "I couldn't think of a quote to fit this moment."

"Here's what I think we should do," I say, firmly and decisively. "First, we go after Thatcher's ring so that we'll be able to call on the Guides for help if we end up in a dangerous spot without backup."

"Like a vortex where Reena takes my body again and makes out with Nick?" asks Carson.

"For example," says Nick, grinning.

I swat them both. "How can you joke right now?"

"It's a coping mechanism!" she says.

I clear my throat to get them back on task. "Okay, so step one is: get the ring."

"Makes sense," says Dylan, his face lighting up with enthusiasm. "The ghost emergency call button needs to be secured."

"So we'll go to Eli's house tomorrow while he's at school and find a way in—we've got to search his room," I say. "I trust y'all can figure out your own alibis for missing school."

Everyone nods.

"What if the ring's not there though?" asks Carson.

"We could always try going to where the poltergeist used to live," says Dylan. "If his family still lives in town, maybe he took it there, for safekeeping or something."

"So you're saying he stole it off Eli before I expelled his soul yesterday?" I ask. "Do you think Leo still has that kind of power, now that he's been away from the Prism for so long?"

"I don't know, but I think it's a possibility," says Dylan.

"Okay, so searching Leo's place will be option two," I say, smiling for a moment. But then I glance at Dylan's books and sigh, frustrated. "I haven't figured out what comes next though."

The honeysuckle smell gets even stronger, and it's almost as though Thatcher is giving me a sign of support. It feels really good to have him trusting in me.

"We'll figure it out," says Carson, encouraging me. "Let's just do step one."

Nick runs his hands through his hair. "This is . . . a lot to take in. Last week the only mysterious thing in my life was where the heck my lost socks go."

"I know." I touch his shoulder to convey that I understand how crazy it all sounds. Dylan and Carson are so quick to believe because they've always believed. But Nick . . . he didn't seek out any of this. I look at him pleadingly—we really need his help, especially with Eli Winston.

"We have to try and get the ring back," I say, and when he gazes up at me, I see the commitment in his eyes. He puts his hand over mine, squeezing. It's a pledge to move forward, in so many ways.

"Okay," he says. "I know where the Winstons keep a spare house key."

Twenty

WHEN I WALK IN the door after school, I'm happy to have this quiet moment at home. Tomorrow, the plan begins. Tonight feels like the calm before the storm.

"Callie May?" I hear my dad's voice in the den.

"You're back from work early," I say, popping my head in.

"I took a mental health day," he says. "I have to go to DC tomorrow to give a talk—it's a last-minute fill-in. But I wanted to make sure you're okay with that."

"I've stayed home alone for one night before."

"I know. But not since . . ."

"The coma. Right." I smile at him. "I'm fine, really."

"Okay, I'll be gone less than a day." Dad pats the cushion beside him. "I've been looking through this old album."

I recognize the book instantly. It was a secret album he kept, one that he didn't show me. I only saw it when I was haunting him from the other side, when I was with Thatcher trying to help my father heal.

I curl up next to him on the couch.

As he flips the pages open now, I see my family—me and Mama, Mama and Daddy, the three of us all together. There's a photo of me and Carson, both front-toothless on a swing set, and even a picture of me and Nick from last year, all dressed up in front of the Fishers' fireplace, right before we went to the winter formal.

"How come you never showed me these before?" I ask.

"Oh, you know," he says, smiling. "I guess I was just embarrassed about my sentimental side, or I thought you'd think I was holding on to the past too much or something."

"I would never think that," I tell him. "You're the strongest man I know."

I lower my face, feeling kind of cheesy for saying that, but he reaches out and turns my chin up to him, so he can look me in the eye. Now he speaks clearly, deliberately. "You're healing, you're living your life again, you're not letting what happened this summer get you down—or even slow you down, far as I can tell." He pauses. "I'm proud of you," he adds.

I start to tear up, and my father pulls me closer. He puts his arm around my shoulder, and I lean into him, smelling his clean detergent smell, breathing in the safety and security of home. It's the two of us on the couch, missing Mama, as we've been missing her for years now.

But when I close my eyes, I know she is always with us.

"Your mama knew how to express herself; she knew exactly how to make everyone around her feel loved. I feel like she's still teaching me how, through you. As long as you're here and we're together, Callie May, she is, too."

And then, like a puzzle piece falling into place, I finally understand why she couldn't haunt me the way she wanted to. . . . I was her death spot, a place where spirits are not supposed to return. So she visited Carson instead. She tried to bring peace through my best friend. Mama did her best for me and Daddy. What else could I ask of her?

I meet Carson in her driveway the next morning. "Let's go," she says. "Nick and Dylan are on their way to Eli's."

We're heading toward our friend's house, banking on his parents being at work and Eli being at school. I know I'll get in trouble for skipping again if my father finds out, but this is urgent. Like, life-or-death urgent. Besides, I hid my dad's cell last night, so he'll probably have to call me from the landline and tell me it's missing. I felt a little guilty being sneaky like that, but desperate times call for drastic measures.

Carson parks on the street a few doors down, behind Nick. He drove his parents' van, I notice, as we walk up to greet the boys.

"Those are really awesome," says Dylan. He's admiring the red and yellow kayaks strapped to the top of the van.

"Did you guys carpool?" I ask them.

"It was on the way," says Nick. "Mom let me take the van because I told her the soccer team had a field trip today and needed more vehicles. School might call her, but I'll deal with that later."

"Good thought," I say. "We can all drive together from here."

"It was Carson's idea." Dylan smiles at her adoringly, and I make a note that when this is all over I need to talk to Carson about how perfect Dylan is for her. When I look over, though, I see that she's noticing his grin, and returning it with one of her own.

"You probably should've taken the kayaks off the roof," I say to Nick. "Gas burners."

"My dad's going camping this weekend. He wanted them ready."

I shrug. "Well, I'm glad we have a big car anyway."

When we get up to the porch, there's a bright blue snail-shaped planter in the front filled with red geraniums. Nick gently tilts it back and pulls out a silver key.

"Really?" I say.

"So obvious," mutters Carson.

"Don't look a gift snail in the mouth," says Dylan. He stands behind Nick, who steps in and calls out, "Hello?" just in case.

No response. We all head inside.

Eli's room is easy to spot on the long hallway. There's a dirty-laundry trail spilling out of the door, which is covered with World Cup athlete posters. I peek inside to see his bed isn't made and there's a half-empty bottle of Gatorade on the nightstand.

"Where would he put the ring?" I wonder aloud, as we all crowd in.

Dylan takes in a breath. "He doesn't seem to be the most thoughtful person in the world, does he? I bet if it is here, it's under a pile somewhere. . . ."

Just then, we hear the door creak open and we all freeze. Keys are thrown onto a table, steps start coming down the hallway.

"*Shiiiit*," whispers Nick. He stands in front of the rest of us as Eli walks into his room, totally startled.

"What the hell are y'all doing here?"

"Hey, man," says Nick, cool as a cucumber. "No school today?"

"I'm off for the week. I'm . . . resting," says Eli. Then he seems to remember our situation. "Hey, why am I explaining myself to you? You're the ones in my house."

I step forward from behind Nick.

"Eli, the other day in the hallway—"

"Y'all need to get out of here before I call the cops." Eli's words are strong, but at the sight of me he looks shaken.

Carson goes up to him and links her arms through his. "Eli, we're looking for a ring," says Carson. "Callie was wearing it around her neck when you had your . . . scuffle."

"You already asked me about that," says Eli, turning to me. "I told you I don't have it."

He shakes off Carson's arm and says again, "I'm seriously gonna call the cops if you don't leave."

"I know about the night by the bonfire at Folly Beach, Eli," I say, and it's as if the room stills. "When you heard the ghost girl's voice, and Brian and Hunter didn't believe you."

I was with Reena that day, and we stumbled upon Eli and the others on a summer Saturday night, drinking by the fire pit. Reena had some fun with Eli, knocking a beer from his hand, pulling a cigarette from his mouth, whispering in his ear. Eli was truly freaked out—I know because I saw him run through the woods to escape what was happening.

Eli's eyes are big and round. "I don't know what you're talking about," he says, but it's clear that he does.

And then, suddenly, a gust of wind passes through the room and Eli's bedroom door slams shut.

Our eyes all flick over to the tightly closed windows.

"Weird," says Nick with a smile. I wink at him. It's Thatcher, willing to bend some rules to help us right now.

"Are you sure you don't have it?" I ask Eli again. "Maybe if you think really hard you'll remember something you had no idea you forgot."

"You sound crazy," he says. "You know that, right?"

And then the bulb of his ceiling light shatters above us, showering the floor with pieces of glass.

Eli jumps, but the rest of us stay calm.

"We're not crazy. And we're not the only ones who want to know where the ring is," says Dylan. "As you can see, we have powerful friends."

"Dead-people friends, actually," Carson says, crossing her arms over her chest.

"I really have no idea," says Eli, his voice trembling now. I glance over at his bed and see a stuffed teddy bear there, one he maybe still sleeps with. I feel a pang of guilt that we're here, scaring him.

"Okay, enough," I say. "He really doesn't know. We should go."

We start to file out of Eli's room, but he follows us to the front door. "Are y'all just gonna leave me here?"

"It's your house," Nick says.

"But I'm obviously not alone!" He's pretty freaked out, not that any of us can blame him.

The rest of us look at one another, the same question in our eyes. Eli is as involved in this as any of us. He's been possessed; he's in mortal danger. He deserves to know what's happening, even if he can be a jerk sometimes.

We all seem to understand this in an instant, almost like we're sharing thoughts for a moment. At once, everyone nods.

And then Dylan turns to Eli and says, "Come with us."

Leo Cutler's family still lives in the same place where he grew up, according to Mr. Internet, and when we check the address against Dylan's vortex map, it seems like it's in a safe zone. We looked up Reena's old address, too, just in case, but it seems like her family has moved away because the house she lived in has been sold twice since her death.

As we drive to Leo's, I tell Eli everything. Any normal person would never believe what we recount, but Eli has experienced things for himself—at the bonfire at Folly Beach, on the train tracks during his "dodge," in the hallway just this week, and now at his own house. I almost feel sorry for him, but at the same time I'm glad he's here with us. He's been such a part of this, almost from the beginning.

Eli folds his arms tightly across his chest as he listens to me talk, but he doesn't say a word in response. When I'm done, Carson waves her hand in front of his face, but his eyes just keep staring forward. I see something in his expression, though . . . a spark of understanding.

"I know it's hard to take in, Eli," I say. "But I can see that you know that what I'm telling you is true. And you're involved, too."

He nods but doesn't talk yet.

"Let's give him a sec to get over the shock," says Nick, turning up the radio. "He'll rally soon."

As we approach Leo's small split-level home, for some reason the first thing I notice is the chain-link fence around the backyard, which looks broken and sad. There are no cars in the driveway, so I figure we'll try the door, maybe find an open window. The front screen is off its hinges, I notice, as we walk up to it.

Eli stays in the van, though. I guess he's still in a state of shock.

As I reach for the Cutlers' doorknob, I hear a shout from around the side of the house, where Carson went to scout. "Over here! Window!"

I turn the knob just in case, but it's locked, so we head to the window, where Carson is already hoisting herself inside.

"The girl is fearless," says Dylan admiringly.

I look around to see if any neighbors might be watching, but I don't see anyone. "I think we're all being pretty brave right now," I say, wondering how I got to the point where I had enough courage to commit trespassing or breaking and entering or whatever official crime we're guilty of right now.

Nick goes in next, and he pulls me up and in through the window. I know instantly that this was Leo's bedroom—it's crazy, but I can still sense some of his energy here. It kind of feels like being lightly pricked by a thorn, but over and over again. This isn't his room anymore, of course. There's a sewing machine in the corner, and off to the side there's an exercise bike with laundry draped over it. The closet has no door, and I see a folded-up ironing board and a few winter coats hanging in there.

But on the walls, I see Leo.

There's a bulletin board with photos of him in football uniforms, starting at around age five, it looks like. There's a third-place certificate from a school talent show, for singing! He wore a blue tux to a junior high dance. I have to smile at the personality I see in these photos. It's the Leo I met, but the good side. The funny, jocular, loyal friend Thatcher must have known before he became a crazy poltergeist.

On one wall is a huge pen-and-ink drawing of a tree, with branches and roots spreading out in all directions.

"Leo was an artist?" asks Dylan.

"I don't think so," I say. "I'm sure that's someone else's."

Dylan leans in to the lower right corner of the drawing. "Well, he signed it."

I lean back and stare at his creation. *Leo was an artist.* It's hard to imagine. In the Prism he was all about destruction, not creation.

"I don't really know where to look," says Carson. She's rifling through the sewing basket. "Oh, this is cool."

She picks up a gold cuff link. "LC," she says.

"His initials." I take it from her and turn it over in my palm. And when I hold it in my hand, I have this gut feeling that Leo has not been back here for a long time. That it would hurt him, somehow, to remember what he used to be.

"The ring's not here," I tell them, handing the cuff link back to Carson.

"How do you know?" Dylan is starting to open the drawers of a wooden dresser along the wall, but I put my hand on his arm.

"No," I say. "Don't. This family has suffered enough."

The feeling of thorns is becoming more intense, and I want to get out of here, to leave the Cutlers alone. Just as I'm about to swing one leg out of the window, I hear a low growl from the ground below us.

Nick, Carson, Dylan, and I all lean out to look.

Doberman. I should have figured. Such a Leo dog.

"Nice puppy," whispers Nick.

The dog is not amused. He barks once, loudly, and bares his sharp teeth.

"Front door," whispers Carson.

We back away from the window, hoping the dog isn't smart enough to figure out where the other exits are.

"One . . . two . . . three!" yells Dylan as we burst open the front door and start running toward the car where Eli's waiting.

"Go, go, go!" shouts Nick, who's bringing up the rear.

The dog spots us, but we're already down the driveway and we have a lead on him. We are screaming for Eli to open the doors. He's in the backseat of Nick's van, and when he sees us running, he does open one large sliding door. We all cram in on top of him and slam it shut in the dog's face.

Eli groans from the bottom of the heap.

Nick, Carson, Dylan, and I all mumble some form of *sorry*

and move into our own seats. The dog is still barking outside the driver's-side window. Nick presses the lock button.

"Just in case," he says, and it makes me laugh.

"'There is no fear in chasing. There is fear in being chased.' Jack Nicklaus."

"The golfer?" asks Eli.

"Yes," says Dylan. "I know he was talking about leading on the course, but it feels appropriate anyway."

"You spoke!" I say to Eli.

"Well, y'all piled up on me!" he says. "It kinda snapped me out of it."

I grin at him and then I look around the van. Carson is panting from the run, her cheeks red with effort. Nick is sweating up a storm. Dylan looks surprisingly cool for just having sprinted for his life. His glasses even stayed in place. And Eli . . . well, he still seems a little dazed, but that's okay. The prickling sensation from inside the house is gone, and I realize that I feel a happiness deep down that I haven't felt since . . . I don't know when. I feel less alone than I have in years.

I let out a little *yawp*, almost involuntarily, and everyone looks at me funny. "Sorry," I say. Then I smile at the Doberman, who's making his way back to his house. "But that was kind of fun."

Carson pulls me in for a hug and says, "That's my Callie! Now let's get back to being the chasers and not the chasees."

Nick starts up the car. "Where to next?"

"Something is telling me that Leo still has the ring with him," I say. "Wherever he and Reena are."

Dylan nods. "I think you're right."

"So what do we do?" Carson sighs.

I close my eyes and try to tune in to Thatcher, to see if he's with us. I don't feel that warm impression of his soul, just a cool emptiness.

But maybe it's good that he's not here, because even though he seems to understand why I can't just sit home and wait for this whole mess to be resolved, I know he wouldn't approve of what I'm about to do, what I *have* to do.

So I look at Nick, and I don't ask. I just tell him, "Take me to a vortex."

Twenty-one

I'M STANDING ON THE east side of the same cemetery that I visited before, but I'm across the grounds from where Thatcher is buried. The last time I came here with Carson, I felt my energy being taken; I felt the poltergeists testing me. I know it's a vortex, and it's also up on a hill, so if I stand in the right spot, my friends can still see me. Plus it's the least populated area I could think of.

Nick's van is parked down the hill and across the street. They're watching, but I've told them not to interfere, no matter what they see happening.

Carson and Nick argued with me, and Eli sat in confused silence when I tried to explain why I *had* to get to a vortex to confront Leo. "I know he'll come if I'm there. I need to go alone, so they can't attempt a possession. Reena and Leo will show—I'm sure of it. And I'll be able to get the ring."

"What makes you think you'll be able to take the ring from that guy?" asked Nick. "In those photos his neck looked as thick as a tree trunk."

"They're losing energy," I told him. "They're becoming weaker by the day, and they haven't been back to the Prism to recharge—that's important. I can do it."

Dylan was the only one who supported me from the start. "Callie's right. We need the ring back—they obviously took it for a reason, so that she'd be without protection when they attempt possession. Her going alone is our best shot."

And so here I am. At first I just wait, listening to the chirping of the birds and the rustle of the squirrels under the few trees planted in the middle of the hill. *It's not a bad place to be buried*, I think. I sit down in the grass and run my hands over its soft texture, focusing on the living world around me instead of looking at the individual stones. I mapped out Leo's grave, and Reena's. They're close together, and I wonder if their families, and Thatcher's, all went to the same church. Probably.

I pick a yellow dandelion and play with its petals. It always seemed strange to me that these bright yellow dots of sun are considered weeds.

After a few minutes, a plane flies overhead and with its sound comes the sensation I've been waiting for. I feel a jolt, a charge, and a rush of energy. Despite the fact that I expected this, fear starts to creep into my skin. The atmosphere feels suddenly cold as ice, like a frost has fallen over me. An August freeze in Charleston? Not likely. Then I hear a rumble, like approaching thunder.

The sky darkens; the sun is hiding behind a fast-approaching storm cloud. Before I can even stand, the heavens open up and a hard rain begins to fall, drenching me and the hallowed ground at my feet. A flash of lightning streaks across the clouds, illuminating the silhouettes of two figures who are striding toward me with purpose and determination.

Reena. Leo.

I look to where the van is parked, down the hill and across the street. My friends should be safe.

This is good. The poltergeists don't have a body to take, and I can fight them off. I know I can. I practiced at the bookstore—I am capable of a lot in these high-energy spots. As I rise to meet them, I wonder at the fact that not very long ago, I thought these two were my friends. I even considered them more helpful than Thatcher when I was haunting, especially when they showed me how to manipulate energy to touch and control the weather. But it was all wrong—it was the wrong method for the wrong reasons.

I straighten my back and give them a smile that I hope is convincingly confident.

When they get within a few feet of me, I'm surprised at how clearly I can see them. Their bodies look almost as solid as mine—their eyes glow with an energy that surprises and intimidates me.

"I *knew* this was a vortex," I say under my breath.

"What was that, Callie?" asks Reena, her shiny black hair dry and full, despite the sheets of harsh rain all around us.

"This spot," I say. "It's a vortex."

Leo laughs. "She's learned a lot," he says. Then he turns to me.

"Of course, Callie. Our bodies are buried here, aren't they? The bodies of ghosts like us have powerful energy, even after death."

"Poltergeists like you, you mean," I say. "And I doubt there's much left of your bodies." *Ashes to ashes, dust to dust.* "Whatever's crumbling under the ground there won't look like your yearbook photo anymore after ten years."

Reena grins at me, big and broad. It's a smile that I've seen before, but I'd forgotten just how enchanting—and bone-chilling—it is. "I'm not worried about my old body," she says wickedly. "I'll have a new one soon enough. Someone young, someone energetic . . . someone like—"

"Don't you say her name!" I snap at Reena.

"You're not afraid," she says, a hint of admiration in her voice. "I've always liked that about you. It's endearing. Stupid, but endearing."

I snort, letting her insult roll off me like the raindrops, which I know are soaking my skin. I barely feel them. My energy is heightened, my physical body ready. They may be using this vortex for its powers, but I'm using it too. And I'm stronger.

I see two more figures emerging from the rain. A girl with a mass of wild curls, a lanky guy with a long face—Delia and Norris, more poltergeists from the Prism. Souls who can't let go of what they used to be.

"What a reunion," says Delia, waving at me. I'd almost think she was being friendly, if it weren't for the steely glint behind her eyes.

"Together at last," says Reena in a singsong voice. "Soon we'll all be able to sit and enjoy the sunshine like Callie was doing a minute ago, basking in the warmth of a late summer day, smelling the grass and the flowers in the air."

Her eyes move to the dandelion that I realize I'm still holding. "How sweet," she says. "Planning to leave that on Thatcher's grave?"

I turn away, not wanting to engage in her taunting. I know she's baiting me. The question is, what for?

"Eli, isn't that a pretty flower?" Reena is addressing Leo . . . and I'm confused for a moment.

"It is, Carson," he says. "So very vibrant and alive."

And then I know what they're doing.

"You'll never take them fully," I say.

"Of course we will." Reena's voice doesn't contain a hint of doubt.

"Over my dead body."

Reena shrugs. "If it has to be that way," she says. "But I'd rather we stay friends. Best friends, even. Right, Cal?"

I feel anger swell within me. My eyes burn with rage.

"So emotional," says Reena, her dark ponytail swishing to the side to reveal the charred moon on her neck, the one that marks her as a poltergeist who can't merge with Solus. "Your energy is still strong, but anger makes you weaker."

I snarl at her, sick of her talking. "You have no idea what I'm capable of," I say.

Leo laughs, a big hearty guffaw that rivals the rolling thunder. As he does, I see more of them, more poltergeists, marching toward us. The dark marks on their necks move in unison as they climb.

I try to count them—one, two, four . . . ten at least. My heartbeat quickens.

"There it is," says Reena, smiling. "I knew the fear would hit."

I glare at her. "I'm not afraid."

"You should be," she says, gesturing to the ghosts around her. "We have an army of followers, ghosts who don't believe in Solus. Leo and I will show them how to achieve possession, one body at a time."

"I'll fight back. I'll fight every one of you."

"We're not here to fight you, Callie," she says, her eyes darkening. "We're here to take you."

The last thing I see is her hand reaching out toward me, snatching the space between us with the speed of a snake's strike.

In a swirl of light and color, I lose consciousness. Something inside me latches on, though. It's like I've thrown a rope around a high peak to keep myself tethered to my own body even as I feel my soul spinning into somewhere dark and remote, a cavern in the farthest reaches of the deepest ocean depths. I'm going down, down, down, past the limits of space and time, and I feel more distant from my body than I was when I was nearly dead. But there's a part of me that knows I'm still holding on.

"She can't take you this way. . . . Hold fast, Callie." I can hear a voice, but not with my ears. Something inside my soul echoes, rumbles and shakes, like I'm reading the vibrations on a train track. I'm a cello whose strings are being played perfectly. I hear, I understand, I do.

And suddenly the heavy boulder that was crushing me, the

suffocating blanket I was underneath, nearly swallowed by, is thrown off. I'm uncovered, my eyes adjusting to the bright sky, which no longer rages with a storm but is instead cloudless and sunny, as it was in the initial minutes I spent here.

The first thing I see glimmering in the new sunlight is the ring. It's on Leo's finger. I lunge for it without thought, grasping its metal in my hand and crying into the sky, "*Thatcher!*"

In what seems like less than a heartbeat, the Guides arrive.

A tall brunette Guide named Sarah takes Delia; they're circling each other like they're in a boxing ring, but it's energy that they're using to fight. I see blasts of light fly between them, and I realize that these flashes are coming from all over the hill atop this cemetery. I'm standing in the middle of a giant vortex, and suddenly there's a hell of a fight going on. Guides and poltergeists, dueling with energy. The Guides outnumber them, I see as I quickly assess the scene. But the poltergeists are wilder, more willing to do *anything* to win.

Leo shakes me off of his hand and moves in another direction— he still has the ring! I try to see where he's going but when I turn my head I feel the strain of a monster headache. I attempt a step but my legs feel weighed down and leaden. My eyes take a minute to catch up with my gaze; the scene blurs and then sharpens.

I spot an older man, a living man, holding an umbrella above his head as he starts to climb the hill toward us, and a poltergeist advances in his direction. They're not above hurting the living; this I know for sure. But a short, stocky Guide, Ryan, rushes in and diverts the man with his energy—I see a translucent shield emanating from Ryan, causing the man to slowly move away from the vortex, out of the poltergeists' reach. Then Ryan turns toward the evil ghost and begins to fight.

It feels like I'm standing in the middle of an energy tsunami, being pushed and pulled in every direction.

And then I see him—Thatcher. Leo is locked in battle with him, their energies colliding in a firestorm of darkness and light. I can hardly tell who's who, and I race to help, my body moving at a pace that starts slow, but picks up quickly.

"No!" says Thatcher when I get closer. He holds Leo at bay for a moment and shouts, "Finish her!"

Reena. I look back to where I was, and I see her lying on the ground, starting to crawl to her knees. She's weakened after trying to possess me, her energy depleted. I can feel my own life force returning now; the weighed-down feeling has left my legs. I know I'm capable of doing what he's asked.

"You're sure?" I say this to Thatcher quietly, and he shouldn't be able to hear me, not in the midst of this chaos. But he does. And what I'm asking him is this: Does he truly want me to try to destroy the girl Reena once was? His first love, the one who died by his side.

He seems to understand all of this, even in my whisper, and he nods without hesitation.

I lunge at her. She's barely on her feet when I reach her, but she manages to dart to the side, zigzagging among the headstones as I track her. I am strong and full of energy, but my physical body has to move around objects, over the ground in a way that her soul doesn't—it holds me back. Reena's weakened but not weak by a long shot, fast and cunning as she avoids my pursuit, dodging each move I make as if she sees it coming.

But then, as Reena swerves to the right when I reach for her arm, she hesitates. It's a millisecond, but it's enough. I make contact, and when I grab her, a deafening *crack* echoes in the air. I can feel myself using her the way she used me in the Prism, taking her energy and making it my own.

Ryan falls next to me then, thrown down by a blow from poltergeist Norris, and my hold on Reena is broken. She wrangles her arm out of my grasp, and she turns to run, but my reflexes are on point in this moment—and I'm close enough to do what Dylan showed me. My arms flash out at the speed of light, and they jolt through her soul, maiming her energy field. I know it worked—her entire being is rocked.

She looks back at me, shocked, and her face fades slowly in front of me. As she pales, so low on energy, she whispers, "Carson is mine." And then she flickers, almost invisible.

"Rage, rage against the dying of the light."

The line from a poem by Dylan Thomas, one my father loves, runs through my mind as I watch her disappear, this girl who has caused me so much pain and fear.

In that instant, Leo lets out a yowl, eerie and earsplitting. It rallies the poltergeists, and they all start fading, exiting through portals and retreating into another dimension.

When they're gone completely, I look down to see where I'm standing, what made Reena pause when she'd been so artfully avoiding my pursuit.

REENA BELL, BELOVED DAUGHTER AND SISTER.

Her grave.

I look away before any emotion can hit. I didn't kill Reena Bell. I fought off a poltergeist who was hell-bent on destroying me.

I'm left standing with Thatcher and a band of Guides, tired from the clash but still strong. I can see them in full color, their auras blazing in the sunny skies—their energy visible as it ebbs and flows between their spirits, uniting them.

"I can't believe we weren't able to capture them," Ryan says, shaking his head.

"Their powers were more intact than I thought they'd be," Sarah replies.

"Yes, but we've dealt them a hard blow," Thatcher reassures them. Then he moves to my side, his eyebrows arching with concern. "Did she hurt you?" he asks.

"No. But I feel . . . violated," I say. "The possession made me feel completely out of control." I look up at him. "But a voice . . . it coached me back. It sounded like . . . my mom."

"That's your inner strength," he says. "You may recognize it as your mom, but it's you, Callie."

"Did I . . . kill Reena?" I whisper.

"No, not kill," he says. "But this battle definitely rattled them and depleted their energy reserves. Especially Reena, and that's key. Without her and Leo brainwashing the others, we can help the rest of them see the light, get them to change."

He gazes at me with wonder in his eyes. "You were amazing."

The other Guides gather around me, still glowing from the

fight—despite Ryan's disappointment, it's clear that they're counting it as a win.

"Does this mean they're . . . gone?" I ask, still unsure of what just happened, and a little shaken by Reena's parting words.

"It won't be long before they'll have to come back to the Prism now—I'm sure of it. We'll sense it the second they reenter, and then they'll be our problem. They won't bother anyone on Earth, ever again," Thatcher says.

The rest of the Guides take this news with sober faces as Thatcher motions to the bottom of the hill. I know they'll be responsible for the poltergeists once they get back to the Prism. They'll have to make sure they don't ever return to Earth to finish off their sick plans. It doesn't seem fair. There *must* be a way to banish them for good. But if there were, wouldn't Thatcher and the Guides already know that?

"Hold out your hand," says Thatcher. I do, and he drops his grandfather's ring into my palm. "Here."

"Just in time."

"You won't need it for long," he says. "They'll be running scared tonight and now their energy is way down. I could feel it in the way Leo was fighting. My guess is that they'll have to return to the Prism by tomorrow."

"Tonight's their last chance at possession. . . ."

"Right. So get to the bookstore," says Thatcher. "Call your dad, tell him you're with Carson, whatever you need to, but stay there with her, and Eli, too. It isn't safe for you to be anywhere else tonight."

I smile slightly. It would be easy to do what Thatcher says.

But I don't think I'm going to.

"Callie . . ." Thatcher's voice is suspicious. "Call your father."

"He's away tonight on business," I tell Thatcher. "He won't know I'm not home."

"Good," says Thatcher. "My energy needs replenishing. I have to go back to the Prism until my levels are back to normal. . . . Do you understand?"

"Yes, I do."

"Use the ring to call to me if you see any signs of the poltergeists, but *stay* at Dixon's, out of danger."

"Okay," I say. I stand there, lingering in this vortex where I can see him and hear him, almost as if he's alive. If I focused enough energy I could touch his face, just for a second.

"Callie," he says softly, sadness in his eyes, "go."

I nod, and I walk slowly down the hill.

When I get to the van, all of my friends are standing outside, practically bursting with emotion.

"Callie, are you okay?" Carson gasps, coming up to me and taking my hand.

"I'm fine," I tell her, but I watch her eyes run over my body in shock. I look down at myself and I realize that I'm soaked from the rainstorm; my clothes are tattered and covered in mud. I've been so inside my head that I haven't even felt my physical body or taken note of the disastrous shape I'm in.

"Let me get you some clothes," says Nick, opening up the back doors and bringing out a black hoodie. "This is all I have."

I duck into the van and take off my wet, dirty T-shirt. Carson follows me and whispers, "Are you really okay?"

I do a once-over of my body, too, to be sure. I'm filthy, but incredibly unbruised. "I'm fine, don't worry," I say, zipping the sweatshirt over my bra.

Then the rest of my friends get back into the van, and they all look at me with the same question in their eyes.

"I fought the poltergeists," I tell them.

"All we could see was a rainstorm on the hill," says Dylan, his eyes as wide as saucers.

Then they listen, rapt, as I explain the feeling I had being possessed, the way Reena took me before I struck back. "I used your move," I tell Dylan. "I don't think I've ever hit anyone so fast." Then I hold up the ring. "And I got this back."

Dylan pumps a fist in the air. "Amazing!"

"You're like a superhero!" screams Carson.

"Guys, this isn't a video game," says Nick.

"He's right," I say. "There were at least a half dozen Guides fighting, all in hand-to-hand combat with poltergeists who have no conscience."

"Wow," says Carson. Dylan's eyes are blazing with emotion—excitement, fear . . . I can't tell. Nick just leans over the middle console and gives me a hug. There's nothing romantic in it, but it's full of comfort and protection.

"I'm sorry I couldn't help," he says.

"You are helping. Just by being here," I whisper, squeezing back tighter.

This embrace, this physical connection, is something Thatcher can't give me. It's something I need from Nick, because even if he's not my love anymore, he's still one of the people I care about most in the world.

We stay like that for another few seconds, and then I back up into my seat. "We still have work to do. The Guides believe the poltergeists only have one night left before they'll have to return to the Prism. But I want to banish them for good before morning."

Eli chuckles and runs his hand over his face. "How are we going to do that?" he asks. I like the way he says *we*.

"Seems like we should just go to Dixon's where they can't get to us and wait it out," says Nick, thinking like Thatcher.

"We *should* go to Dixon's now," I say. "But not to wait it out. To find out how to destroy the poltergeists."

"But if they have to leave Earth tomorrow, why get ourselves in deeper?" asks Eli.

"If the poltergeists go back to the Prism, the Guides will be responsible for them," I explain. "Instead of doing their haunting and helping people move on, they'll have to track the poltergeists forever to be sure that they don't come back to Earth. Don't you see? The whole balance of the Prism and Earth is at stake here. That's why we have to find a way to expel the poltergeists from both dimensions."

"Why wouldn't Thatcher have mentioned that, though?" Carson asks.

"Maybe there are methods Thatcher and the Guides aren't aware of," Dylan suggests. "Special spells and things that sensitive people like my grandfather were able to pinpoint, but kept secret from the spirit world, as a way to protect the living."

"What are we waiting for then?" I say.

And then all of a sudden, Eli puts his hand in the center of our group. Carson piles on. Then Nick. Then Dylan. I grin and put my hand on top with a smack.

"Go, Ghostbusters?" says Eli.

We all break up laughing, and then Nick starts the car.

Twenty-two

BACK AT THE MAIN table at Dixon's, we're ready to focus. We're in a safe zone for the moment, and we have Thatcher's ring.

Eli makes jokes about the dusty surfaces. Then he asks whether there's a house-elf around to tidy things up.

"Think of it as a nontraditional space touched by the wisdom of time," I tell him.

"Nontraditional dust is more like it," he says. "Is this place ever open to customers?"

"It's always open," says Dylan.

"You don't find it—it finds you," I tell Eli, and Carson winks at me.

Part of me knows I should do what Thatcher said and stay here tonight. It would mean keeping my friends safe. The poltergeists will only get more desperate, and more violent.

But another part of me knows that if we have a chance to banish the poltergeists for good, then we need to do it together. There's no way I can figure it all out on my own.

I look at the stacks that Dylan has put out on the center table. "Are these the books we need?"

"I think so," he says.

Nick picks up a musty brown book with two fingers. "What are we looking for?"

Eli sinks into a chair. "How can I help?" he asks.

"Now that's a sentence I never thought I'd hear from you," I say to him, smirking.

"I think he's still in shock," says Nick.

"I figure I'm in a dream, or maybe a nightmare." Eli grins for the first time today. "So I'm just gonna go with it."

"Okay, let's do this," says Dylan, joining us at the table. "We know that incantations can at least reach the other side, because of the way Carson's worked on Callie this summer. We just have to find the right *one*."

Dylan looks at me. "Callie, do we know everything—really *everything*—about your near-death? About your time in the Prism?"

I know what Dylan is getting at. The other night he asked me a question about being *physically* close to someone who died, and I was so taken aback by what my father had revealed to me about my mother that I couldn't bring myself to admit the truth to him. It was just too painful to reveal to a stranger.

But if we're going to succeed in this, I have to bare every

personal detail of mine, no matter how much it might hurt to talk about.

"Well, there is something I haven't told you. It's not about my time in the Prism, but . . ."

When I bite my lip, Dylan sees me getting emotional.

"It's okay, Callie," he says gently. "Take your time."

A tear runs down my cheek before I even begin to tell them about my mother and how she died in my arms.

When I finally start talking, telling them the story, the room gets so quiet, it feels like I'm speaking in outer space, where the only sound that exists is my voice.

"My father just told me about this," I say. "I didn't remember any of it. But somehow, I think I've always known."

By the time I'm done, everyone's eyes are glistening. Carson is holding my hand and Nick kneels next to my chair, his arm around my shoulder. Even Eli is leaning in sympathetically.

"You're a death spot," says Dylan, understanding just as quickly as Thatcher had. "Of course." He pushes up his glasses and bounds to the back of the bookstore, behind three rows of shelves and up a tall ladder, which he scales quickly. He reaches for a dark-green volume, and when he brings it back to the table, he lays it in front of me.

On the cover are two symbols: a glowing green moon, similar to the tattoo that ghosts who are preparing to merge with Solus have, and a charred dark spot, which appears on the necks of the poltergeists.

I stiffen at the sight of them.

"You know these marks," says Dylan, reading me.

"Yes," I say.

"Then this book is the one." Dylan turns back to the book-shelves with renewed ardor, like all the wonders of the world are in this room, and maybe they are. When he looks at us again, he smiles. "I've read this book before; let me just . . ."

He starts to flip through the pages, and in ten seconds, he's found what he needs.

Carson's looking over his shoulder. "An incantation," she says.

"Ancient words to move energy," says Dylan. "The first set-tlers in Charleston used this technique to banish evil spirits, which I'm convinced were the same as the poltergeists we're dealing with now—though they weren't called that in the past."

"That's it?" says Eli. "Well, let's go ahead and say the magic words."

"It's not that simple." Dylan glances down at the book again. "It says here that the incantation has to be a calling of energy—we have to target the specific poltergeists we want to banish."

"If we can get rid of Reena and Leo, the rest of them will fall apart," I tell him. "They're the ringleaders."

"Right," says Dylan. "Callie, do you know where they died?"

On the upper Wando. With Thatcher. "Yes."

"Good. The incantation requires that we be in a place of great energy for them. Death spots qualify. So we have to go to each of their death spots, and—"

"They share a death spot," I interrupt.

Dylan stares at me. "They share one?" he says.

I nod. "They drowned in the upper Wando River," I tell him. "On homecoming night."

"Yikes," says Eli. "That sounds like one of those bad horror movies. *Death at the River* or whatever."

I can feel him grinning in my direction, but I don't meet his eyes. I don't mention Thatcher, how he also died there. There's a part of me that wants to keep him separate from the poltergeists in my friends' eyes. He's not like them.

"Okay!" Dylan claps his hands together, like we're about to run out onto the football field for a big game. "The upper Wando it is."

"Y'all . . . ," I say. I don't want to tell them that the last time we were there, Thatcher possessed Nick. That might make them suspicious of Thatcher, when it was my fault for calling him to me that day. "I think the river is also a vortex."

"A vortex and a death spot . . ." Dylan rubs his chin like he's thinking. "The energy will be really powerful there."

"We should go now," says Carson, "before it gets dark."

I shake my head. "I'm nervous," I say. "I think I should go alone." We can't risk Carson and Eli being there.

"We need Carson," says Dylan. "She's the only one who's been able to use an incantation effectively. She has to read the words."

I look over at Nick to back me up—but he doesn't. "Dylan's right," he says.

Eli stands up and walks to the tiny window in the front of the bookstore. He looks out for a long moment, and we all stare at his back, wondering if he's going to break from us and leave. I couldn't blame him if he did.

I walk up to him and touch his shoulder gently. "Eli, you don't have to—"

He turns around with a small grin on his face. "If you think I'm going to sit in a bookstore while there's a poltergeist asswhuppin' going on, you're crazy, Callie."

I smile as he puts his arm around me and walks back to join the group. I'm encouraged, but I'm also scared. I don't know if he truly understands the danger, if any of them do.

"We're wasting time, Callie," says Carson. "You said that tonight might be our last shot."

I lock eyes with Dylan, and I see his wisdom, his caution. Eli is already by the door, ready to go. I look at Nick, so strong and kind, willing to help in any way he can. And Carson, my Carson, unafraid even though she's in so much peril.

But maybe us all being there is the key. I haven't felt this strong, this determined . . . ever. What we're dealing with is an invisible energy, a magic, a chemistry. And I feel something powerful when we're all together.

"Okay," I say. "Let's do this."

"There's something else we need," says Dylan.

"What?" asks Nick.

"Personal items of Reena's and Leo's . . . something from when they were alive."

"Oh yeah!" says Carson. "Callie, when we called to you in the séance, I used the amber pendant Nick gave you—the heart-shaped one."

My hand goes up to my neck automatically, but it's not there. It hasn't been since Thatcher gave me the ring.

"I know—and it almost worked." I frown. "I guess we do need something of theirs. But we can't find an address for Reena's family now . . . and Leo's . . ." We all shudder collectively at the memory of the Doberman.

"Good thing I pocketed this," says Carson, dropping the LC-engraved cuff link on the table. It moves for a few seconds and then spins to a stop.

"You stole that?" I asked.

"We were looking for Thatcher's talisman," says Carson. "I just had a feeling we might need something of Leo's."

Dylan beams. "Brilliant instincts," he says. "What about Reena? How can we get something of hers?"

"Her family moved," says Carson. "I'm not sure what we can do to—"

I interrupt and stop her with one word: "Wendy."

"Wendy?" Dylan raises an eyebrow.

"Thatcher's sister," I say, nodding at Carson, whose eyes light up. "She knew Reena, too."

"Hey, Callie." Wendy's voice on the phone is friendlier than I expect. "I've been thinking about you."

"Same here," I say. "How are you?"

Carson, listening in, rolls her eyes at me and makes a hurry-up motion with her hands. Small talk is not on the poltergeist-fighting timetable.

"Better," says Wendy. "It's funny. I think . . . I think something is shifting in me. I feel . . ."

"More peaceful?"

"Maybe," she says.

"Wendy, Thatcher has been there with you. He only wants the best for you, and for you to move on from his death."

"It's hard to forget what happened after he died," she says, her voice hardening a little. "But I'm trying. I heard what you said, that he probably wasn't himself. I'm actually home this week, helping my parents clean out his room. It was my idea. I . . . I just thought it was time."

A lump forms in my throat and I have to swallow it down before I respond. Even though I still don't know what happened between Wendy and Thatcher—or what kind of threat she felt from him— what I do know is Thatcher has been splitting his time, trying to protect me and go to Wendy, helping her heal—all the while searching every corner of our Charleston for the poltergeists.

"I'm so happy to hear things are getting better," I say, emotion quivering in my voice. And then I realize that what she's doing dovetails with what I have to ask her.

"Wendy," I say, "I called because I need a favor."

"Okay," she says cautiously.

"It's going to sound strange."

"Callie, since we've met, everything you've said to me has sounded strange."

"I'm sorry," I say, realizing that's true. "You know those

friends of Thatcher's, Reena and Leo?"

I hear Wendy's sharp intake of breath. "Yes. Of course. They . . . that night . . . they died, too."

"I know," I say. "I'm calling because I need something that belonged to Reena. It can be anything. Maybe Thatcher had something in his room, or—"

"What is this for?" she asks.

"I can't tell you. But please, just trust me. This is for Thatcher."

I hear her sigh into the phone. "I'll look," she says. "When do you need it?"

Carson is pointing her finger down and mouthing "now, now, now" at me.

"Now?" I say.

"Now?" Wendy echoes my question.

"Yes," I say. "I'm sorry, it's really important. I could come—"

"This is for Thatcher?" says Wendy, interrupting me.

"Yes," I say. "I promise."

"I'm trusting you," says Wendy, giving me her parents' address. "So don't screw with me."

The house is modest and tidy—a single-floor ranch with brown shingles, a green door, and a big picture window through which I can see Wendy as Carson and I step out of her VW Bug.

Nick, Dylan, and Eli took us to pick up Carson's car, and then they drove Nick's van to the upper Wando—we're supposed to meet them there as soon as we can.

Wendy frowns at us from the window, and I ask Carson to hang back by the car.

"Hey," says Wendy when she opens up the front door. We stand there awkwardly for a moment, but I see something softer than usual in her eyes. I go in for a hug and she grips me firmly, in a real embrace.

When we part, she glances at Carson in the driveway.

"Sorry I didn't come alone," I say. "I needed a ride. And I guess we're all kind of in this together."

"What is *this* exactly?" asks Wendy, her lip ring causing her to lisp a little.

"Believe me when I tell you that you don't want to know," I say. "But it's important."

Wendy nods, and Carson gives her an enthusiastic wave.

"Not her," she says. She must remember Carson from campus.

"Only me?" I ask her.

"Yeah," she says. "Sorry to be weird but his room is . . . sacred to me. I guess that sounds stupid."

"No, it doesn't," I tell her, giving Carson the *stay put* hand gesture. I don't want to risk anything tipping Wendy's emotional scale, and it seems like she's opening up more, like she's not as upset and moody as she was when I last saw her. Is that because Thatcher's been here, haunting her in a loving way?

I follow Wendy into Thatcher's home.

The first thing I see is a framed photo on the mantel, a picture of a boy kneeling in a football uniform and holding a ball under his arm. He looks so all-American, so normal, so bright. And it's Thatcher. My intense and brooding, lovely ghost. The sight of him as a child takes my breath away and I gasp.

Wendy turns at the sound. "I forgot that this might be awkward for you."

I nod, too overcome to speak for a moment.

"My parents are out," she tells me, and I'm glad they're not around. I'm not sure I could handle more sensory experiences of Thatcher right now, since I'm at my fill when I imagine him sitting on this beige couch, eating at this teak dining table, leaning against the granite counter in their spotless kitchen.

"It's down here, space cadet," she says, when I stand too long in the doorway of the kitchen.

I shake my head. "Sorry," I tell her. "I'm a little overwhelmed."

She smiles. "It's okay."

We walk through the carpeted hallway, lined with photos of Wendy and Thatcher as babies, family portraits of four, black-and-white young-grandparent shots.

As we reach the door to Thatcher's room, I have the sense of being on a precipice, an entrance into another world. But when I walk in, I see that the cleanout has already begun in earnest, and I wonder if I should be disappointed or grateful.

There are boxes all around the twin bed in the corner, and a desk on the opposite wall has only a couple of items on top of it. One of them catches my eye and I walk across the room to pick it up.

It's another framed photograph, this time of three friends, high school seniors with their arms around one another, laughing.

Leo's face is open and joyful—he looks a thousand years younger without the shadows of bitterness that cover his deep-set eyes and hang from the corners of his mouth. Reena, too, is a picture of innocence. Her soft brown eyes are warm and welcoming, her smile brimming with happiness. She looks like a Disney Channel star, one who bounces around singing about dreams and stardust and best friends forever.

And the third friend. *Thatcher.* His gorgeous full lips are holding back a grin that's on the verge of bursting through, like someone just told him the funniest joke of all time. His blue eyes, unclouded by the storms I've seen in them, shine like the open sky, full of promise and wonder.

"They're so . . ." I don't know how to finish my thought.

"They are," agrees Wendy, coming up behind me, and I know she understands the words that are unsaid but still hang in the air. *Alive. Untouched. Hopeful.*

We stare at the picture for another minute, and then Wendy clears her throat.

"You can keep it if you want," she says.

"You're sure?"

"Yeah," she says. "We have a bunch."

I take the photo out of the frame and put it in my pocket. "Thank you." I shake the emotional cobweb from my voice with a cough.

"I found something that may help you," says Wendy, switching gears.

"Great."

She reaches for a shoe box that's resting on top of a bigger card-board box, and she pulls out a shoelace. I give her a curious smile.

"It was Reena's," she says. Then she sits on the end of the bed and stares at the white string for a moment. "It's funny. I have a distinct memory of sitting with her in Thatcher's room—over there by the closet—and helping her change out her shoelaces for cheerleading practice. She had these white ones, but she wanted to swap them for red and gold, the school colors. There was a pep rally that night."

She lets out a little laugh, lost in the past. "I remember Thatcher joking around with her, saying her school spirit was out of control. But I was twelve, and I thought she was so cool."

"*You* thought cheerleading was cool?" I laugh.

"It was before I knew who I really was. And before these." She points to her piercings, and then she shakes her head, clearing the memory. "Anyway, I found this on the floor of Thatcher's closet," she says. "It's definitely hers."

She hands it to me and I look at it in my palm. This piece of string was once on Reena's sneakers. Back when she was a girl, like me. Before she was . . . the vengeful creature she is now. I stuff the shoelace into my pocket.

"Thank you," I say.

"I also found this." She reaches back into the box and pulls out a small round pin with an intricate drawing of a tree on it—it's tiny but you can see the texture of the bark, a delicate knothole, the detailed roots. Just like the drawing in Leo's room.

"Did Leo make this?" I ask.

"Yeah," she says. "He used to draw all the time and he pressed buttons too. It was on the strap of Thatcher's last backpack."

I take the circle in my hand and finger it gently.

"Thank you," I say to Wendy. "I like knowing that this side of Leo existed once."

"What do you mean?"

"He changed," I say. "In the Prism, Leo's so angry. He can't come to terms with what happened to him."

"Like Thatcher," says Wendy, looking down at the carpet.

"No," I tell her. "Not like Thatcher at all."

She glances up at me, and I can sense a secret in her face, one that is longing to come out. Her eyes are asking if she can trust me.

"What is it?" I ask.

"You know that feeling when you're bodysurfing and you get trapped under a wave and rolled along the sand?"

I nod, not sure where she's going with this. Anyone who's gone in the ocean has had that happen at some point—that feeling of panic just before you come up to the surface and breathe again, coughing and choking.

"Yeah," I say. "It's scary."

"Right," says Wendy. "It is. And it's even scarier if someone holds you down."

"What do you mean?"

"It was the first time after Thatcher's death that Mom and Dad let me go off with a friend's family. Jen and I spent the day in the sun, reading magazines and digging our feet into the sand. And when we went in the ocean, Thatcher was waiting."

My eyes grow large and I take a breath in.

"The boy in the ocean wasn't like my brother. He was bitter and mean. Reena and Leo were with him."

I nod, encouraging her to go on.

"Thatcher waited for a wave to take me, and when I ducked under, he held me down."

I'm shaking my head now, *nonononono*, but she's nodding yes.

"He was in a rage, churning like the ocean itself."

"It was a hallucination," I say. "Maybe you hit your head on the bottom, maybe—"

"No," says Wendy, interrupting me.

"It was Leo, then; I'm sure of it. I know he was different when he was alive, but Wendy, you don't know what he's capable of now. He's—"

"It. Was. My. Brother." She says it staccato style, and her intense stare makes me go quiet again. "I know it was. Just before I broke the surface, Thatcher whispered, 'Always remember, *this* is what it feels like to drown.'"

I look up at her, shocked, and her kohl-rimmed eyes are filled with tears.

"My brother blamed me, almost enough to want me dead. So how can I not blame myself, too?"

I stand up and move closer to her, sitting on the edge of the bed. I stroke her back for a minute as her shoulders shudder, trying to process this information myself. Is it possible that Thatcher did this to his sister? That he held her under water and scared her half to death? I shake my head. It can't be.

"I don't know what happened that day at the beach," I tell her honestly. "But I do know that Thatcher loves you very much. He always has. You can't hold on to the guilt you're carrying—you've got to let it go."

"I've tried," she says, drying her tears and pulling away from my touch. She stands up quickly and crosses her arms in front of her chest. "I go to church, I went to therapy, I do all the things they say can ease grief. I even kept a journal about my feelings for a year. But I keep reliving that day, under the water, when Thatcher's words were full of hate and I wasn't sure I'd see the sun again."

My heart goes cold. I can't believe what I've just heard.

Was Thatcher once a poltergeist, like Leo and Reena?

Twenty-three

WHEN CARSON AND I step out onto the beach where we pic-
nicked the day Thatcher possessed Nick, my mind is not thinking
the way I want it to. I'm supposed to be focused on using this
incantation to expel Reena and Leo from the universe, but Wendy's
confession has me reeling. The thought of Thatcher trying to hurt
his own sister—the realization that I don't know everything about
his past and what kind of spirit he used to be—is so unfathom-
able to me that I keep trying to make sense of it, running through
possible alternate scenarios in my head, and my balance is totally
off-kilter.

I haven't said anything to Carson, but of course she senses
something's wrong. As we close in on Dylan, Eli, and Nick, who are
assembled in a little triangle about a hundred feet away on a mound
of wet sand, she gives me a sharp look.

"So are you going to tell me?" she asks.

"Tell you what?"

"Don't play dumb. Something happened at Wendy's house. Something that really has you spooked."

I shrug. "It was weird being there. In his room, with some of his stuff. I just . . . I can't shake the feeling."

It's all true, but I'm afraid to mention what Wendy told me about her brother, how he held her down under water so he could show her how horrible it felt to drown. I don't want my friends to mistrust Thatcher, especially not now. I hate to admit it, but my trust in him is wavering a bit.

"There's more to it than that," Carson says, stopping for a second. "Your eyes were totally glazed over when you left their house."

I tug her along by the wrist, so that she doesn't lag behind me. "Please, let it go. We have to focus on the incantation."

"That's what I'm worried about. You know better than anyone that stuff like this doesn't work unless you're spiritually centered. If you're not focused, it can backfire," she warns.

"I'll be fine; I just need another minute to settle down, okay?"

"If you say so," Carson says skeptically.

"Hello, ladies," says Dylan, waving us over and smiling from ear to ear. Eli, on the other hand, still looks puzzled, while Nick appears to be scanning the beach, for what I'm not exactly sure.

"Do you still think you're dreaming?" I ask Eli.

He scratches his head. "There's a lot of logistics in this dream," he says. "A lot of driving."

I glance around, too, scoping out the area carefully. It's almost dark and the beach is empty, so no one will see what we're up to. There's also a buffer of trees all around us so that if someone pulls into the parking lot we'll have advance warning.

"There," says Carson, pointing to the floating dock out on the water. "That's the perfect spot."

"Really?" I ask her. It's only about twenty feet out, not far at all, but still . . . I pictured a simple circle on the beach.

"Please don't question the master of incantations," Dylan says, winking at her.

"Thanks, Dyl. Anyway, the incantation mentions water, so I think we'll have more power out there on the dock," she says.

"Who's calling those kayaks gas burners now?" asks Nick with a grin. I suddenly see that he has the two boats all set up to go.

Carson rolls her eyes and reaches into her large bag to bring out a candle in a tall glass votive holder. "Well, I've got to see the book to read the incantation, don't I?" she says, when I let out a soft giggle. "I took it from Dixon's."

Eli shoves his hands into his pockets and turns to Dylan. "Walk me through this again?"

But Carson steps in, like the good host she is, and plays Martha Stewart to our poltergeist-expulsion party. Seems like she's doing what I asked her to—letting go of her suspicions that something is bothering me.

I let out a small sigh, hoping that what I said was true. That in a minute I'll be fine, I'll be centered and ready.

"We're going to do an incantation that is meant to call these two poltergeists—Reena and Leo—to us," she says. "Once they're here, the incantation will draw out their energy—hopefully all of it—and force them to move on from the Prism to merge into another dimension and leave the Earth, and the Prism, alone for good."

Eli pales a little.

"'There is a real magic in enthusiasm. It spells the difference between mediocrity and accomplishment.' Norman Vincent Peale," Dylan says out of the blue.

"Is that supposed to make me get excited?" asks Eli.

"Don't worry," says Dylan. "The whole thing sounds a lot weirder than it is."

"I'm not so sure about that," Nick whispers under his breath, and I give his arm a squeeze.

"Okay, y'all!" says Carson. "Let's go."

The two kayaks from the van are already halfway in the water, but they're both two-seaters.

"Who's riding three?"

I see an opportunity here, a chance to thank Carson for not pressing me too hard. "Eli, you get in the back of that one. Dylan, you sit up front, and Carson can be on your lap."

Dylan's face reddens instantly. "Y'all are the littlest," I explain.

"Why don't you and Carson sit up front together and then Dylan and I can take this one?" asks Nick, totally not getting my goal here. I kick him in the shin.

"Because I want to kayak with you, Nick," I say, sitting in kayak number two so there can be no argument.

We push off and I watch Carson navigate Dylan's lap as he blushes and adjusts his arms to rest around her. I can tell they're both into it, and it warms me up a little on this shadowy, still night. I need that reassurance that two people can be a perfect fit for each other—and not have any secrets between them.

It takes about a minute to paddle to the dock, where we tie up and sit in a circle on the wooden planks. I place Reena's shoestring and Leo's cuff link in the center, willing myself not to hear Wendy's voice echoing in my ear, but it doesn't work. The sound of chirping crickets can't even drown her out.

Thatcher waited for a wave to take me, and when I ducked under, he held me down.

My brother blamed me, almost enough to want me dead.

Carson snaps her fingers in front of my face when she notices I'm in a bit of a trance. "You concentrating, Cal?"

I clear my throat, hoping it will also clear my mind. "Yeah, I'm good."

"Do we hold hands?" asks Nick.

"No," says Dylan. "Once Carson starts saying the words, the energy will flow between us without us having to touch."

He opens up the book, placing it in front of Carson. Her voice kicks into serious mode, and she begins to say the words we hope will stop the poltergeists, as the rest of us close our eyes.

"I call to you, Reena Bell and Leo Cutler,
I appeal to you
On the wings of words that fly,
Whatever the distance,

Traverse time and space, water and earth,
And appear in our presence on this moonlit night."

The first time she says the incantation, nothing feels different. It's like we're kids at a basement slumber party, playing "Light as a feather, stiff as a board" and wishing something would happen without any real results. But my thoughts are here, with my friends, free of distractions and feelings that might threaten this whole process.

Then Carson repeats the words. . . .

"I call to you, Reena Bell and Leo Cutler,
I appeal to you
On the wings of words that fly,
Whatever the distance,
Traverse time and space, water and earth,
And appear in our presence on this moonlit night."

This time, I can feel energy starting to swim around us, like we're under water, surrounded by an element that's thicker than air, heavy and pressing. I hear a cackle from behind me, so I peek a little and see streaks of light hovering between me, Dylan, Nick, Eli, and Carson. When I open my own eyes fully, the others do, too—it feels like all of our senses are connected right now. The light looks pretty at first, like the twinkling of tiny stars dancing above us. But the sound of laughter grows louder, and the stars begin to flicker—light to dark, dark to light.

When I turn my head to the right, I can see them.

Reena and Leo.

They're hovering on top of the river, clear as day—at least to me. Their mouths are curved into ghoulish shapes as they sneer and continue to laugh.

"Can you believe this?" Leo says to Reena. "They're trying a spell on us!"

"It's pathetic, isn't it?" she replies, but when she locks eyes with me, Reena realizes this isn't a joke. All of us mean business and we won't stop until they're gone.

"Carson, part two!" shouts Dylan, and Carson switches gears, moving on to the second step, which is ridding the poltergeists of everything that gives them power.

> *"Energy, I summon thee,*
> *Black to white,*
> *Dark to light,*
> *I call to thee,*
> *Precious energy,*
> *Leave these souls*
> *And come to me."*

"It's not working," says Dylan abruptly, his voice sounding shaky and uncertain for the first time.

"It is," I tell him. "They're here. I can see them over the water."

"I can sense their presence, too," he says, closing his eyes for a moment. "But we're not in control . . . they're not losing energy. In fact, they feel—"

"Stronger than ever?" says Leo, filling in the rest of Dylan's sentence and booming over Carson's second chant of the incantation.

Carson's head whips toward Leo. "I see them now, too," she says, her eyes glowing with anticipation. Once Reena notices Carson's attention, she tilts her head affectionately at my best friend, which makes my stomach tie into knots.

I look around at the rest of our circle—Dylan, Nick, Eli. Dylan is concentrating hard, still focusing his attention on the spell, and trying to get Carson to return to her chant. Nick looks thoroughly confused.

"What's happening?" whispers Nick. He can't see them yet, and Dylan can't either. But I don't have time to fill him in.

I glance over at Eli. His face is frozen in fear—he's looking directly at Leo.

"Can you *see* him?" I ask Eli.

"Uh, yeah. Dude's standing right there on the water and he's not exactly small."

"Callie," says Dylan. "What's happening? I can't see anything."

"I thought you were smarter than this, Callie. Letting that idiot lead you out here, convincing you that this might make us go away," says Reena.

"Hey!" shouts Carson. "He's not an idiot!"

Leo growls at her, and I see Carson's skin go completely white, like she's just now realized what deep trouble we're in. I nudge her with my foot and mouth the words "the ring" to her, reassuring her that we can get backup here at any time. Carson nods, her shoulders loosening.

"You seem a little frightened, Carson," says Reena, smiling with all of her teeth. "That's disappointing. I expected that you'd be energized by your glimpse of us, of the other side."

Carson shrinks back a little bit, and I move toward her protectively.

"Callie, who is that?" Eli's still staring at Leo, who's giving him a menacing grin.

I feel a panic grip me. If Leo takes Eli now, it'll be the third possession. The one that will destroy Eli's soul and allow Leo to keep his body . . . forever.

I have to think fast. "Eli, that's Leo!" I say fake-cheerfully. "What would a party be without Leo?"

"What are you doing?" whispers Nick.

But I don't answer him. I'm too busy trying to stall so I can try to figure out why the second part of the incantation is failing, and deciding whether or not to call Thatcher. Suddenly it feels like they called us here instead of the other way around and I'm worried that we're in way over our heads.

Especially now that Reena is staring at Carson like a starving lion eyeing an antelope.

"Aren't you wondering why you and Eli can see us and hear us right now?" she asks Carson patiently, like an adult patronizing a little kid.

"I've always been perceptive," says Carson, her voice even despite her saucer-sized eyes.

"Too true," says Reena. "But the reason you can both see and hear me now, in this instant, is because you're both ready for the final possession."

Then Reena glares at me. "Say good-bye to Carson, Callie. You'll be seeing me from now on."

I grab hold of Thatcher's ring and stand up, breaking the energy of the circle. Every fiber of my being vibrates with the bellowing call I make, the wind shifting around me like a storm.

"*Thaaaatcheeeer!*" I scream, so hard my vocal cords are nearly shredded.

And then I hear something that sounds like streams of air being sucked out of the sky.

"Stop!" Thatcher's voice echoes from the woods and I see him emerge on the beach, clear as day. His muscular arms are taut and ready—I can see he's poised to spring out into the water, ready to battle, and it pushes away the seeds of doubt that Wendy planted within me earlier.

How could this selfless person ever hurt a soul?

"Oh my gosh!" says Carson, turning to see him. "Thatcher." She glances back at me. "Callie, is this . . . him?"

Reena's laugh carries across the sand. "Aw, the gang's all back together," she says with a fake-friendly lilt. Then she fixes her attention on Nick. "Better tell your living boyfriend to be careful, Callie. We know how Thatcher gets . . . overcome by emotions."

"Reena, enough. Leo may be able to own Eli tonight, but you'll be left without a body—taking Carson a second time will just weaken you even more," says Thatcher over the water. I have to admit, I was expecting him to attack her and Leo right away, but of course he wants to try and talk them out of this first—that's his way. "Then you'll have to return to the Prism, and we will never let you come back here."

He gestures behind him and I see the other Guides, their figures glowing on the beach with him. I feel a wave of relief wash over me, but as quickly as it comes, it goes with the sound of Reena's voice.

"Oh, Thatcher," she says, acting sickly sweet. "I think you missed possession number two."

My heart speeds up, regret charging through me. "What do you mean?"

Reena spins toward me. "While you and your true love were canoodling out in the water on Sunday, I took the opportunity to use Carson the way he was using Nick."

I feel like I've been punched. The energy pull . . . the one I thought was happening because Thatcher was using my energy to possess Nick. It was Reena taking Carson's body, back on the beach. I think about Carson mentioning how tired she was feeling from her day in the sun. Why didn't I make the connection then? Why didn't I see the signs?

Maybe because the only person I was thinking of in that moment was Thatcher.

I don't think the consequences of our relationship have ever been greater.

Before I can explain or say anything to Carson, she's standing up to face Reena in her take-no-bull way, despite the fear I know she feels. She sways a little on the dock but stays steady on her feet. "You're so full of crap, Reena. Everyone here knows you're bluffing. Callie told us what Thatcher knows. That you're almost out of energy."

"Oh, Carson," purrs Reena, stepping from the water to the dock now. "I admire your fire. So very much . . . too bad you're dead wrong."

Reena reaches out a hand to touch one of Carson's glossy brown curls, and I hear Thatcher shout, "Nooooo!"

I lunge toward Reena, but the moment I move, a piercing pain hits me, like someone has driven a pair of scissors through my skull. A blazing flash of light blinds me and I roll off the dock, my head in my hands. The sting is excruciating, and I must black out for a minute, because when I come to again, water is filling my lungs and I'm sinking down to the bottom of the river.

Suddenly, I feel someone reach under my arms and pull me up to the surface, where I spit up liquid and choke down air. Nick has me—he's dragging me to the beach.

When he pulls me to the sand, I don't see Reena or Leo. But I see Thatcher and the Guides, now standing on the beach around me in a protective circle.

I slowly sit up and my vision clears. Nick is next to me. Dylan is pulling up the yellow kayak nearby—he kept the book dry. Carson. Eli. They're sitting on the beach next to the red kayak—they must have paddled back together when I went under.

"Did it work?" My voice is a whisper.

I look over at Carson, whose eyes are closed. Eli's are too.

But then they both blink at once.

"Yes," they say in unison.

And the way they say it makes the blood in my veins turn to ice.

I look at Thatcher, hoping he'll shake his head, tell me that my worst fear hasn't happened, hoping he'll say that our incantation worked, that Reena and Leo are gone.

But what I see is pure rage in his face as he stares at Eli. When Thatcher runs at him to attack, I know there's no time to waste. I have to get Reena out of Carson's body before she fully attaches.

I spring to my feet and tackle my best friend, driving her into the sand and trying to draw on my energy, reach inside myself and find the depths of my power—if ever there was a time to call on every ounce of strength I have, it is now. I'm trying to push her energy—trying to move Reena's soul from Carson. What I end up doing is some messed-up kind of CPR, banging on her chest and screaming like a banshee.

"Callie, you're only hurting her physically," says a voice beneath me. It sounds just like Carson, it's coming from her mouth, but isn't her. And I lift my head toward the sky and let out a ferocious scream as I realize, truly realize, what has happened.

Reena has taken her for a third time. Carson's soul has vanished. Turned to dust.

It's too much to bear.

"Callie, what are you doing?" It's Dylan. He clearly doesn't know what's going on, but he's pulling me off Carson, confused by this bizarre scene.

"Dylan, help!" says Reena, deceiving him from inside Carson's body. It must look like I'm crazy, like I just attacked my best friend. But Dylan knows better than that.

He glances at Carson, but then, holding my shoulders tightly in his hands and shaking me until I lock eyes with him, he just says, "Reena?"

Tears stream down my face. "She's taken Carson for a third time," I say. "I can't move her soul. It's latched into the body and—"

He doesn't let me finish, just drops my shoulders and turns to Carson, staring at her with a gaping, horror-filled gaze. She smiles back at him, but the smile isn't Carson's. It's sinister and tight and void of any compassion or love. Dylan panics, diving for the book he left in the kayak.

"There's got to be a way . . . ," he whispers, rifling through the pages frantically.

Nick is standing next to Eli, gazing down at him in horrified wonder after Thatcher's assault. Does Nick know that the person he's looking at isn't his soccer teammate? Eli is dead, vanished, and Leo has taken him.

And all this happened because of me.

I'm the one who organized this whole plan. The one who brought everyone to a vortex without knowing if the incantation would really work. I'm to blame, for all of this. If I had just listened to Thatcher and waited . . .

The guilt ravages my mind and Thatcher must hear it somehow, because he's there, by my side. His face is a picture of dread. The other Guides stand, helpless, at the edge of the woods. The battle they were ready to fight cannot take place. Because the enemy now walks among the living, inside the physical shells of our friends.

"Don't punish yourself," he murmurs, but nothing he can say can make this awful ache inside me go away. "Your intentions to banish them were all good . . . but . . ."

The look in his eyes says it all.

"It's over," I say, translating his expression. "They've won."

He sinks to the sand, where Carson's and Eli's bodies still lie, regaining strength. His ghostly form flickers like he might disappear from devastation. I long to reach out to him, to hold him, but I can't. We are all lost, unable to save our friends.

I drop to my knees next to Carson, who is now going to live a life that Reena dictates. Will she leave Carson's family and find her own? Will she treasure my best friend's world, so full of light and laughter and friendship and love? Or will Reena create her own existence, living carelessly and doing whatever she pleases? It doesn't matter, I realize. Even if she does follow in Carson's footsteps, it won't be Carson. It'll be an impostor.

I lie on the ground, unable to face the new world around me. I find some comfort in the cold, wet grains of sand that stick to my cheek. I focus on them, not on the anguish I'm feeling. These billions of tiny specks broken up by water, washed away with years of patient energy and careful erosion, are my universe right now.

Then I hear a jangle of keys behind me. "Sweet!" It's Carson's voice, but Reena's tone. "A VW Bug? I've always wanted one."

I lift my head to see Reena and Leo near me on the beach, smiling at each other, holding hands. Carson and Eli reimagined. Reborn in a way so wrong I can't accept it. I won't.

I push myself to my feet and stand over them as they revel in their victory.

"You can't do this," I say, and my voice sounds almost pleading.

"It's already done, Callie." Eli's mouth speaks Leo's words.

Reena shoots her hand up into the air, lifting Carson's keys like a trophy and letting out a rebel yell that echoes through the woods and out onto the water. Then she races down the path to the parking lot with Leo at her heels, and I hear the two of them rev the engine and drive off into the night.

I falter, almost faint with grief, and I shift my feet to keep my balance. I feel Nick's arms before I see him come up behind me. He envelops me in the hug I want from Thatcher, and I turn to him, burying my face in his warm chest. That's when I cry. I let my body shake, heaving with sobs for my best friend, who's suffered a fate worse than death—she's been taken. Turned to dust. And someone else is going to assume her identity. Her family will always wonder why their sweet, loving girl suddenly changed, and all of us will know the horrifying truth.

A truth that I couldn't prevent. A truth that I brought upon all of us.

My body is racked with sadness and I don't hold a single sound back as I wail into Nick's shirt. Crying for Carson, for Eli, for . . . me.

When my tears dry and my blurry vision clears, I stare down for a moment and focus on two objects that catch my eye. The shoe-string and the cuff link. They're lying in the bottom of the yellow kayak. I let go of Nick and reach down to pick them up.

Then I turn, and I see Thatcher, still bent down in the sand.

The upper Wando is a vortex, a powerful place, a death spot even, and I can see Thatcher here. I can talk to him. Who knows, this might be the last time.

I walk over to him slowly, and each step feels like my feet are leaden and dragging.

"What do we do?" I ask him, my voice vacant and detached. I don't sound like me at all.

"There's nothing," he says. "Nothing can be done."

"Thatcher?" a voice calls from the woods, and I turn to see Wendy, finding her way through the deepening darkness.

"What's she doing here?" asks Thatcher, startled.

"I don't know. I'll go talk to her." I jog over to Wendy, wondering what she saw and, if she did, if she's okay.

"Hey," I say, coming to a stop at the edge of the forest and the sand.

"Don't be mad; I just had to see why you wanted Reena's and Leo's stuff, so I followed you. I was in the woods, watching," she says, looking over my shoulder, as if she's still trying to spy on us. "I'm not sure what I saw happen. Is everyone all right? Your friends ran past me just now. . . . They seemed weird."

"It's complicated" is all I can say without breaking down again. Until I realize that there's someone here that she desperately needs to see. "Come with me."

I lead her to where he's still kneeling in the sand, and he looks up at me with a world of torment in his stormy blue eyes.

"It's time for you both to talk," I say.

Then I turn to Wendy. "Your brother is right here," I tell her. "He can see and hear you."

Wendy takes in a breath, her eyes starting to fill with tears. I see a flicker of doubt, but I say, "Trust me. Everything's going to be okay."

Thankfully she does, standing still, waiting for what she's always hoped for and feared.

"Wendy," says Thatcher. And I can tell he's using all of his remaining energy to push through the boundaries of the Prism and Earth so that she can listen to the sound of his voice.

Tears streak down her cheeks instantly, and I know she's heard him.

"Thatch. It's you," she says.

"It's me," he replies, standing up to face her.

Wendy wipes at her eyes. "I've missed you. I've missed you so much."

"I know," says Thatcher.

"I thought . . . you hated me," she murmurs. "That you felt the accident was somehow my fault."

"No, nothing is your fault. Not my death. Not what happened at the beach."

My breath catches when I hear him admit it. He did hold her under the water that day. He had threatened his own sister.

Thatcher looks at my face, and the way his lips are tightening sends a surge of sympathy through me. "I was angry, misguided, as vengeful as Reena and Leo are . . . once," he says, his eyes trained on me, as though he's trying to explain his behavior to both of us. "But it was wrong, and I let go of all that bitterness, and I tried to haunt you the right way, Wendy, I did. I tried to help you grieve . . . and heal."

His face turns to hers, and though I know she can't see him, it's almost as if she's looking into his eyes.

"Oh, Thatcher," Wendy says. "I've wanted to believe that you were with me, but I've been so afraid since that day. I—"

Thatcher puts his hand up close to her mouth, and Wendy's words quiet. She can sense him there; the energy connection is clear.

"Shhh . . . ," he says. "I'm so, so sorry. I would do anything to take it back. I want you to live without guilt, without regret."

Her head drops and two tears fall, hitting the sand gently.

I back away, letting the two of them share this moment of forgiveness. I burn the scene into my memory, one that I'll turn to when I wonder if there is still any light in the world. In the midst of the horror, at least there is this one piece of good.

But the second I feel a small bit of relief, I'm smacked back down again by the truth.

The more Wendy's burden begins to lighten, the more peace she lets into her heart, the closer Thatcher gets to Solus.

The hope that's brimming in Wendy's eyes is secretly killing me. Thatcher is going to merge and I'll be all alone, with this blood on my hands.

Well, not entirely alone. Nick is sitting on the beach still, his head hanging low. Dylan won't stop frantically reading the book we were using. There are silent tears spilling down his face as he bites his lip, obviously hoping that there's some kind of Hail Mary pass in the pages in front of him.

Then all of a sudden, he stands. "Guys!" he says. "Listen to this: 'In the case of a third possession, the host soul will grow smaller and smaller, fading over a period of one sun cycle, from which point the occupying or possessing spirit shall inherit full control of the body and the host soul will vanish.'"

I'm excited by his enthusiasm, but I have no idea what he's saying.

"What does it mean?" I ask.

"It means that there's a timetable for the soul attachment," says Dylan. "It means that Carson's and Eli's souls may still be in their bodies, but by dawn, they'll be gone and the takeover will be complete."

"You're saying they're alive?" I ask, hope starting to swell in my chest.

"There's a chance, yes," he mutters.

"But they'll be dead, or whatever, by morning?" asks Nick.

"Right . . . for now, they're just barely hanging on."

I stare at the book in Dylan's hand, and the hope I was just feeling transforms into frustration, and anger. "So what do we do now?" I shout. "Each time one of these books gives us some answers, it gives us even more questions! Meanwhile our friends are disappearing while we sit here and *read*!"

"It's all I know how to do, dammit!" Dylan stands up and throws the book across the sand, and it nearly lands in the water.

His hands are balled into fists. His optimism, his hope, is faltering. Just like mine. I lean down to pick up the book, sorry I lashed out, and the photo I took from Wendy's house falls to the ground. The wind picks it up, blowing it straight to Dylan's leg, and he reaches out to grab it.

My instinct is to take it back, to keep it close because I can almost feel Wendy sending Thatcher away from us. But I don't, because of the intense way Dylan is studying it. Staring at Reena, Leo, and Thatcher, together.

"Is that Reena and Leo?" he asks me.

I look down, afraid that if I tell him, he'll tear up the photo. "And Thatcher," I say softly.

"Wait," says Dylan, and his voice demands attention. "They were all friends?"

"Yes," I say. "A long time ago." I look around and a chill rushes through me. "They all died here."

Dylan whips his head up, his eyes locking with mine.

"All three of them at the same time?" he asks.

I nod.

Dylan grabs the book from my hands. He opens it up, flips to the middle, and starts to read.

"'When banishing a poltergeist from a death spot, it is important to note that all souls who were present and taken in the moment of said poltergeist's passing must be called as well. One soul shall not move without the presence of other souls in the case of multiple or simultaneous deaths.'"

"English!" Nick yells, getting impatient.

"It means that the three of them are tied—they died in the same spot at the same time. In order to send the two away from the here and now, all three have to move from these dimensions together."

"But we tried the incantation with Leo and Reena, and it didn't work."

"Maybe it *did*," says Dylan. "We may have primed their energy for banishment, but without including Thatcher's merge, the action couldn't complete!"

From the corner of my eye, I see Wendy walking toward us. Thatcher is by her side.

"Is he still here?" asks Dylan.

"Yes," I say.

"He has to merge with Solus," he says, his voice rising. "Tell him he has to go *now*."

I nod, knowing Dylan is right, but when Thatcher takes his place next to me and I see the outline of his face, which looks more radiant than ever, I hesitate a little, not wanting to send him away just yet.

How horrible does that make me?

"Wendy's okay?" I ask him.

"Yes, finally," Thatcher says. He turns to look at his sister lovingly and I can see all the hurt between them has disappeared. "Thank you, for helping bring us back together."

"You're welcome," I say, even though they did most of the real work. It took a lot of courage, to be vulnerable and let each other back in, to forgive and move on.

The same courage that I'm going to need to lean on this moment.

"Thatcher, Dylan thinks there's a way to get Eli's and Carson's spirits back," I say, my breath catching a bit at the thought of everything that's going to come next.

"What?" he says, completely confused. "How?"

"Oh, wow. I can hear him," says Dylan, his face lighting up. Thatcher is now using his energy to speak to everyone here, not just me. But a part of me wonders why I'm the only one he'll reveal himself to physically—is it because he was planning on saying good-bye to me tonight, regardless of what happened at the river?

"Thatcher, listen to this," Dylan says, not missing a beat. He reads the passages again, the ones about the timing of soul attachment and the all-souls-present aspect of merging and banishment. Nick bounces with excitement, clearly willing to do whatever it takes to finish this mission, while Wendy's serenity cracks a little, knowing that her reunion with her brother might soon be over.

I watch Thatcher's face change as Dylan reads, as understanding dawns. When Dylan is done, he says, "How come I never knew any of this was possible? Why don't any of the Guides know?"

"The books in my bookstore go back hundreds of years and have been written by obscure members of the living," Dylan explains. "They've been kept safe from the spirit dimension as a means of protection, so I'm not surprised that no one in the Prism knew."

Thatcher turns to me, his eyes brightening. "Well, if Dylan is right—if the earlier work you did primed Reena's and Leo's souls for banishment—their souls might be vanquished when I merge with Solus. But . . ."

"But what?"

"Before I go, there's one more person I have to bring peace to," he says.

"Wendy seems ready," I say, glancing at her.

"I am," she says, her voice strong and certain. But then I see something else in her eyes. A sadness that isn't her own.

"Then you're truly ready to merge," I say, turning to Thatcher, a lump lodged in my throat. I raise my eyes to meet his—I can catch glimpses of their light when he moves closer.

So close I almost feel his energy inside of me.

"No, I'm not." Thatcher shakes his head. "There's someone else holding on to my soul."

Without having to ask, I know it's me.

I'm the one who won't let him go.

Can't let him go.

Must let him go.

Twenty-four

"I DON'T KNOW IF I can do this."

Although that thought did just cross my mind, Thatcher is the one to say it, out loud and in front of everyone.

Dylan throws his hands up in the air, completely exasperated. "We don't have much time, Thatcher," he says. "Please, you have to—"

Nick holds a hand up to stop Dylan. "Callie, explain to me again how this works?" he asks me.

"Everyone who . . . loves Thatcher has to accept his death; that's how haunting works," I say, casting my eyes down to the sand. While Nick and I aren't together anymore, it's still a little strange to tell the boy I've been with for so long that I love someone else—someone who I have to give up if I want to save my best friend.

"Once the soul has eased each loved one into a place of acceptance, once they've all let go, then the soul can merge."

"So everyone has to get over his death," repeats Nick, not fumbling over the fact that I just admitted to my feelings, which just goes to show what an incredible friend he is.

"Yes." I pause and then say the truth that's killing me: "*I* have to let him go."

"But I have to let you go, too," says Thatcher, his voice cracking. "It's not just a one-way street, like you might think."

"So you have to choose, too?" I ask, my chest feeling heavy and sore.

Dylan grabs me by the shoulders. "There is no *choice*! You both have to do this, don't you get that?"

"Yes!" I shout. "I love Carson just as much as you do! Actually, *more* than you do. So back off, okay?"

I'm shaking, but I know that underneath my anger is a sadness that I'm not sure anyone besides Thatcher and me can understand.

"Callie knows what has to be done. Let's give her a minute," Nick says to Dylan and Wendy.

Dylan huffs. "Nick, there isn't time for—"

"Now," Nick says forcefully. And I love him for letting me have this moment.

The three of them head into the woods, and I'm alone on the beach with Thatcher. He's just a silhouette I can't fully see or touch, but he's here. For the very last time.

"I wish I could hold you," I whisper.

"Me, too," says Thatcher, and he puts his hand out to stroke my cheek, but when I can't feel his touch I begin to cry. I can't believe there are more tears left in my body, but there they are, streaking my face and blurring my vision. I can hardly see him at all now. Thatcher is fading and this is the last time we'll be together for the rest of my existence. I fall to my knees, completely overcome with hurt.

And then I feel a hand under my arm, lifting me. I wipe at my tears, and I see Nick at my side.

"You're going to be okay, Callie," he says.

"No, I don't think I am," I say, sniffling.

"You will, trust me. Tell Thatcher," says Nick. "Tell him he can use me again to say good-bye. Maybe it will, you know, allow you both to heal."

My eyes widen. "Wait, how long have you—"

"Known that your ghost boyfriend possessed me?" Nick says, winking to lighten the mood. "I figured it out a little while ago, but I didn't want to . . . I don't know, embarrass you."

"I'm so sorry." Again that thought was just in my head, but Thatcher is the one speaking, and I think both Nick and I can feel his overflowing anguish about what he did at the river.

"I am, too," I say, taking Nick's hand. "We never meant to take advantage of you."

"I know that," Nick says to me. Then he looks up to the sky. "And I know it's not easy to let her go, Thatcher. But for Carson's and Eli's sakes you have to, and if I can help, then I will."

"I can't leave you, Callie," says Thatcher. "It's almost impossible for me to go . . . and this . . . Nick is giving me the chance to hold you one more time."

I feel faint with anticipation as I glance back at Nick, and I nod. "Are you sure?" I ask him.

"Yes," he says, squeezing my hand.

And then the outline of Thatcher vanishes from thin air and Nick's eyes become a beautiful, unforgettable blue.

There is no one else in the world, the universe, all of the dimensions that exist, known and unknown. I am holding onto Nick, yet breathing Thatcher in. All I feel is the boy I love, will always love. Elation rushes through me as we sink to our knees in the sand and his kisses rain down on my face. When our lips finally meet, everything falls away and the distance that's always been between us is gone. I don't want to stop tasting him or clinging to him, but I do, just to say these words:

"Stay with me."

"Callie, I can't—"

I place a finger on his lips. "Let's pretend that you can. Just for a minute, okay?"

"Okay," says Thatcher, smiling at me as his hands glide down my back.

"Want to go to an amusement park on Saturday?" I ask him, gazing into his eyes. "The state fair is coming soon."

"Sure. I've always loved the livestock competitions," he jokes.

I laugh, a sound that surprises us both. "Great; I'll buy you a chicken."

"The next day we'll fly to Europe," says Thatcher.

"Paris!" I say excitedly. "I've always wanted to go. Is that a cliché?"

"Only because it's a worthy one." Thatcher rubs my waist. "We'll buy you a beautiful new dress and walk hand in hand down the tree-lined streets eating croissants and saying *'Bonjour!'* to everyone we see."

"And then we'll hop a flight to Venice," I say, taking his hand and kissing his palm.

"Ah, yes, the canals," he says. "I'll wear a striped shirt and row you around!"

"No, I'll row *you* around."

"Only until we catch our train to Spain," says Thatcher.

"Barcelona and then Madrid!" I say.

"Maybe the beach, too? Southern Spain is amazing this time of year."

"And then Africa," I say. "It's just a ferry ride away, right?"

"How worldly you are," says Thatcher. "Yes! We'll spring for rugs and teapots in Morocco before we head to Egypt to see the Pyramids."

"Heaven!" I say, wrapping my arms around his neck.

And then we both realize what I said. *Heaven.*

My heart sinks and then bursts into flames—I try to stop it, but I can't. This fantasy isn't real. What's real is Thatcher leaving. That he has to leave in order to help Carson and Eli, and save countless others from the ringleaders of the poltergeists.

"You won't forget me?" I ask.

He leans his forehead against mine. "Never."

We kiss again, and I know that this moment will play over and over again for the rest of my life, into the Prism, into Solus, where maybe I might finally see him again.

If that's what Solus is really for. Thatcher is about to find out for sure.

I pull back from him, and Thatcher gives me a knowing look. It's full of pain and regret, but also peace and love. Maybe one extreme can't exist without the other.

"Callie, I have things to tell you," says Thatcher.

"Please don't stop touching me," I say to him, as he runs his fingers through my hair and pulls me in for another kiss.

I'm pressed against him as we shiver in the warm night. Then he slowly kisses his way across my cheek, and I treasure the soft breath on my skin. Thatcher's breath. Through Nick.

"You brought me back to life in so many ways," he whispers.

"Not in the one that matters," I murmur, choking back tears.

Then he leans away and I can gaze into his gorgeous, soulful eyes.

"You, Calpurnia May McPhee, have saved me. Never forget it," he says. "You'll save Carson. And Eli. And the other poltergeists—they won't have anyone to follow once Leo and Reena are gone. They'll come with me when I merge. This will work."

"It has to."

"It *will*." Thatcher's voice is confident, his face resolute. When I stare into his eyes, I see the storms that have haunted his gaze calming and quieting. He looks more like the boy in the old photo I got from Wendy than the ghost I've come to know.

"What's happening?" I ask him.

"Peace," he whispers. "Can you feel it?"

I look at his face and it's no longer Nick's. I see Thatcher's bristled jawline, his full pink lips, his blond hair. Seeing him like this should tear me up inside, but, like Thatcher, all I can feel is a peace I haven't known since Mama would whisper a lullaby into my ear when I was a baby.

Good night, you moonlight ladies. Rockabye, sweet Callie May. . . .

"Solus is waiting. Leo and Reena will make it there, too." Thatcher's voice rises above the song, and I kiss his lips once more. I close my eyes, letting my vision of him go, and I feel his smile under my kiss, and the happiness spreads into my body as well, touching every part of me as I am filled with overwhelming contentment and warmth.

And then, suddenly I hear him say it. . . .

"I love you."

But when I open my eyes, Nick is holding me tightly, his face hovering close to mine, Thatcher's soul already just a memory.

I cast my eyes downward, but Nick gently lifts my chin.

"He'll always be with you, Callie," he says, grinning. "Even though you said good-bye."

I reach down into my pocket and put Thatcher's ring on my finger, knowing that what Nick just said couldn't be more true.

Then I look back up at him and his trusting brown eyes.

"Let's go find Carson and Eli, okay?"

Twenty-five

THE MBIRAS ARE PLAYING their rain-like music and the glow of white-gold light is everywhere. I'm walking behind someone tall and strong, with broad shoulders pulled back straight. Without hesitation, he strides toward the source of the incandescent brightness, sure of himself and about what he must do.

He doesn't turn around to look at me. He's too focused on the face of the person standing in front of him, welcoming him into the light.

"Welcome to Solus, Thatcher Larson. We've been waiting for you for a long time."

My mother. Her voice is like honey, her smile like the sun, her long hair cascading down to almost her waist.

Then she steps to the side so she can get a glimpse of me. Our eyes meet and my heart is racing. She doesn't say anything, but I can hear her thoughts as if they are my own.

We'll be here for you, Callie May. We'll be right here.

I reach out, wanting to touch her. . . .

And I wake up with a start. My arm is outstretched, angled toward the window seat in my bedroom. I pull it back, my head sinking into my pillow, and I wonder about the dream.

The details are still in my mind, sharp and clear, warm and comforting. Most dreams fade in the morning light, the emotions they brought on growing quickly cold. This one, I think, will stay with me, though.

"*Caaaallie!*" Carson's voice echoes in the hallway outside my bedroom as she bounds up the stairs. "Come on," she says, rushing in and pulling off my covers. "We have to get going if we don't want to be late for our spot on *Good Morning America.*"

"What?" I sit straight up in bed.

"Kidding!" says Carson, a gleam in her eye. "Though they would *love* our story. Can you *imagine?*" She grins. "I'm just here to drive you to school. Like always."

"How long have I been asleep?"

"A few hours, just like the rest of us," she says. "Are you having trouble remembering everything? Dylan said that might happen because of your emotional trauma and all that."

I sit up and take a deep breath, convincing myself that my mind isn't back where it was months ago, when I came out of the coma. I do remember the last twenty-four hours, but when I search my thoughts, everything isn't 100 percent crystal clear.

It's the important things that come trickling back—like rescuing Carson and Eli.

"I'm good, really," I say. "The bigger question is: How are you feeling?"

"Just peachy," she says, smiling. "I'm going to need a *major* debriefing on the drive, though. The guys tried to recount what happened on the way over here, but you know how they always leave out good details, and I don't quite remember how I ended up at the wheel of my car with Eli in the passenger seat parked on Folly Beach, so . . ."

Knock-knock. Nick, Eli, and Dylan emerge in the doorway behind Carson, all of their faces bright and chipper despite the time on the clock—it's only 6:30 a.m.

"Come in, y'all," says Carson. "She's awake."

"Hey there." Nick moves to sit on the side of my bed and wrap me in a hug. I think I remember him driving me home last night, but I'm not entirely sure.

"How did I . . . ?" I whisper into his shoulder, not quite able to finish my thought, because other pieces of our search for Carson and Eli are beginning to fit together in my head.

Like finding them asleep in the VW at Folly Beach . . .

Nick pulls back and looks into my eyes. "I brought you. You were so exhausted that you were asleep before your head hit the pillow."

Dylan takes a step forward, his hands in his pockets. "You've been through a lot, Callie. More than all of us combined."

His sweetness makes me smile and I look at Carson.

"Did Dylan tell you how we were able to locate you and Eli?" I ask her.

When she shakes her head, I go on, hoping to score him extra points with her. "He remembered what I'd said to Eli—that some ghosts had messed with him at Folly Beach. He figured maybe it was a favorite spot of Reena and Leo's . . . from before."

Carson grins at Dylan. "You're pretty smart, you know that?"

"'Intellectuals solve problems; geniuses prevent them.' Albert Einstein," he says, leaning back on his heels.

"Well, solving or preventing, you're a genius to me," says Carson, wrapping an arm around Dylan's shoulder and giving him a kiss on the cheek. "You saved us."

Dylan looks so love-struck, I'm surprised I don't see comic-book cartoon hearts in his eyes.

Eli lurks at the end of the bed with a close-mouthed sarcastic grin that's all his own, and I break into a smile. I stand up in my pajamas to hug each one of my friends close.

"Whoa, what's this? A coed pajama party?"

My father is standing in the doorway to my room, still holding his overnight bag. His cheeks are flushed and his lips are pursed, signs that he's not really happy with what he's come home to after an early-morning drive home.

"We just got here, Captain McPhee," says Nick, trying to smooth things over. "We're all . . . um . . . driving Callie to school?"

Then Dylan steps forward with his hand out. "Sir, I'm Dylan Mason Dixon. The five of us are working on a science project together involving kinetic energy, and we wanted to get an early start today."

Dad grins in spite of himself—science gets him every time, and so does a firm handshake. He obviously hasn't found his cell phone yet with messages from school about how I was absent again yesterday, but I'll handle that later.

"Fine. I'll leave you to it, then," says my dad. "Callie, I'm staying home today. Maybe after school, can you help me look for my phone? I can't find it anywhere."

"Sure," I tell him.

"Have a good day, everyone." He walks out and Carson pushes my door almost closed.

When she does, we all break into this weird fit of laughter, our faces plastered with smiles, our hearts filled with happiness and relief. We did it. The threat against us is gone and we're all alive, safe and together. Actually, together . . . with an exception.

"Wendy said to thank you," says Nick.

Dylan raises a finger. "I believe what she said was that she cannot ever imagine being able to thank you enough. And that she'll call you this weekend."

I feel a bittersweet pang in my heart. It'll be nice to know Wendy, to keep a connection to Thatcher's life and remember him in the way his family does. I feel pretty lucky to have that—a link to the people who loved him before I did.

"Thanks, y'all," I say. Then I look down at my pajamas. "So I should probably . . ."

"Get dressed? Yeah, that would be good," says Carson.

"Are we really going to *school* today?" asks Nick. "That seems so . . . lame."

Carson frowns. "Yes! Do you think we can afford another absence? I certainly can't. Mama's already mad as a horsefly about yesterday, and she still doesn't believe what I told her."

"What'd you tell her?" asks Dylan.

"That they got Carson Jenkins confused with Caitlin Johnson and that I was actually at school all day."

"Weak," says Eli.

"I know, I know." Carson points to the door. "But we do need to go to school. Would y'all excuse us so Callie can get ready?"

The guys go downstairs to wait and Carson sits on my bed as I grab my towel and start for the shower.

In the doorway to the bathroom, I pause to look at my best friend. Here. Alive. In front of me. Out of danger. And, if I'm reading her right, about to have her first boyfriend. I expect something to ache inside of me at that thought, but instead I'm unable to contain my smile.

"You don't have to do that, you know," she says.

"Do what?"

"Pretend like you're okay. I know you miss him already."

"I'm not pretending," I say. "I do miss him, but I feel . . . like everything is how it should be."

"I know you had to let him go to save me," she says, her eyes welling up. "Nick told me. I'm . . . I'm so sorry, Callie."

I walk back over to the bed and wrap her up in a hug. "Don't be. I'd do it again in a heartbeat. Thatcher would, too."

"Thank you," she says, holding me tight. "I know I would have done it for you."

Suddenly there's a gust of air in the room, which catches the curtains over my window seat, blowing them apart to reveal the prism hanging in the front of the glass, sparkling and twirling in the morning light. For just an instant, it casts rainbows around the room, dancing like the lights of joyous souls among fading shadows, reminding me that Thatcher's ring is still on my finger.

Epilogue

One Month Later

"UH-OH, WE BROUGHT THE same flowers!" I hear Wendy's voice behind me, and it's the sound of tinkling bells instead of heartache and pain.

I turn around and look at her radiant smile, and I grin back at her, still seeing a part of him in all of her features. We're both holding bouquets of white daisies with yellow centers, laughing at the coincidence.

"It just seems like a Thatcher flower," I say.

"Right? Simple and pure," Wendy agrees.

We look down at the same time, staring at the gray headstone in front of us.

"It's kind of strange," she says.

"What is?"

"Being here without . . . I don't know, wanting to die myself," she says. "Even though I know he isn't with us anymore, it feels good to know that he's someplace safe."

I nod, remembering the dream of him and my mom together as I play with the ring on my finger. "I know what you mean."

Then we hear a tree branch snap on the ground behind us. When I turn, I see Nurse K. She's just a few feet away, walking along the grass and carrying three white roses. I raise my eyebrows in wonder.

"Hi, Callie," she says, looking just as surprised as I am.

Wendy gasps. "Hayley? Is that you?"

Nurse K brushes her hair from her eyes, and suddenly one last puzzle piece drops into place.

"Nurse Hayley Krzysiek . . . ," I whisper.

The girl who survived Thatcher's accident in the Wando River.

She and Wendy quickly move into a hug and when they part, Wendy says, "I haven't seen you since . . ." She pauses. "You just . . ."

"Disappeared," says Nurse K, her voice cracking. "I know. After graduation I went to college up north. I tried to forget what happened. It was so awful, I . . ."

She can't bring herself to finish her thought, so Wendy reaches out to touch her arm. "It took me years to come home to Charleston," Nurse K continues. "I wanted to give people time to forget, and so I took a job in another school district. I just didn't want to be the girl who survived."

"We understand," I say.

Nurse K steps away from Wendy and places one white rose on

Thatcher's grave. I look at the other two flowers she's holding, and then up into her kind, gentle face.

"They're okay," I say to her. "All three of them." And though there's no reason she should believe me, or even be sure what I mean, I can feel a bond of trust forming between us.

"I know," she says. "That's why I'm here. Somehow, I felt it." Then she smiles and tilts her head at me. "But wait. Callie, how do *you* know that?"

Wendy puts her arm around me. "Callie's an old family friend," she tells Nurse K, who gives me a sly grin.

"You're a mysterious girl," she says.

"Takes one to know one," I reply.

Nurse K squeezes my shoulder affectionately before she walks away to leave two more white roses for her old friends. She never got to say good-bye to them, and neither did I, but I think we've both come to terms with that, for very different reasons. Hopefully someone was there to meet them after their souls were forced out of Carson and Eli. Hopefully, they've let go of the things that made them fight against their destiny and all the love and peace that had always been waiting for them. Since Nurse K is here, I have to believe that.

We stay for a little longer, Thatcher's sister and I. And when we leave, we agree to see each other again at Thanksgiving break. "Maybe at a café next time though?" she says. "This place, it's not where he'd want us to remember him."

"You're right," I say, smiling.

We walk back to the entrance and when we part to go to our

respective cars, Wendy reaches out and takes my hand, giving it an affectionate squeeze. I hold on for a moment, Thatcher's ring pressing against our skin, and I can feel a warmth between us that I have a feeling will be there for life.

Acknowledgments

Thank you, thank you, thank you to the people who participated in this book's creation: Morgan Baden, Claudia Gabel, Sara Lyle, Sarah MacLean, Lauren Mechling, Melissa Miller, Micol Ostow, Doug Stewart, and the entire team at Katherine Tegen Books!

This story will haunt you."

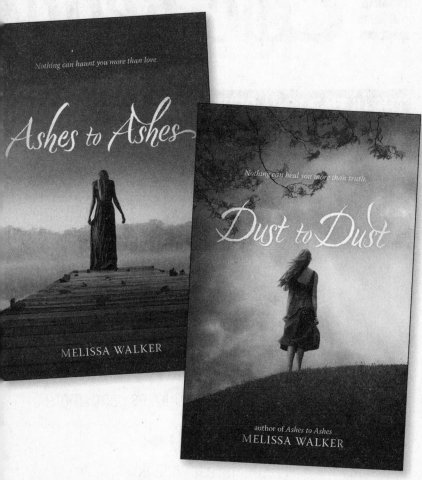

Don't miss MELISSA WALKER'S sweeping, romantic,
and emotionally rich duology about the things that
torment us, even from the Great Beyond.

An Imprint of HarperCollins Publishers

www.epicreads.com

JOIN THE

Epic Reads

COMMUNITY

THE ULTIMATE YA DESTINATION

◀ **DISCOVER** ▶
your next favorite read

◀ **MEET** ▶
new authors to love

◀ **WIN** ▶
free books

◀ **SHARE** ▶
infographics, playlists, quizzes, and more

◀ **WATCH** ▶
the latest videos

◀ **TUNE IN** ▶
to Tea Time with Team Epic Reads

   Find us at **www.epicreads.com**
and **@epicreads**